# TWICE DEAD

# CLIFFORD ROSS

and

# MATTHEW JENNER

ISBN: 9781549643217

To our loved ones.

# PROLOGUE

In the winter of 1982 a joint operation between the CIA and the American military was wiped clean from the records. 'Project P' had been created to perfect the internal capabilities of the human being. It was the latest of several attempts by the Americans to get ahead of the Soviet Union in Cold Warfare. During this time the threat of nuclear war had reached heights not seen since the Cuban Missile Crisis, and just as in the early 1960s the American Military and Intelligence where once again exploring the advantage of psychochemical warfare.

Following the disastrous experimentation of the 1960's, testing on humans was thought to have ceased. With subsequent developments in science and technology it was only a matter of time before a new hope emerged in the search for the ultimate combatant. Opinion in both the CIA and the American military was mixed, but by the early 1980s the US was desperate for the next step in military capability. Tensions between East and West were escalating, yet both sides understood that nuclear warfare would be suicidal. The head of the American military stated in a meeting with the CIA that 'nuclear warfare would be two countries in a bath of gasoline. One nation with three matches, the other with five'. What the Americans needed was something, or someone, to extinguish the enemy's matches.

During a secret meeting in 1981 between the military and the CIA, a leading scientist put forward the idea of Project P for a second time. It was made clear that although it was still not tested fully, there was confidence in avoiding the disaster of the 1960's, and that success could be achieved within twelve months. The intention would be to dispatch successful test subjects behind enemy lines and eliminate leading KGB officers and Soviet officials. The military argued that the proposed time scale was not urgent enough and so a four-month deadline was put in place.

What followed was another catastrophic failure. The hugely expensive and inhumane project involved administration of the drug SU1 to experienced secret service agents, who had volunteered in the pursuit of becoming next-generation heroes and the epitome of modern warfare. The drug was administered in three doses over a three-month period to allow the agents time to adapt to their emerging capabilities.

Initial results were remarkable. The SU1 chemical ignited dormant synapses in the brains and muscles of the test candidates. After only two doses one subject's IQ had increased by a staggering 35%, and continued to increase by the time of the third dose. The ability to solve equations and mental arithmetic had halved in time and had doubled in success rate. A CIA official described one candidate as 'the million-dollar mind'. Three days after administration of the third and final dose, severe side effects were noted. Subjects began to suffer from aggressive migraines, vision became distorted, and blindness ensued as the drug-swollen brains began to lose basic function.

Early signs had also been exciting for strength development. The notion of creating men of steel from flesh and bone was proving a reality when agents with only athletic physiques began displaying herculean power. Excitement turned to anguish once more as several test candidates experienced massive heart attacks after the final dose. No reports exist on the outcome of other secret service agents involved in the trials but they are thought to have received a quick and painless death, with assistance.

In one final attempt to prove the project successful a candidate was chosen for his average IQ and physical ability. A much weaker dose of SU1 was administered. Results were positive, and the candidate showed significant improvement in mental and physical capacity. In the absence of any adverse effects the project entered the surgical enhancement phase. Nerve endings were severed to lessen pain sensations. Bones were broken at strategic points so that they would heal stronger and provide biomechanical reinforcement. The eyes and visual cortex were operated on to increase the vision above the 20/20 mark. The overall result was that whilst the subject still looked like the average man, he was internally far more capable and durable.

Two weeks after the candidate entered the advanced training phase he was found dead in his room. It had been an act of suicide. The head of Special Warfare operations at the time made a statement to both the CIA and the military claiming that 'the biggest strength and weakness of the human condition was the human mind. It could both advance and undermine the fundamental development of the human species'. Project P was discontinued indefinitely.

A confidential file regarding the later stages of Project P found its way across the Atlantic and into the hands of the then Prime Minister of Great Britain. It was believed that the file had been given to her by an enthusiast of SU1 who was eager for its research to continue in a more reasoned and methodical manner. In the presence of a select few government officials the Prime Minister reviewed the file. At this time the British government's priorities were on the rising unrest of coal miners and the newly declared war over the Falkland Islands. On hearing that British paratroopers had defeated a larger Argentinian force at the Battle of Goose Green, the Prime Minister rejected Project P as inhumane and unnecessary.

Filled with pride over British military tenacity the PM was claimed to have questioned 'why the steel from which our soldiers were forged needed any synthetic reinforcement'. The discussion was ended once and for all when she proclaimed that 'we are a nation of great power and responsibility and under international pressure from those opposed to the acts of this government, we will not succumb to this level of experimentation. We are an example to the world of human resilience and the strength of the human condition'. She ordered the file to be destroyed and for all dialogue on the matter to cease permanently.

The file was taken by the British Intelligence services to be destroyed.

Confirmation of this was never reported.

# ONE

Alex Black sat behind the wheel of his Ford Fiesta looking out onto the narrow road ahead. His left hand sat on the steering wheel, his right arm cocked and laid down on the open window frame. Still wearing the lycra cycling gear he had put on six hours earlier, he was enjoying how his body temperature was finally beginning to drop as the heat of intense exercise began to depart on the cool breeze flowing through one window and out the other. He shifted from side to side in his seat, trying to shake off the damp discomfort in the small of his back.

The day had been hot and the sun intense, causing him to become soaked in his own sweat after only two miles of physical exertion. And that had only been the warm-up. The rest of the ride had severely depleted his hydration levels as his body leaked an abnormal amount of fluid in the midday heat. The loss of essential electrolytes from his system was now evident in the cramps building in his calf muscles. Alex's skin felt like it was drawn tightly over the bony contours of his face and the slightest change in his expression reminded him that ignoring his wife's suggestion to bring sun cream had been a mistake. His short black hair had dried quickly after removing his cycling helmet and now his thick crop was being whipped in all directions by the high pressured breeze that passed through the cab of the car. Alex felt utterly exhausted, but liberated.

It had been far too long since the last time Alex had found the opportunity to push the physical limits of his body in healthy rivalry with friends, and he was pleased to still be able to keep up with them as they hammered the paths and trails of the Welsh Brecon Beacons. The spectacular scenery of the sandstone mountain range had reignited his passion for the outdoors and had provided a welcome contrast to his usual grey surroundings of inner-city work. Every peak they reached gave Alex a view he had become alien to, reminding him of long-forgotten aspirations to explore the world and extend the boundaries of his own existence. Hills carpeted in green contrasted the crystal blue waters of the valley lakes and rivers, reflecting wide open skies above. Life had seemed limitless when he was a regular visitor to such vistas. Now his world was a concrete dreariness; grey buildings, black roads and narrow strips of sunlight filling his days and dreams. Somewhere in his journey he had convinced himself that it was his duty to enter a noble and worthwhile profession and that there would be no better challenge than being a teacher in a fast paced and competitive city such as London. But the excitement had soon worn off and somehow he had managed to sustain ten years in the teaching profession.

The Monday Blues were already darkening the

horizon of his mind as he thought about some of the little shits he would face the next day. Disobedient and increasingly dangerous. It had been only a few months since one of his colleagues had been stabbed by a problematic pupil and although he had been expelled and convicted, there seemed to be plenty more of the testy bastards to take his place. Forget classroom control, this was conflict resolution on a daily basis. Alex however was not concerned for his own safety. Unlike many of his colleagues he didn't fear the violence; he feared what he might do in response to such a threat. Anyway, he'd worry more about that when he turned up at school in the morning and instead he tuned his mind back in to the events of the day.

Alex had left Tunbridge Wells for the Brecon Beacons as the sun was cresting the distant horizon. His wife and two young children remained asleep in their beds as he pulled off the driveway, noticing in his rear-view mirror the faded blue paint of the front door to their home. *Another job for the list*, he thought. South Wales seemed to be experiencing a heat wave by the time Alex arrived at his destination. It was half past eleven and the sun was fierce, but not as fierce as the welcome from his old university friends. Apparently the first signs of grey hair was a big deal, and his lack of attendance at the annual get-togethers hadn't gone un-noticed. The location suited the majority of the group who had all randomly settled in the west of England and therefore met regularly to relive their prime. Eventually they acknowledged his efforts to make the trip and by midday the six of them were riding hard under a baking sun. Endless fields and hills were eaten up by the quick pace of the riders and Alex lead for the majority of the route as he stamped on the pedals to attack every challenge the course could throw at him. It felt good to be back in his natural environment. What had he given up for a life more ordinary?

Alex was in a world of his own as he pushed on, unhindered by the burning sun and the searing lactic acid in his legs. In his mind he was racing against his former self and nothing else mattered in that moment. But all too soon the day was over and the pact was once again made to meet in another twelve months. Alex nodded in agreement, and this time he meant it. Sweaty embraces and farewells were exchanged once all the gear was stacked on cars or thrown in to the back of them amongst child safety seats littered with food wrappers. Once the sun had set on their reunion and they were back in their beds next to their wives the usual tick-tock of family and work would resume. Alex felt bittersweet about the prospect of returning to normality.

The country roads were quiet, occasionally punctuated by rising revs from gear changes to negotiate the numerous twists and turns ahead of Alex. Birdsong that had provided the daytime soundtrack was beginning to fade-out as it went with the light. Orange and pink painted the clouds above as the colour of the day clung on for a final hour, while the shadows on the road grew in length. Away with his thoughts and hypnotised by the stillness of the landscape and the sky, Alex removed his arm from the window and pressed the button to close it, making sure he left a small gap between the glass and the frame for fresh air to displace his sweaty aroma.

Miles of hedgerows flanked the car and the green flew past in a blur so that Alex became oblivious to the passing of time and distance. The serenity of his surroundings and the peace of mind he had found seemed to warp his sense of reality. Sat alone with his thoughts he felt reconnected with his old self and he was enjoying the rare solitude. It was only for the occasional bump in the road that he did not completely zone out and forget where he was.

The journey home seemed to take forever and Alex wondered whether his stiffened body would be able to break free from the car-seat mould. To his left the sky was turning to a dark navy that seemed infinite with space. Alex looked up through the windscreen, feeling his forehead tighten as he strained to see the first few stars pop out against the black velvet above him. The noise outside which had filled the fields with life had now gone completely and the only living things were the bugs dancing in the beams of the head lights. The air coming through the window had turned cold and bit Alex's skin, prompting him to close it completely. His legs had gone from a comfortable ache to an irritating throb, and the inside of his thighs felt raw from rubbing. He fought hard to maintain his alertness against the hypnotic rocking of the car's chassis. Alex stepped on the accelerator, desperate to get home.

The force of impact completely disabled Alex's

senses the instant the Volkswagen Golf punched headlong into the right side of the flimsy Fiesta flying unknowingly across the blind junction. The young guy driving home from his girlfriend's was speeding and had no time to slow as the smaller car flew out in front of him. The instant the cars collided the seatbelt-less youth was flung through the windscreen, sending him skidding along the tarmac and tearing skin away from the parts of his body exposed to the road. He died the instant his fragile head hit the hard road surface and broke open.

The brutal force delivered unconsciousness swiftly to Alex and his limp body rattled around the crumpling cab until finally he was pinned in place by the driver's door folded against his right flank. The door frame squeezed violently on his chest and several ribs snapped like dry twigs under a heavy foot. The sharp blow pierced his chest wall and punctured his right lung. Alex's head snapped backwards and then forwards detaching one of his retinas before his skull thumped bluntly against the depressed roof. Glass from the driver-side window shattered and several razor-sharp fragments flew into his right cheek, burrowing themselves deep into the flesh like insects scurrying into soil. The fleshy muscle of his right thigh that hours earlier had powered Alex up the steepest of inclines was skewered by a strand of exposed metal, slicing through his quad like a hot knife through butter. A deep wound opened up and instantly filled with warm aerated blood.

Both cars skidded in unison for about ten metres

before they hit a hedge and the Fiesta ripped itself away from the heavier Volkswagen and somersaulted into an adjacent field. The Golf stood its ground and sat motionless with no driver behind the wheel. The chaotic sound of the two vehicles violently locking and unlocking was enormous and it forced a black cloud of frightened birds to explode into the night sky, shading the scene from any moon or star light. Once the Fiesta had completed its airborne routine it finally came to rest, tearing up grass and mud before doing so. The mass of birds quickly cleared the night air and the true damage could be seen under the serene light of the moon. Silence fell all around. Alex had been secured in place by the numerous bits of chassis entering his body and his flaccid frame was bent and twisted like something only a trained contortionist should attempt.

Two hours later Alex responded to the faintest spark of life and slowly peeled back his eye lids to see the expanse of black above him. An infinite number of stars swarmed in the night with only the faint wisp of his breath seemingly between him and them. With his spine in shock and complete paralysis below his abdomen Alex was oblivious to the soiled mess soaking through his trousers. The pain however was finding alternate ways to his brain and with the adrenaline surge long gone the first signals of tissue damage were flooding his sensory cortex. The sensation was overwhelming and caused Alex's system to shut down but the acrid smell of burnt rubber and petrol filled his nostrils and roused him like pungent smelling salts. Nausea washed over him and the short and panic stricken breaths forced his shattered ribs to move out of step with the rest of his chest. Alex's skin, which before had felt crisp and taut from the heat of the day, had become ice cold under the moon's gaze. The cloudless sky had released the Earth's warmth into space and with it the last of Alex's core temperature.

He drifted in and out of consciousness over the next twenty minutes as life oozed out of the open wounds. Images of his children filled his mind and he longed for his wife's embrace to keep him warm. An icy tear formed in the corner of Alex's eye before disappearing instantly into the pool of red liquid by his feet.

In the distance, a faint siren sounded and Alex's spirits lifted with each rising decibel. The Doppler Effect suggested help was on its way. His painful loneliness was coming to an end. Within minutes a police car and an ambulance screeched to a halt alongside the mangled Golf and the wrecked and ripped-up corpse of its driver. It was he they had been looking for after an anxious emergency call made by his desperate mother. She would shortly be receiving a gut wrenching visit from a police officer wearing a sympathetic look. But what was Alex's fate?

The emergency crews finally found the gaping hole in the hedgerow and immediately started work on extracting the Fiesta's passenger from its deformed remains. The firefighters worked tirelessly like a team of surgeons making precision cuts in the car's steel ribcage, but as the sands of time drained away so too did Alex's chances of survival. His bruised and broken body was skilfully lifted from the battered vehicle and trained professionals busied around the scene in a clinical and coordinated fashion.

As they did so the faint and stuttering tempo of Alex's heartbeat gave way to an empty stillness.

# TWO

Never before had she ignored her children's cries for so long but there was only one thing on her mind, and that was Alex. Emma and Joseph were strapped in the back of the car bleary eyed and totally dazed as Amy used every bit of the available speed limit from Tunbridge Wells to the trauma centre at St George's Hospital. Alex had been passing through the Surrey Hills at the time of the collision and the area of outstanding natural beauty had lulled his weary mind and body into a trance-like state. He had been so close to home, as was the way with most road traffic incidents. Now his grief stricken wife was making her way up the vacant A23 with two children who had been wrenched from their innocent slumber. Despite their young ages they both seemed acutely aware of their mother's agony.

'Mummy, I left Bear at home and I really need him,' whined Emma. Amy wiped the tracks of her tears from both cheeks and cleared her throat before replying.

'Bear will still be in your room when we get back, just don't worry about it for now, Sweetheart.' The sentence ended with a tone sharper than Amy had intended but she was struggling to conceal her anguish.

Emma's pleas had been the first sound out of either child since they had been dumped into their car seats and hastily fastened in place.

Perhaps it had been their curiosity of the night life unfolding outside of their windows that had kept them quiet, or perhaps they had picked up on their mother's vibes and knew better than to make a scene. Emma had realised the instant she was dragged from her bed that Bear was not by her side and she had tried hard to cope without her favourite teddy, but she needed some comfort now in the cold harsh night. Amy sensed her daughter's sadness and tried to comfort her.

'Just be a big girl for a little bit longer darling,' she said as she gave the bravest smile she could into the rear-view mirror.

Emma did her best to be brave but at four years of age that was difficult.

'Mummy, I'm sad,' she said, sounding like she might cry any minute. Her unrest caught on and Joseph started a low whine that quickly escalated into an ear shattering cry. As he kicked and screamed for attention his comfort blanket fell to the foot-well and the volume of the cry rose a few decibels more. The whole scene unsettled Emma further and she too began to cry. The noise thundered in Amy's ears and her senses were overloaded. She felt nauseous. Her mouth dried up and she found it hard to swallow-down the sick at the back of her throat. She was on the verge of losing it with the kids and in her silent rage the speedometer tumbled in to the high 80s. In her head Amy wanted to scream at the children, to scream at Alex, and to not stop screaming until her lungs gave out. She took a deep breath, brought her temper and the car back under control and calmed both children with a combination of soothing words and tone. All this while barely containing her own need to breakdown and weep for her situation.

'Whatever happens,' she told herself, 'these two beauties come first.' She choked on her own words, then putting her own needs to one side she focused on the road ahead and considered what might await them at the hospital.

Amy could not have imagined what she would face. Alex was her rock. To take a call in the late evening and hear the words 'severe' and 'road traffic collision' in the same sentence had tipped her whole world on its head. And now her head was in a spin as the words still echoed in her ears and she tried to give reason to them. Questions like 'why Alex?' 'Why us?' presented themselves to her as if life was ever some sort of level playing field. She felt hard done to. But then life wasn't fair; it was full of bad people and bad happenings, things that you heard on the news but seemed detached from in the safety of your own little bubble. The bubble had well and truly burst for the Black family and all Amy could do was to keep it together long enough to establish how bad things could be. She saw the signs for the hospital and pulled off the A24, taking a long deep breath as she did so. The sight of the hospital forced out a lonely tear that slowly found its way down her face using the channels worn by the many tears that had gone before it.

Despite being physically and emotionally shattered Amy navigated the hospital corridors and departments like a powered-up Pacman. The adrenaline was keeping her on high-alert and she guided her children silently under the gloomy strip lights, never taking a wrong turn. Each corridor took her closer to finding out the answer. When she finally reached the Emergency Department her self-control vanished the instant she saw the illuminated signs marking her arrival. Stood there in her baggy tracksuit bottoms and her husband's oversized sweatshirt with 'York University' emblazoned on the front and personalised with 'Black' on the rear her outward appearance embodied the shrinking feeling she had inside of her. Her legs shook uncontrollably and her heartbeat felt hard; so hard that she could feel it reverberate in her throat. Amy squeezed on Emma's dainty hand and led her forwards into the unknown.

The automatic sliding doors revealed a sea of sickness. Bloodied noses and crooked arms littered the waiting area. As Amy passed deftly through the matrix of plastic chairs and its morbid occupants she pulled both of her children close, wanting to shield their innocence from the hurt and pain all around. She'd half expected the place to be empty, with a nurse on standby awaiting her arrival but the reality of the situation could not have been more different. Amy wondered how it was that people acquired injuries like those around her at such an obscure time of day. Why weren't these people all tucked up in bed, like her husband should now have been? Amy scanned the sad and pained faces of those awaiting medical attention and hoped to see her husband among them, but her optimism soon dissolved when she remembered it had not been Alex who had made the call but instead a nurse urging her to attend quickly. When the realisation caught up with Amy she ushered Joseph and Emma to the reception desk.

'Hi, I'm looking for my husband, Alex Black?' said Amy through the Perspex partition. 'I'm his wife, Amy.' She placed Joseph down beside her, his weight and fidgeting becoming difficult to contain, and placed both of her hands palm-down on the counter. The laminated surface felt cool under her clammy skin.

'Wait a second, I will just have a look,' replied a tired looking receptionist nonchalantly. Amy stared at the woman typing on the computer, her gaze so intense it could have burnt a hole in the side of the receptionist's face. The woman's expression gave nothing away.

'If you would please take a seat, someone will be with you shortly,' she said finally, not bothering to look up from the monitor screen. Amy wanted to scream at the bitch and shake her until she told her where and how Alex was.

'What? No, I need someone now. I need to know what is going on!'

Joseph began to cry again and his big sister did her best to comfort him with an over-enthusiastic hug that the boy instantly tried to shake off. Emma looked completely dejected and in need of comfort herself. Perceptive to her children's needs Amy swept them both up and squeezed them tight. The embrace forced out a tear that clung to Amy's raw cheek. The receptionist finally showed some compassion and decided to concern herself with Amy's situation. She nodded to a nurse colleague who was stood nearby. The uniformed woman in her late forties stopped flicking through a file of patient paperwork and tactfully approached Amy.

'Please Miss, someone will be with you shortly. Take a seat,' said the nurse in a soft tone as she placed a comforting arm around Amy and guided her to a row of three empty seats.

The mother of two reluctantly accepted the offer and resigned herself to waiting amongst the walking dead. Emma and Joseph somehow fell asleep the instant their weary heads rested on Amy's lap. Cocooned once again in their angelic slumber the children were oblivious to the chaos all around them and to the turbulent thump of their mother's breaking heart. Lost in a thousand possible outcomes Amy started to slowly zone out of the world around her, her pulse slowed and her eyes fell heavy. She was exhausted and emotionally empty.

'Mrs Black?' said the voice several times before it stole into her dreams. Amy woke with a start to see a male nurse stood over her.

'My name's Tony,' said the man in a quiet voice, 'If you'd like to follow me I'll take you to see your husband.' For a brief second Amy was dazed and confused but as the nurse gestured to his colleague the horror came flooding back.

'I can watch your children for you,' said the second nurse, 'we have a family room I can take them to. They can sleep in there and I'll be with them the whole time.' The woman's face was warm and friendly, a lifetime of caring for others was etched into her features revealing her years like rings in the trunk of a fallen tree. Amy nodded and between the three adults they managed to get the two children, who were now dead-weights, to the peace and tranquillity of a softly furnished room adorned with leaflets and posters about the grieving process. The room had bad-news written all over it and Amy felt sick to her stomach. She gave a lingering kiss on the forehead of each child and left with the male nurse to face the fate of her family.

After passing through another maze of gloomy corridors the male nurse handed Amy over to a shorter and older man stood by the door to a side room.

'Hello, I'm Doctor Baker,' said the man in an obvious Scottish accent, but the exact dialect was lost to a refined education and a prestigious career. He extended his hand and while Amy expected gentle compassion his touch felt cold and disconnected. The doctor got straight down to business.

'Before we enter the room I need to discuss your husband's condition with you.' Amy felt the sick rise inside of her. Baker was wearing the standard attire of any hospital doctor and it hung off him loosely, as if it had fitted him twenty years prior when his back was a little straighter and his limbs a little thicker with muscle mass.

'Where's my husband? I want to see Alex,' snapped Amy impatiently. She wiped away a few more tears that had gathered in the corners of her eyes and a look of determination spread over her fatigued face. The doctor took the cue that she was ready and turned to press an identity card against a pad above the door handle. The pad beeped and a green light pulsed. Dr Baker pushed open the door and gestured with his free arm for Amy to step forward into the sterile scene before her.

It was a large room, but with the myriad pieces of sophisticated equipment around the bed it looked cramped and not big enough for a patient in Alex's condition. Everywhere there were sounds bouncing off each other as the machines made a variety of noises; not one of them looking like they weren't important. The only machine that Amy recognised displayed the hopeful trace of Alex's heartbeat. Amy did her best to take it all in but through the tears she could see clearly that her beloved husband and the father of her children was little more than a piece of meat being pumped with air and given an unsustainable pulse. He was void of personality and his existence had been distilled to the most basic definition of living. The corpse laying in front of Amy seemed to her like a shell discarded by a snail. Empty and redundant.

The doctor's voice played out as background music to the images all around Amy. She had mostly tuned out but his words were registering in some small part of her distraught brain.

'Mrs Black, your husband was involved in a severe road traffic collision a few hours ago.' There was a grit in his voice now that underlined the gravity of the situation. 'Alex was found a few hours after the crash.

He lost a lot of blood in that time, and given the severity of his multiple injuries...' Baker's words petered out. He was now stating the obvious and Amy's expression said that she understood where the conversation was going.

'What now?' she asked. The doctor shifted his weight between his legs and then stepped into Amy's peripheral vision. She could see a sympathetic look forming on his face.

'When Alex arrived he was in a very bad way. He had suffered head trauma and some damage to his brain. His lungs were punctured and many of the bones on his right-hand side were broken.' Amy's shoulders began to shake and she started to sob heavily as the reality finally hit home.

Alex's skin shimmered with an unnatural pink texture and as he lay there motionless he resembled a painted doll neatly presented in its packaging. The only part of him that moved was the steady rise and fall of his chest as the positive air pressure forced it up and down in parallel with a machine to his right. It took Amy a long while to build up the courage to touch his fragile swollen skin. She thought of all the things she wished she could say to him. The love she had for him, the gratitude she had for being their children's father. Instead she said nothing for the thirty minutes she spent by the man's side. The only sound was the soft cry that she intermittently let out. Her sorrow had no bottom and she could not even begin to comprehend the cruel twist of fortune that had befallen the Black family.

*

'This is the one,' exclaimed Baker, 'I believe he will be perfect for your needs.' The doctor spoke hurriedly, keen to impress the man stood alongside him.

'First of all *Baker*, it is not my needs we are here to discuss. It is the needs of a project that is no concern of yours. Secondly, this man looks to be far from perfect. Did I, or did I not, give you an exact description of the candidate profile?' The doctor's pleased expression drained from his furrowed features. His voice now a little shaky.

'Aye, you did indeed, but we're talking about opportunities here. What comes through our doors is a lottery and what you have here is the closest match to your profile in the whole time we have been searching.'

'Listen to me Baker and listen well. You were approached because you are fortunate enough to be close to the right people, in the right condition. Despite this, you kept me waiting for three years, and then after all that time this is what you get me out of bed for?' The man was taller than Baker, with a thick build and a worldly face. Doctor Baker had indeed called the man in the late hours but he doubted he had disturbed his sleep. In his professional medical opinion Baker thought the man looked like he never slept, and if he did then the creases in his jacket and trousers suggested that he did so in his dark grey suit. The man's ill-looking skin complemented his crumpled attire.

'Let's not forget the third reason you were recruited

to help with this project.' The doctor flushed a deep red and pulled at his shirt collar with a single bony finger. He looked barely strong enough to loosen the half-hearted knot in his tie.

'We met our end of the deal and paid off those debts of yours, meaning that you got to keep your knee caps. But what do we get in return – this pile of broken shit!' The grey man was livid. Baker felt his shame begin to simmer. He had worked hard to control his gambling addiction since the mystery man had turned up and offered to wipe-clean his insurmountable debts, but at times like this he felt the need to hit the bookies again for that one-last win that could transport him out of this hell. His knees physically ached as he remembered the numerous threats to his health from the lone-sharks.

'I will always be grateful for your assistance, but I have done my best for you and I believe this is the best you will find. It's not easy making things like this happen. My career is on the line. I could go to prison for this, and if I was to mention your name...' Baker realised as soon as the words escaped him that he had gone too far. The man leaned in so close that his ash-tray breath overpowered Baker's senses.

'Are you threatening me, Doctor?' his voice loaded with aggression. Baker's head recoiled and for a moment it looked like his scrawny head and neck might disappear into his loosened collar like a turtle receding into its shell.

'I'm sorry,' stuttered the Scot, his r's now clipped and flat. 'But you must understand that I can only offer you what comes to us.'

The man snatched the clipboard from the timid doctor and surveyed its contents.

'Alex Black,' he said out loud as he continued to skim the candidate's credentials. 'This is not even close to what we want, let alone need. You know I am not a man of humour, so don't you fucking joke with me. Are you telling me that this is the best you can offer us?' The doctor nodded encouragingly, his confidence building with the increasing possibility of closing a deal.

'Alex Black,' repeated the suited man, 'age: 34. Married. Two children; aged four and two. No past medical history. Physically fit.' His tone was objective and unsympathetic. He could not have cared any less for the barely-living body before him whose whole life had been summarised on a single side of A4 paper.

'Six foot and three inches tall. Weighing thirteen stone and five pounds,' he continued from the clipboard. The man paced around the bedside surveying every aspect of the human wreckage whose skin tone was now almost indistinct from the crisp white sheets beneath him. He sucked air in through his pursed lips as he contemplated his limited options. Finally, he nodded in the doctor's direction.

'Ok, he'll do for now. I will have someone come to collect him in exactly one hour,' he declared.

Baker was quick to reply and conclude proceedings, 'I will make all the necessary arrangements for you,' he said. 'I'm sure you won't be disappointed.'

'We'll see about that Baker. In the meantime, keep watch for something more suitable.'

'But…but our deal was one candidate,' contested the doctor with great trepidation.

'Just make sure you sign him off as a dead man and we'll take it from there.' The man checked his watch and turned to leave without even looking at the doctor. Over the sound of his hard-heeled shoes clanking against the polished floor he gave his last order; 'one hour Baker!'

\*

Alex's body was collected exactly an hour after their conversation. It had been only a brief tea-break but by the time the nurse returned to tend to Alex he was gone. The doctor handed her a clipboard with an attached sheet confirming the man's death. Doctor Kenneth Baker's signature was scrawled across the bottom of the sheet, and after thrusting the clipboard in her direction he left the nurse standing there in the middle of the room trying to fathom what she had missed. Outside of the hospital a team of medical professionals in uniform scrubs worked busily around a body and its numerous medical adjuncts. The trolley on which Alex lay was eased up the ramp and into the back of the unmarked private ambulance. The black rear-doors to the ambulance closed the instant he was inside and the tinted windows obscured Alex from the living world.

The medical facility was pristine and loaded with technology and expertise. The body of Alex Black, along with the faintest signs of the soul that occupied it, arrived no worse for the journey. On the edge of England's Capital, ironically close to where he had crashed, Alex Black was being prepped for his final act. The room bustled with anticipation and professionalism.

'Are we ready?' asked the surgeon, looking round the room full of masked professionals. He was greeted with eager nods of affirmation. 'Let us begin.'

# THREE

The room was three metres by four metres, enclosed by walls of concrete block covered in a thin veneer of white paint. The space was stark. The centre piece was a table and two chairs, made of a light-weight metal and grey in colour. Two individuals sat facing one another under a gloomy fluorescent light that cast shadows beneath their brows. The whites of their eyes shone intensely through the shadow's umbra and their gaze was locked. The pair had met many times in this room over the last few months, going through the same routine but this time there was a sense of change in the encounter. For several moments there was silence as both of them waited for their opposition to offer the first word. A woman in her late twenties was sat perfectly upright with a flawless posture that pushed her pert breasts against her blouse and fitted suit jacket. Her only motion was to lay a clipboard on the metal table top, leaving her left hand rested on top and her fingers lightly tapping on the surface. In her right hand she spun a plastic biro pen between her fingers; neither task in themselves difficult but it was impressive to see them both being performed simultaneously.

'Can you confirm your name please?' The words left

her mouth with a prolonged exhalation. Her dark brown hair was tied tightly in a ponytail, the tip of which came to rest at the base of her neck and didn't move an inch as she spoke.

The man who was sitting opposite her studied her features and was committing several of her characteristics to memory, as he did every time they met. He did it with every person he met, a habit of his intense training. He noted that in an academic sort of way the woman had attractive features; a symmetrical face with a small straight nose that ended in full lips set across a dainty jaw. His analysis of her beauty was more objective than subjective; it was a fact that by conventional standards she had aesthetic value. He considered how many times they had played this ridiculous game. Finally, he answered the woman's question.

'My name is Adam,' he said. 'Adam Newman.'

From behind her thick rimmed spectacles the woman's clear blue eyes scanned the man's features as he spoke.

'But then you already know that Dr Quickfall,' he continued. Although his expression was dry she could tell instantly that he was playing with her. She fought the urge to rise to it. The man sat before her had developed the ability to get under her skin and it irked Grace Quickfall, a Psychology post-Doctorate, that he could unpick her so easily. Over the course of their meetings she had found his gravitas difficult to resist, and his handsome features were an added distraction. She refocussed her attention.

'Well then, as you will know already,' started Dr Quickfall, 'my role is to monitor and analyse your psychological performance and general wellbeing during your recovery and training. You will also be aware that my reports go directly to the Director of the Special Operations Unit, who will have the final say on whether or not you are ready for active duty.' She fired a look straight into the man's eyes, instantly regaining authority. Adam Newman conceded with a wry smile.

For the next ten minutes the two engaged in their usual dance of questions and answers. Adam had learnt not to push the interviewer too far and today he mostly played along, keen to get signed off and progress through his training.

'What is your role within the Secret Intelligence Service?' she asked.

'Well Doctor, it would hardly be a secret if I told you,' he answered. Quickfall ignored him and looked down at the clipboard that was now resting on her thighs. She waited for the correct response.

Adam obliged; 'to serve Her Majesty's Government and protect the interests of the United Kingdom by any means necessary.'

'Thank you Adam. And do you feel you are ready to take up your role?'

'More than ready,' he replied with a hint of arrogance. Grace Quickfall looked up from her notes.

'Really?' she asked. 'And what makes you so sure?' Adam's eyes narrowed and the boyish charm evaporated from his expression.

'I have trained non-stop for six months, pushing

myself to master any situation you have thrown me in to.' He leaned forwards and placed his forearms on the table as if to reinforce the following point, 'so yes, I am sure. Get me *back* on active duty.' His choice of words triggered Dr Quickfall's next question.

'Adam. What do you remember from before your accident?' He shifted in his chair and then came to support himself against the back rest. He massaged his temples between the thumb and second finger of his left hand.

'You know the answer to this,' he said.

'Tell me again,' she insisted.

Adam wracked his brain, and finally replied, 'I don't remember anything.' Quickfall continued, using the momentum of his thoughts to her advantage.

'You don't remember a single thing?'

'No,' snapped Adam. 'Nothing,' he said again, this time his answer calm and measured. The woman made a note of something on her clipboard.

The wall to the right of Grace Quickfall was covered in a large mirror that reflected the room's sickly glow. Adam fully expected that it concealed a viewing room where more likely than not his responses were being observed. He could sense the eyes on him, analytical and critical. Perhaps he was being paranoid, but his instincts told him otherwise.

Behind the mirror stood a man in a heavily creased grey suit, his face was ashen and furrowed. The man was Richard Palmer, Director of the Special Operations Unit within the British Secret Intelligence Service. He studied his subject intensely through the glass, noting his responses like on every other occasion he had watched in secret. As always, he sported a look of dissatisfaction on his face.

'Ok Quickfall,' muttered Palmer in to a microphone, 'wrap it up. Let's just see how he gets on in the final phase shall we?' Dr Quickfall didn't flinch as the tinny sound rolled down the canal of her right ear.

'Thank you Adam, that will be all for now,' she said as she pushed back her chair and stood to leave. 'Get some rest, it's a big day for you tomorrow. We want you on active service too.'

'Who's *we?*' he asked. It was a question he had asked increasingly over the last few weeks. Quickfall gave her usual response.

'SIS, of course. See you tomorrow.' Her smile was sincere and striking. Adam smiled back and nodded to acknowledge her departure.

Quickfall had barely walked a few yards from the door of the interview room when she was greeted by the overbearing presence of the Head of the Special Operations Unit. She couldn't tell whether it was the entrenched aroma of stale cigarette smoke or his lack of personality that made her feel nauseous, but she concluded it was likely a combination of the two.

'I'm still not convinced,' he started. 'What the hell was he playing at in there? We haven't spent six months training him for University Challenge!' continued Palmer who had now taken a step further in to Quickfall's personal space. She felt uneasy in Palmer's presence. He lacked any emotional intelligence or sensitivity to social convention. The doctor tried to stand tall and meet his stare but his rancid breath and bad attitude were making it difficult for her to look him in the eye.

'I think he's ready,' she said with commitment. 'His recovery has been remarkable and he shows no signs of physical or emotional trauma following his experience. In my professional opinion you should progress him to the final phase.' Her opposition didn't look convinced.

'You have no idea what's at stake here. We've invested a significant amount of time and resources in this man and I don't feel he's met the expectations of the project.' Quickfall contemplated a response but thought better of it.

'Yes Sir, I understand your concerns. If you feel he isn't ready then I will accept your judgement. All I can offer you is my professional opinion, and my opinion is that he has the resilience to progress from training to active service.' Her reverse psychology was subtle but effective as Palmer's expression softened.

'Fine,' he muttered. 'But any fuck-ups and you'll be first in the firing line.' Grace swallowed hard at the level of accountability being pushed her way. *He's the bloody Head of SOU*, she thought, *he should be responsible for this one!* She straightened up, looked her superior square in the eye and took ownership of her decision.

'Right then,' said Palmer, 'you're dismissed for now. I'll meet with you tomorrow.'

Palmer ogled Grace Quickfall's slender outline as she disappeared along the corridor. He waited until she was out of sight before he pulled out his sleek iPhone and scrolled through the address book for a familiar name.

The phone rang five times before being answered.

'Yeah, good, and you?' he said in response to the voice on the other end of the line. 'Listen, I need to know I can rely on you if something I'm working on goes tits-up.' He listened while the voice offered the reassurance he was looking for. 'It's big,' he said. 'It could be my ticket to the top but if it goes bad I need you to make it disappear like piss in the rain. Can I count on you old friend?' Again he was reassured. The voice asked questions but Palmer was reluctant to give much away.

'We are fighting a secret war with most of the world and we can't even wipe our own arses overseas without specific authorisation from the foreign secretary. I can't be waiting around all day for some shit-for-brains minister to make a decision on whether or not we can call for the SAS to come out and play. We need someone who doesn't exist, who does whatever we want, whenever we want without being bound by UK Law.' His voice was becoming louder and his tone more exasperated. With his rant over he uttered a brief goodbye in to the phone and then killed the call. With the iPhone still warm in his hand he made a second call.

'You can collect him now and escort him back to the training quarters.' Palmer ended the call, slipped the phone back in to the inside pocket of his jacket, and made his way above ground for a mixture of fresh air and nicotine.

The reverberations created by Palmer's outburst had been minimal as they reached the outer wall of the interview room. Adam had his hands cupped against the wall to create a funnel against which he pressed the left side of his jaw bone. The cone shape formed by his hands drew in the vibrations of air from the wall and channelled them to his mandible. The tiny movements of gas and solid particles transmitted the vibrations to the small bones of his inner ear and as they thumped on his ear drum they beat out a rhythm for his brain to interpret. The conversation between the mystery man and Quickfall had been brief but Adam had understood the gist of it. He needed to prove himself. Adam couldn't recall a time before his accident, the one that he had reportedly suffered in the line of duty, but he was certain of one thing in his constitution; he never, ever, failed at anything. He would get on active service and fulfil his duties, and he would do so at any cost.

*

The digital display flicked to 05:00 and the melody of the alarm began to slowly ramp up in volume. Adam's bed was neatly made and the building volume of the alarm was now echoing around his empty cell-like quarters.

'For Christ's sake, where is he?' spat Richard Palmer as he paced the mezzanine above the killing room.

Dr Quickfall took a nervous glance at her slim Armani watch and noted that it was now 06:08. Their multi-million pound killing machine was now eight minutes behind schedule. She also noted that her hands were shaking a little. She intensely disliked the bastard stood over her and deeply resented the way he made her feel. Quickfall stole a second glance at her watch and hoped that Adam would turn up any moment and demonstrate how good at killing he was with a bullet to Palmer's swollen head. Instead, Adam was now nine minutes late.

'I hope he hasn't gone AWOL,' growled Palmer. Quickfall adopted her standard rational approach to the situation.

'I shouldn't think so Sir. He hasn't missed a single session in the last six months, I can't see any reason why he would start now. He's been totally focused on active duty for the last month, he wouldn't jeopardise that.' Her words hadn't registered with the Head of SOU who now looked like a cardiac arrest waiting to happen. It crossed Quickfall's mind that such an event might be a silver lining in an otherwise thundery storm cloud. Another two minutes of pacing and cursing passed before the limits of Palmer's patience had been exceeded.

'Get me an armed security team down here now. He's finished!'

'Yes Sir,' replied Quickfall. A trace of reluctance tainted her response. 'Right away.'

Brad Hargreaves strode down the concrete lined corridor, his pace quickening once he had finished buttoning his shirt and throwing on his suit jacket. He had a rugby player's build and a face to match following his long-service as a prop.

'Morning Brad, what's the score?' said a voice to his left.

'Morning Si. I'll brief you when we've assembled at the armoury but in short it's in-house and it's a single target'. Si Walker was a seasoned MI6 officer but like the rest of the team being raised from their slumber his role rarely included Office security.

'Must be serious to need us instead of internal security. Who called it?' asked Si, who looked as equally well turned-out as Hargreaves given that they had been woken only five minutes earlier.

'Palmer,' said Hargreaves, his tone giving nothing away.

'Jesus,' replied Si, 'someone must have a death wish to upset that nasty bastard!'

Before the pair of them could crack out a few funnies about the SOU Director they reached the armoury of the training facility, located two floors underground along with the facility's indoor firing range.

'Good morning chaps, thank you for assembling quickly,' started Hargreaves, who had been designated Team Leader. Marc Sanders, Phil Henderson, and Daniel Hills were all waiting in anticipation of the brief. All of them were decent men, and highly experienced field operatives. They had been resident at the training facility on a weapons course and were confident about putting their new skills to the test if required.

Hargreaves continued, 'our target is a fellow officer who is believed to still be on the premises. He failed to report for a training session 20 minutes ago and Richard Palmer, Director of SOU, believes the man to be a potential threat to the Office. The target's name is

Adam Newman.'

Trevor Collins was the armourer on duty; an ex-British Army Staff Sergeant that knew his way expertly around every weapon held at the training facility but also made it his business to know everything happening on his range. It was for that reason he was listening in to the brief being given by Hargreaves whilst stood only a few meters away waiting to issue the men with their handguns. All officers had called ahead to make ready their requests, which included two older but highly reliable Browning Hi Power pistols and three Sig Sauer P226 9mm for the rest of the team following their recent training on the firearm.

'You won't need to look far,' interrupted Collins, 'he's on the range and has been for most of the night.'

Adam studied the grouping of his last round of fire. He had emptied the magazine of the Sig Sauer P226 from 75 metres away but now, stood close to the target, he could see clearly the five-inch group created by all 15 rounds in the centre of the target's chest. He had achieved similar results that morning with the Browning HP and the Sig Sauer P230 between a distance of 60 and 70 meters, whilst getting an even tighter group with the Walther P99. But he liked the feel of the P226 and could see why it was being used by both the British SAS and the SBS. It had been a long night of practice and now Adam could sense that the opportunity to prove himself was upon him. The thrill of the fight pushed his fatiguing nervous system back in to overdrive. He was more than ready to validate his readiness for active service.

There were three rings on the black iPhone before the call was answered.

'Yes?' said Palmer, noting the smooth feel of the aluminium case in his roughened hand. Dr Quickfall was still by his side and was anxious to know the outcome of six months' worth of work. She was using all of her training to read his reaction to the call but Palmer hadn't gotten to his position in MI6 without developing an expert poker face.

'I'll be there in less than five minutes. Do not approach him until I get there. And if he engages you or tries to escape then use whatever force necessary to stop him,' and with that Palmer killed the line.

'Have they located him?' enquired Quickfall with a feigned nonchalance. The Director flashed her a smug grin.

'Yes. Yes they have. And it could prove to be some showdown. I'm going to the indoor range but when we've finished there you and I will need to discuss your situation.' She suddenly felt exposed and vulnerable and her face flushed with a mixture of anxiety and anger.

'Of course Sir. What specifically will we be discussing and is there anything I can prepare for it?' she asked.

'Dr Quickfall, only you and I know what became of Alex Black and I must be sure that all loose ends are tied up if this gets messy.' He could see she was uncomfortable. 'It may sound like I'm threatening you but really I'm not,' he said. The fact that he needed to say it meant that he clearly was threatening her and she got the message loud and clear. She watched him while he turned and strode away, only releasing her breath when he was finally out of sight. *Bastard*, she thought. Grace Quickfall was beginning to wish she had never been recruited to Project ADAM.

The armed security team stood in the air-locked corridor that sound-proofed the range and waited for Adam to discharge the magazine in the Sig Sauer P226 that was cradled in his right hand.

'Did he just do what I think he just did?' asked Hills, himself a highly proficient marksman.

'Yeah,' replied Walker in astonishment, 'all 15 shots in the centre of the chest and he's got to be 70 meters away.'

'I didn't realise the effective range extended that far,' added Henderson who had just recently been acquainted with the Sig P226. There was an edginess amongst the quintet and a few of the men shot nervous glances at one another. Marc Sanders, known to his friends as 'Colonel', because of a fried chicken restaurant chain rather than any previous military rank, started to question his leader about the nature of their task. Hills was now looking equally concerned as the pre-fight seed of doubt began to germinate in his mind.

'Listen-up,' snapped Hargreaves, 'what's possible is that five highly skilled operatives are about to go on to that range and secure a single target who has just spent a full magazine and is now unarmed. Is that understood?' The response was unanimous as the remaining four men kicked in to battle mode, their default setting following thousands of hours of specialised training.

Hargreaves' tone was firm and assertive; 'Adam Newman, place your weapon on the ground and come with us.' Adam looked up to acknowledge the five men but he had noted their presence and intent from the moment they had stepped out of the air-lock. Brad was cradling the Browning Hi Power in his right hand, which was hanging by his right hip. Although Hargreaves was a quarter turned to Adam in an attempt to conceal the weapon, Adam had recognised that the safety catch was still on. He had also noted that the lead figure was the heaviest of the bunch and was at least 16 stone of fatty muscle, giving him a 3 stone weight advantage over Adam. The other guys looked to range from 12 to 14 stone, mostly athletic, and all carrying holstered pistols under their suit jackets.

'For what purpose?' asked Adam. He could see that his use of a neutral tone had momentarily deflated the team leader's follow-up command.

'We have orders to escort you immediately to a secure room. Now slowly place your weapon on the ground and move away from it.' If he was nervous it didn't show and Adam appreciated the fact that they had sent an experienced team to deal with him.

By now the security team had stopped six feet from Adam and had formed an arc which penned him in to the back of the firing range.

'Who gave you that order?' asked Adam, buying himself time and also keen to know who was pulling the strings.

'Put down your weapon,' reiterated Hargreaves, his

voice becoming louder and stronger. Adam took a step forward, and then another. Hargreaves raised his pistol and levelled it at Adam's chest.

'Drop it,' he commanded.

Adam took one step more and was now one foot away from the muzzle of the loaded firearm. At this distance a round would hit him in under one thousandth of a second after discharge but the fact that Hargreaves had not removed the safety was in Adam's favour. His forward movement had also caused the team's arc to close, meaning that the men where now in each other's line of fire. Adam knew that their ability to think clearly was being hijacked by the adrenaline surging through their bodies.

'Who sent you?' he persisted. He could sense that the other men where reaching for their side-arms. His action was immediate and decisive.

If Palmer was surprised by what he was witnessing on the CCTV monitor in the armoury then he did not show it. As he stood alone looking up at the small coloured display a smirk contorted his thin dry lips.

Adam threw his empty pistol sideways with such force that Hills collapsed the instant it struck his face. Within a fraction of a second Adam crashed forward into Hargreaves, the top of his head colliding with the team leader's nose. Hargreaves tried to resist the lunge but Adam had hoped he would and used the man's forward momentum to drive him up and over his shoulder before his 16 stone came crashing down on Si Walker. Adam was levered round by the force of the falling opponent and as he spun he launched a rapid fist strike to 'Colonel' Sander's windpipe, causing him to crumple in a flaccid heap. Henderson drew his Sig pistol, which felt natural in his hand given the recent training on the weapon. By the time the Sig had been levelled Adam had side-stepped his opponent's outstretched arm rendering the readied firearm useless. A hard fist strike to the outside of Henderson's upper arm caused an explosion of tingling and hurt to radiate down to the man's hand. His grip on the pistol instantly loosened. Before the falling pistol had hit the ground Adam followed up the attack with a sharp open hand strike to the corner of Henderson's jaw causing his head to swivel round. Adam swung his other arm low and grabbed the falling weapon. In the same moment Hargreaves jumped to his feet and turned to face Adam. The Sig stopped dead between Brad Hargreaves' eyes, Adam's hand steady, and his expression promising every intention of using the pistol. Hargreaves closed his eyes in anticipation of the bullet burrowing deep into his head. The noise echoed in his ears and it took what seemed like an age for Hargreaves to recognise the voice from his earpiece.

'Stand down man,' urged the voice. From his remote viewing position Palmer had seen all he needed to and was ordering his men to back off before someone got seriously hurt.

Hargreaves opened his eyes as he backed slowly away from the scene of devastation. His team were in ruins. Every one of his men had been incapacitated sufficiently for them not to be able to fight back.

'Tell him I'm ready,' said Adam with fire in his voice.

He was breathing quietly and keeping the pistol trained on the heavy rugby man, who looked like he'd just been raked over by the entire All Black squad. Hargreaves nodded to show that he had received the message.

Back in the armoury Palmer nodded also as the same words played out of the CCTV monitor.

'You'll do for now, Adam.'

# FOUR

The four-tonner military wagon seemed to hit every bump in the road on the long drive from Hereford to the Brecon Beacons. Each jolt forced a moan from any one of the men who were cocooned in their sleeping bags, conserving every ounce of their strength for the test that lay ahead. Adam sat alone, away from the other men, their subdued conversations fading into the engine noise. The wind blew through the truck as if there was nothing separating them from the bitterness of winter, forcing Adam to blow into his hands and rub them together to revive his circulation. Though he sat in silence, his mind was awash with conversation. He had fully expected the usual debrief following his actions back at the training facility. The content of the debriefing, however, still rung in his ears.

'Do you realise you could have killed those men?' was how Dr Quickfall had started the session back in their usual box room.

'Yes,' he replied dryly, 'I could have easily killed them.' It had not been arrogant of him to say so; in his opinion he was stating the obvious. She had not looked impressed with his answer. Adam felt obliged to defend his position on the matter.

'Would you rather I had surrendered,' he had

continued, noticing a slight reaction from the doctor. 'Is that what you've been training me for?' He could tell that she was choosing her words carefully and had guessed the man behind the mirror would be paying attention to the language she used. Grace could almost feel Palmer's breath on her neck, seeping through the mirrored window. But she was also struggling with her own thoughts and feelings on the situation.

'What I mean is, despite your skills, you have been given...,' she paused momentarily, 'certain attributes; physical characteristics.' She looked flustered and was scrambling at words that might explain herself yet not give away too much of the top secret information that her been bestowed to her. Adam had leaned in, his curiosity getting the better of him. He gave a slight nod, encouraging the doctor to continue. Grace was deep in thought and although she was looking right at him she didn't see his gesture. Keen to hear what she meant he brushed the back of his fingers against her slender arm as it lay out across the table that separated them. Her heart fluttered and missed a beat. She cleared her throat, and her mind.

'Following your accident, you were badly injured. You know this already from your file. What we haven't yet had the... opportunity...to tell you is that parts of you were reconstructed; augmented even,' Quickfall said. Adam grinned believing her to be playing her own joke on him at last, and in response he frowned and gestured to the space between the tops of his thighs.

'Oh, no. No,' spluttered Quickfall as her face flushed

with colour before composing herself to continue. 'Please Adam, be serious for one moment. What I mean, specifically, is that the bones of your right arm, leg and chest wall were completely shattered in places and we used high-technology materials in their place. Although you have not yet had cause to use it, you have phenomenal strength in those limbs, which could, as I said, have killed those men instantly.'

Adam recalled how he had shifted back in his chair trying to formulate the numerous questions he wanted answers to. His first question was not what Grace Quickfall had expected.

'What happened to me,' he asked, 'in the accident?' She hesitated and waited for an instruction to come down the wire from behind the mirror. To her surprise there was no answer from beyond the room. Was Palmer testing her, or did the question leave him equally lost for words?

Quickfall's mind was whirling, partly because in all honesty she did not know the whole truth.

'I'm sorry Adam, that information is now regarded as classified and if you are unable to recall the events then we are not at liberty to discuss them.' It was a good recovery on her part. She had not lied to him and he could tell that much. Then the next words fell from her before she could check herself.

'Your body has endured so much trauma and pain, it is incredible that you have survived. Not only have you survived it but you have thrived on it and you have met every expectation we had of you.' Quickfall struggled to conceal her embarrassment when she realised what she had mindlessly blurted out. She blushed for the second time.

In the background Adam could feel the wagon beginning to slow as his mind replayed the last of the conversation.

'Adam, were you in control during the confrontation?' she had asked. He had leaned forward again, emphasising the point with his direct body language. There was almost skin contact again between his hand and her bare arm.

'I'm always in control,' he said. 'If I kill someone it's because I mean to, and if I don't kill them then that was my intention. I never intended to kill those officers. I was making a point. I'm ready for active duty. Let me get out there.' Quickfall met his eyes and gave a reassuring smile.

'Yes, you are ready Adam,' she had acknowledged. 'There's one last test, but I have every confidence you will pass. Good luck.'

\*

The still waters of the Talybont Reservoir lay underneath a thin blanket of mist, making it look eerie and mysterious, reflecting the sense of unknown amongst the men. A bitterness lingered in the air and all around the thirty Special Forces candidates a cloud of fog surrounded them, created by their own breath. Each one of them had a look of absolute seriousness, keeping speech to one another specifically about the task at hand as they prepared for the long and treacherous march through the Brecon Beacons.

Adam stood alone checking that every piece of his kit was in order, doing it in his usual disciplined rhythm. His Bergen rucksack was tightened at the straps so they cut under his arms and his waist strap was secured firmly around his front. Every single one of the numerous adjustments you could make to the rucksack had been done, making the fifty-five pound bag as compact as possible. In his arms was his rifle, a C8 Diemaco Carbine, a standard issue in the Special Forces. He recognised every feature of the rifle from his time at the training facility and like most weapons he had handled he felt confident in using it to its fullest potential. He reacquainted himself with its balance and feel, judging how best to cradle it over the 40-mile route march that lay ahead.

Adam surveyed the men around him, all of which were Selection candidates for British Special Forces. Some men looked more prepared than others. A few already had defeat on their minds and it showed in their faces. An undercurrent of apprehension simmered below the buzz but no one wanted to be the first to verbalise it. Despite this the general mood amongst the thirty potential SAS and SBS men was one of excitement. Some of the guys looked overly keen to walk out in to the freezing January night. For others the weather was clearly playing on their mind as they looked to the clear night sky for a sign of things to come. The temperature was already at a chilling two degrees Celsius and with the lack of cloud above them it was only going to get colder before the inevitable storm hit. A slight breeze flew around the men, biting into their skin and showing no sympathy for their endeavours. Tonight, the bitter winter would end the dreams of many of the men stood before Adam. He was determined not to give in to the Long Drag.

The noise fell to low-level chatter as many of the guys turned their attention inward in quiet contemplation. Adam was also staring into the distance, not for an external sign to put his faith in, or for any sort of weather forecast. The scene of rolling green felt strangely familiar to him. He felt a sense of peace and belonging around this landscape and the idea of testing himself on this terrain excited a part of him.

A voice stowed into his thoughts. 'Are you Regiment?' Adam looked down at the fit-looking soldier in front of him. The man was about five feet ten inches with a gritstone expression. He looked perfect Special Forces material. From the additional kit he was wearing Adam could tell instantly that the man was no stranger to outdoor pursuits. He wasn't sure where he knew it from but he recognised the Keela branded jacket being sported by the squaddie, although he had never seen it in the multi-terrain pattern before.

'No, I'm not Regiment,' he replied. Adam extended his right hand and briefly introduced himself. 'I'm being tested on the Drag with you guys tonight.'

'Johnny Clark,' replied the man as he accepted Adam's handshake. Adam was too focused to make small-talk and Johnny soon got the hint after his attempts at conversation were frozen out by a cold shoulder and the winter night. The two men wished each other luck and Johnny melted back in to the huddle.

'I think he's a bit nervous,' said a voice off to Adam's right, 'but Johnny's a good lad, and a good soldier. He'll skip over these hills like a mountain goat.' A second man now stood beside Adam. Slightly shorter in height at six feet tall, the newcomer was of a similar structure and although his battle hardened features denied it, he was seven years younger.

'What's your name?' asked the man.

Adam replied reluctantly.

'I'm Tom Austin,' said the man without waiting for an invitation, 'Second Battalion Parachute Regiment.' His handshake was firm and reassuring and Adam found himself receptive to his new comrade. Austin looked every bit the professional soldier. His kit was moulded to his body like it was tailor-made and a thick dark beard gave the appearance of a Special Forces veteran. He scratched at the coarse blanket of facial hair.

'This should keep me warm out there tonight,' he said with smiling grey-blue eyes. Adam acknowledged him with a nod.

'Looks like it could be rough. Be careful out there.' Both men used the opportunity to study the night sky and the looming storm clouds, and as they did so a comfortable silence fell between them.

A loud voice immediately in front of them broke their reverie.

'Who is that?' asked Adam flicking his gaze in the direction of the voice. Austin rolled his eyes.

'Don't get me started on that guy,' he said. But the temptation was too great. 'That's Gaz Roberts. I had to put up with his bullshit in the wagon on the ride over here. Claims he sniped a few kills in Iraq, but I don't believe a word of it. He can't even get his gear right for a night like this. What a tosser,' ranted Austin. 'If he doesn't end up freezing to death tonight I'll be surprised.' He let out a sigh of disapproval. The corner of Adam's mouth had folded upwards in a boyish grin.

'Friend of yours then?'

Austin laughed at his own seriousness. He looked like he was about to have another go at the gob-shite when a different voice sounded out above all others.

'Right then gents, gather round.' It was a member of the elite forces Directing Staff, or DS, readying for the final brief.

'This is it,' whispered Austin.

'Good luck,' said Adam initiating a final handshake.

'You too.'

The thirty-one men stood in a large cluster next to the body of still-water and simmered to a cold silence. For just a moment, the only sound was that of the wind-formed ripples of the reservoir lapping against the banks. The men looked around at each other, knowing that 'The Long Drag' was about to begin; the nerves beginning to burrow into their stomachs.

'Welcome to Endurance,' continued the chief instructor. 'The weather is expected to be grim, so when it comes in hard please try not to die out there. If you do die, then you've failed selection.' A gentle laugh rolled through the group. 'But it also means we have to mobilise the standby squadron to drag your frozen corpse off the hills. So it's a lose-lose situation.' He let the importance of his warning sink in allowing any man with less than full commitment to back out now. There were no takers for a hot bath and an early night.

'Okay, it's twenty-three hundred hours; best of luck and we'll see you all back here in twenty hours!'

As the directing staff called out each of the thirty-one names the men filed out into the freezing January night. Gaz Roberts shoved past Adam within the first few minutes, confirming his first impressions of the man as he raced off in pursuit of his next target. The ground crunched underfoot and the rhythm of heavy footsteps and laboured breathing could be heard through the blackness. Adam could feel his skin beginning to leak and the wetness that formed at the nape of his neck started to trickle down his back, slowly at first and then in torrents. After a few hours of testing terrain, the mixture of moisture and friction from the weighted Bergen soon became painful and Adam could feel his skin breaking down under the repetitive trauma. His legs felt heavy and the lactic acid that accumulated in his thighs was fierce. He wondered to himself why they were putting him through this without any real training and queried whether they were actually testing the man or the machinery they had used to rebuild him. Either way it didn't matter. Adam was not a man to give up and he had no intention of failing his final test. As he took in a lung-full of the fresh Welsh air he could feel his second wind kicking in. Despite his lack of training on the hills Adam's body seemed to remember this sort of physical punishment. A faint smile cracked across his wind-beaten face.

By the time they reached a route feature called Torpontu the men were spread across the landscape like the beads of a pearl necklace, glistening under the flickers of moonlight. The wind had dropped again and there was a stillness in the air, as if it were holding its breath in anticipation of things to come. It didn't take long before the men reached the first checkpoint, an outdoor activity centre called The Storey Arms. So far the pace and the terrain had been manageable but as Adam disappeared back into the darkness he felt a strong gust of icy wind from the East and he knew that things were about to get a lot worse.

Adam was tabbing hard to maintain an average pace of just under four kilometres per hour and had overtaken about ten men, the first of which had been Gaz Roberts. He had looked in a sorry state as they ascended Jacob's Ladder on the approach to Pen-Y-Fan. The climb was brutal and Adam wondered whether Roberts would drop off the shear edge of the ridge line as he staggered about, wiping copious amounts of snot from his contorted face. Adam had not been able to recce the route in person but had researched the terrain before arriving at Sterling Lines, Hereford. It was proving to be far tougher than he had imagined but he told himself it was a test of his will power, and that was a part of him that couldn't be broken.

The path ahead was narrow and cut out of stone and if it were not for it being shaped into a sort of staircase it would have been incredibly slippery and almost impossible to climb. As it was, the rain had made the steps slick and occasionally he would feel a foot slide out from beneath him. This was one place he wouldn't want to slip too far. On each side of him there was a sharp drop which became fatal on the approach to the summit. The climb rose away and Adam's chest jerked up and down as he gasped to expel the stale air from his lungs and replace it with oxygen-rich fresh air. The Bergen straps cut into him and the combination of the heavy constrictive load and steep incline made it almost impossible for him to breathe.

The mist they had seen at the reservoir a few hours prior had followed them and hugged itself around the hill, reducing visibility to only a few meters. The stars which had dotted the sky before were hidden behind the advancing veil and looked as if the heavens themselves were retreating from the impending doom. After another hour of hard tabbing, Adam could no longer hear his own panting over the wintery wind that whistled in his ears. He looked up from the hypnotic rhythm of his marching feet and was surprised to see that he had caught up to Johnny Clark, the so-called mountain goat.

'Alright mate?' asked Johnny as Adam approached him. He looked as fresh as a daisy.

'Fine,' replied Adam between breaths. 'Are you?'

'Yeah mate. I'm feeling good but I'm just making a few kit changes and getting some food and drink in before this weather really hits. When it comes in, the last thing you'll want to do is stop and that's when the low blood sugars and dehydration will cause you to make silly mistakes and lose time.' Adam took the advice and seized the opportunity to refuel himself. He was soaked with sweat and realised that he was probably warm enough to buffer the incoming cold snap. He pressed on, leaving Johnny to make his own final preparations. The four guys that had passed Adam during his brief stop had disappeared into the mist, giving him an incentive of something to chase. He left Johnny Clark enveloped in a swirl of fog, enjoying the last mouthful of a thick chocolate bar. Johnny could hear the violent grunting of Gaz Roberts from beyond the blanket of darkness but he didn't see his approach until the very last second.

The miles passed slowly but the time seemed to slip away from Adam like grains of sand through his fingers. He knew he had to eat up the miles much quicker or he was in danger of failing the Selection test. The pain in his shoulders was becoming unbearable and whichever way he writhed under the straps of his Bergen he could not escape the relentless pressure on the welts forming on his skin.

He had been pleased to reach the 'Turn-Around-Point' but the weather had deteriorated and the thought of covering the same terrain again did not appeal to him. He buried the negative thoughts deep inside of him and forged ahead in pursuit of the finish. *One foot at a time*, he told himself. *Mile by mile.* The rain had turned to a combination of hail and snow which came so thickly that it pushed him around the hillside. Adam used up precious energy to focus more on his balance and footing. Fatigue and the icy blizzard were forcing his eyelids shut and he struggled to see the sharp drops on either side of him. He was physically depleted but his mind would not allow him to give up. Something inside refused to stop and as long he was making the checkpoints in time, he was still in the game.

The sodden earth beneath his boots was slippery and Adam had already stumbled on several sections of lumpy ground. If he had been alert to the warning signs he would have anticipated what was to follow. As he descended a small peak Adam began to pick up speed but his tabbing was getting sloppy and his right foot snagged on a mound of grass. He immediately began to steady his forward momentum but his over-reaching right leg landed on a polished slab of exposed wet rock. He stumbled further to his right and the Bergen load on his back levered him over his ankle and over the drop of the ridge line. With a blind instinct he reacted with flailing arms and he felt an exposed root against his fingertips. Reflexively he clamped his right hand around the vegetation and waited helplessly for his body to plummet. The snag came quickly and his body slammed against the cliff edge, wrenching sharply at his right shoulder. He dangled over a murky abyss. A weaker arm would have buckled under the falling body weight and additional Bergen load but Adam hung tight. His heart raced from the shock of being violently and suddenly plucked from his ambulant reverie. Without so much as a creak one end of the root gave out and Adam fell a foot or more, the contents of his stomach following a split second later. The root and his grip held steady and he hung there for what seemed like forever.

'Grab my hand,' commanded a voice from above, barely audible above the whipping wind. Tom Austin was laid prone on the ridge above, his arm outstretched towards Adam. Adam launched himself upwards and swung his free left arm towards Tom. Their fingertips made the faintest contact but failed to form any sort of grip of each other. Adam slumped again under his own weight and a chunk of loose earth came away from cliff edge and showered him in debris. The cold and moisture worked into Adam's clenched fist and softened his grip on the root. For a second he contemplated the death that waited for him below but in his mind he dreaded the failure more than the loss of life. The directing staff's words echoed in his ears. Another shout from above refocused Adam to the peril and pain he was experiencing.

'Come on man, you can do it!' Adam looked upwards to see Tom's splayed fingers searching around in the blackness. He felt another wave of adrenaline surge through him, igniting an explosion of neural activity in his brain and spinal cord. Thousands of pulses were delivered to the muscles in his right arm in rapid succession causing an immense pull of muscle against a mechanically enhanced skeleton. With one almighty heave Adam thrust himself upwards through the darkness in search of Austin's secure grip.

Both men were exhausted as they tabbed on through the night, neither man mentioning the fall. The silence continued as they reached the infamous 'VW' valley, so called for its popularity as a point for voluntary withdrawal. Adam's legs burned and he frequently tripped on the numerous tufts of elephant grass. By now Tom was suffering equally and cursed intermittently as he lost his footing on the boggy ground below him. The going was tough and time and energy were no longer on their side. All they could do was push on through the pain and fatigue, with nothing but determination and an unspoken camaraderie fuelling their engines.

Dawn was breaking tentatively over the east horizon and for the first time during their ordeal the two men were illuminated by the powerless winter sun. They were now able to take in each other's features and it was no surprise to see that both men wore the same pained expression as they trudged relentlessly over the god-forsaken terrain of the Brecon Beacons. In their own heads they set themselves small targets to strive for, the next peak, the stream in the distance, until finally Talybont reservoir came into view.

'Thank fuck,' muttered Austin through his matted beard. A wide grin cracked over Adam's face. The final check-point, and the knowledge of passing one of the world's toughest Special Forces selection tests lay before them after nearly 20 hours of physical torture. With the end in sight both men picked up the pace, which amounted to no more than a stiff hobble.

There was no great fanfare as they checked in at the finish. Their only reward was a well-earned sign of respect from the directing staff. Adam writhed under his Bergen as he struggled to separate the load from the drenched and damaged skin on his back. It was like trying to slip a straitjacket and when he finally freed himself the pain was like a giant sticking-plaster being ripped from his back. He dumped the load by one of the wagons and headed over to Tom who was cradling a steaming brew. They shook hands and congratulated each other on their achievement.

'There was no way I was getting binned today,' said Tom. 'I just had to keep going and knew it would end eventually.' Adam agreed. A moment of quiet fell between them.

'Thank you, again,' said Adam. 'I owe you one.' Tom looked embarrassed.

'No worries, mate,' he said. 'I hope you would have done the same for me.'

Adam gave a faint grin and turned to leave.

'You never did say what unit you were from,' said Tom inquisitively.

'I'm not military,' replied Adam, 'I'm with British Intelligence.' Tom's face formed an expression of surprise and interest.

'Really? I've got my eye on MI6 if I ever make it out of the Regiment alive. Perhaps we'll work together one day.' Adam didn't think that would be such a bad thing.

He reiterated his promise as he climbed in to the back of the four-tonner, 'I owe you one.'

As Adam's truck pulled away from the scene he saw a delirious and exhausted Roberts make the final checkpoint with minutes to spare. He instantly recognised the Keela multicam jacket. Across the bleak open ground the two men locked eyes.

Tom watched as his newest comrade departed on the back of the wagon, then he turned to a group of finishers stood nearby.

'Alright guys, well done,' he started. The group acknowledged him and briefly praised his efforts before returning to their conversation.

'Yeah bloody tragedy that, I can't believe it. He was a sound bloke and would have done well in the Regiment,' said one of the guys.

'What's going on lads?' asked Tom.

'Bloody hell Tommo, haven't you heard?! Johnny Clark's body was found on the hills. The poor bastard froze to death.'

# FIVE

The document read:

Project ADAM. Candidate One.

ADAM 1.0 to be given the operational identity of Adam Newman.

Biological age: 34. Estimated fitness age: 24.

Previous medical history: Nothing of note. No known allergies.

Blood group: Type O. Rhesus negative.

Pre-surgical status: Heavy trauma resulting in mild to moderate brain damage affecting the memory areas of the hippocampus. His brain injury was not regarded as life threatening.

Multiple fractures to the bony structures of the right upper and lower limbs. The right humerus bone was most affected and compromised the integrity of the right shoulder joint. The associated soft tissue trauma was serious but considered to be surgically repairable. The patient also suffered multiple rib fractures in the right chest wall, causing several flail segments and a right lung pneumothorax.

No severe facial injuries and no long lasting damage to the vertebral column or spinal cord. Blood loss was severe at the time of injury and it is thought that the cold temperature at the scene of the accident reduced cellular activity enough to prevent secondary cell death due to lack of oxygen delivery.

Post-surgical status: Synaptic circuitry diversions between the hippocampus and the prefrontal cortex using 'Neuronic' technology implantation. It is fully anticipated that such technology will prevent the recovery of long term memory due to neural plasticity. Similar technology was also integrated within the patient's limbic system to regulate emotional responses. It is expected that such regulation will limit excessive reactions such as fear, anger, and compassion thus regulating bodily responses in situations that would normally provoke such emotional responses.

Whilst undergoing the above surgical procedures a prototype 'neuro-net' device was also implanted. This is a self-contained database which artificially synapses with the patient's motor cortex area at the front of the brain. When the patient attempts to cognitively process any situation, his brain will search not only his memory but also the programmed memory of the neuro-net device. If the device is found to be lacking any of the necessary information it will automatically log the required information and download it via secure wireless internet connectivity at the next available opportunity. In this way the patient is capable of 'learning' vast quantities of new information by download.

Three days following the above procedures the patient recovered sufficiently and underwent reconstruction and augmentation of his musculoskeletal system. A novel magnesium based alloy was used which presently boasts the highest strength-to-weight ratio and is trialled here as a biomaterial. The unique properties of magnesium as an anti-inflammatory substance are expected to reduce injury and increase repair rates in surrounding soft tissues. The use of an alloy will give great strength and protection to the patient's right arm, leg, and chest wall. The integrated robotics are linked with the aforementioned surgery to the patient's brain in an attempt to increase control and force production of the limbs.

The surgery appeared to be successful and the candidate is healing well. There appears to be no early rejection of the augmentation or any adverse reaction to the substances involved.

\*

Quickfall handed the paper file back to Palmer who was sat behind his expansive desk, smoking a cigarette through a smug grin.

'So, doctor, there you have it. That is the man we

have created,' he said. Quickfall had gravitated to the tall windows along the wall of Palmer's office and found herself gazing out at nothing in particular. She took a deep breath and then exhaled, the warm air from her lungs fogging the glass, causing the River Thames to disappear momentarily from sight. Quickfall became acutely aware of the blemish imparted on the pristine glass. Turning to cover her tracks she found her stare locked in his.

'Sir, why have you shown me this? Why now?' she asked.

Palmer stubbed out the cigarette, wriggling it left to right until the embers died out beneath his thick and tarnished fingers. He stood from behind his desk and the rapid movement and rush of air down his windpipe triggered a barking cough. Keeping eye contact with Quickfall he walked towards her, passing numerous framed achievements that hung on the wall amongst photographs of Palmer with various high profile faces.

'Tell me … Grace,' started Palmer, 'do you truly believe he's ready for active duty?'

'Yes Sir, I do.' The use of her first name had caught her off guard but her answer was sincere. She hadn't been able to find a single fault in his conduct or abilities over the six months she had worked alongside Adam.

'Enough to stake your career on it?' he asked. Quickfall didn't know where this was going, or rather she didn't want to know where it was going.

'All of my reports have concluded the same thing now for several weeks; I believe he is ready.' Her answer was emphatic. 'Is there a specific concern you have?' she asked.

Palmer moved round the desk and stood alongside her at the window. He was far too close for Grace's comfort but she stood fast.

'You and I have created something very special here and I was looking for some reassurance that the finished product is up to scratch.'

'*We* didn't create anything,' fired Quickfall reflexively. 'You recruited me to this project to monitor his psychological state during the recovery and training period. That's all. What you just showed me in that document was nothing to do with me.' Her heart was thumping in her chest now. The notion that she could have created something so cruel and dangerous repulsed her. Then the penny dropped.

'You showed me that information to make me party to it, didn't you, Sir'

Palmer was wearing a smug expression. 'We're in this together doctor. I wanted to make sure you were fully committed to the cause.'

With each briefing and operation that she had played a part in, Palmer had drawn her deeper in to his world. Quickfall was now a slave to the project and not an employee of it. The thought of her predicament made her feel nauseous and a lump formed in her throat. Whatever this project was, it was something she wished she had never heard of.

Palmer pulled out his packet of Marlboro Golds and placed one of the sticks in his mouth. Lighting it up he inhaled the smoke, and after letting it sit on his chest for a few seconds he blew out the thick acrid cloud in

Quickfall's direction. The fumes caused her eyes to water, or at least that's what she told herself.

'Sir, are you aware that passive smoking can kill?' she asked.

'So can misplaced loyalty,' replied Palmer, who was lifting the cigarette to his mouth for another drag. He turned his back on his guest and stood by his desk again. 'Remember what you have read today Grace and think about it the next time you come into contact with Adam. We have created a killer and, if you are correct, it's time to put him to work. I hope your evaluation of him turns out to be accurate, for your sake.' He watched the ash fall from his cigarette and float towards the tray beneath it.

'You can leave now Grace,' he said, without bothering to look up at her. 'And next time, don't fog up my windows.'

*

The walk back to Kings Head Road gave her the space and time she needed to wrestle with her dilemma. There was a sharp wind that whipped around her and caused litter to dance between her feet. She was oblivious to the weather, engulfed in her thoughts and protected by a black cotton scarf and beige trench coat. The sound of her footsteps echoed against the Victorian buildings before ascending into the clear black sky. Every night she had this moment; a mixture of pitiful solitude and the pleasure of her own company. Opening the door to the converted Victorian town house Quickfall checked the shared entrance hall for mail before making her way up the stairs to her third floor flat. The usual soundtrack of her evenings emanated from the other flats. From the floor below came the daily argument between the young couple high on alcohol and jealousy, while the neighbouring flat pumped out nineties dance music into the small hours. She unlocked the door to her flat and was instantly greeted by the familiar scent of lilies, a flower she always kept in a vase on her kitchen table. It may have been surrounded by stormy waters but this was her island and when she closed the door to the outside world she could begin to unwind.

As she passed through the kitchen she fired up the DAB radio that was pre-tuned to BBC radio three. Modern music never had been her thing; she could never relate to the lyrics. She poured herself a generous glass of Châteauneuf-du-Pape and took a long sip of the red liquid as the frequency of Shostakovic's piano concerto calmed her brain waves. The alcohol stung the back of her throat but she felt instantly anaesthetised when it hit her bloodstream. The tremor in her right hand steadied with each gulp of wine until the glass was empty. Grace helped herself to another good measure before crossing her flat to the lounge area and slumping into her favourite possession, a well-worn deep leather chair. With her mind finally in cruise control she let her thoughts wonder as she reflected on the events of the day, and of the last few months. She had worked tirelessly through her undergraduate and doctorate studies to master the neurobiological basis of psychology, but she had never imagined her career would end up like this. When MI6, or specifically Richard Palmer, had recruited her for a 'ground-breaking' project she could not have imagined it would be to work with a brain-damaged assassin. The situation left her moral compass spinning wildly; she wanted out desperately but Palmer had her cornered. There was something else also stopping her from abandoning the project, something deeper and more personal. She could not escape the intrigue of fusing technology and biology in a human brain; and then there was the man himself. Grace Quickfall refused to let her mind roam in that direction.

Sitting curled-up in her chair, Grace was surrounded by memories of her former life. Special moments had been immortalised behind glass and were now suspended against the intense red paint that formed the feature wall of the lounge. The contrasting white frames enclosed younger and happier versions of herself, with friends or family, and even an old lover. Beaches, mountains and dinner parties formed the backdrop to those care-free times and as she studied the images from the comfort of her chair Quickfall felt sadness and loss. She drained the second glass of wine and the pain inside of her eased a little. Another glass would make it all go away she concluded. Walking back through to the kitchen she felt unsteady on her feet as the alcohol got to work on her nervous system. Having skipped lunch Quickfall felt the sudden knock of hunger in her stomach, which was also contributing to the fast-acting inebriation. The visceral response prompted her to make a start on dinner, which amounted to perforating a film of plastic that covered a Waitrose ready-meal, before setting it spinning in the microwave. In the meantime she filled her glass and enjoyed a liquid appetiser.

Having finished both the meal-for-one and the bottle of wine, Quickfall had made it into her pyjamas and was settling down with a peppermint tea and a pre-recorded episode of a popular numbers and letters gameshow. The familiar music that heralded the last few remaining seconds to solve the maths puzzle was suddenly drowned out by the shrill of her ringing phone. Quickfall hit the pause button on the gameshow and checked the phone display before answering.

'Hello darling, it's mum. How are you?' asked the older woman's voice. 'I know it's a little late but I haven't heard from you in a while. Your Father and I were beginning to worry.' Quickfall sobered instantly.

'Mum, hi! That's ok. It's good to hear from you. I'm sorry I haven't returned your last few messages. Busy with work – you know the routine,' replied the daughter. The older and wiser Mrs Quickfall reassured her daughter and the two of them made small talk for a few minutes.

'Dad's been busy with his golf darling. I think he's enjoying retirement too much. I'm busy running around after him as usual.' The two of them laughed. 'Dare I ask about work?' Grace's response was sharp and made it instantly clear that the topic was off-limits.

'Ask me another one,' she said. She regretted giving

the open invitation.

'Found a man yet, darling?' asked mum. Quickfall's eyes rolled skywards and her head slumped back into the soft leather chair. It was the same question every time, but this time she faltered for an answer. The silence prompted further questioning from mum.

'Grace, it sounds like you have something to tell me,' she continued.

'Err, no, not really. Just a work…colleague.' Quickfall Junior could feel herself colouring up.

'Darling come on, tell me more,' coaxed her mum. Grace stumbled and spluttered her way through the next few minutes until finally mum seemed satisfied with the level of detail. 'Well it sounds like trouble to me Grace,' came the verdict. 'If I were you I would leave well alone. Sounds like a married man to me with all of that mystery surrounding him.' The statement seemed so obvious and it was left hanging in the ether while Grace's mind wrestled with the possibility.

'Darling, are you still there?'

'Yes mum,' she said mindlessly just to appease the woman. 'I think you could be right.' She signed off on the conversation and still had the phone to her ear when the line went dead. *What if?* she asked herself. Her mother's stab-in-the-dark comment had torpedoed Grace Quickfall's fantasy.

# SIX

The mission brief had been clear and concise.

'This is a covert operation Adam,' started Quickfall, her tone deeply serious. 'Strictly "black bag". Do you understand?' Adam gave a curt nod. It was a simple enough statement and he thought she was over egging the whole thing. 'You will be flying a false flag on this one, and if you are captured or killed then I'm afraid the British Government will deny all knowledge of you.' *Nothing new there then*, he thought to himself. He flashed Grace his brightest smile, but today she seemed immune to it.

She continued, 'You will surreptitiously enter a military research facility belonging to one of our closest allies, gathering intelligence on some of their research activity, and destroying any technology that you can't take with you.' Resting on Quickfall's lap was a single side of A4 paper secured along its top edge to a clipboard. She glanced down and paraphrased a section of the brief that had been lined with a highlighter pen. The sentence glistened yellow-green. 'Our Intelligence colleagues believe that the testing carried out at the facility is being performed on human subjects, thought to be military personnel.' Adam didn't look phased by the information but the words resonated with

Quickfall.  The proof of such experimentation was sat looking right at her.

*

Adam pulled off Route 70 and from his vantage point he surveyed the US Air Force Base. The air was hot and dry, with the ambient temperature sitting steady at 27 °C. It was fairly typical for a summer day in Dayton, Ohio. Adam noted the sky, its cloudless expanse suggesting his mission wouldn't be hampered by the thunderstorms or light rains that tended to frequent the area. He glanced back at the wide-open croplands behind him before turning to face his target, homing-in through the Nikon binoculars. The research facility was approximately a ten-minute drive from the air base and Adam wanted to know what their mobilisation capabilities would be like if things didn't go to plan. Turning back to the car Adam kicked-up dust from the gravel patch beneath his feet. He reached into the boot of the blue Toyota Camry, a car like most others on the road and one that he had easily obtained for cash in a quick sale. Instead of the obvious night camo combat uniform that would normally lend itself to night-time clandestine operations, Adam took out a neatly pressed US Air Force Blues uniform. He planned to hide in plain sight, making the most obvious entry and exit of the facility as was possible.

The sun was beginning its descent over the distant horizon, the last of the scattered light casting a fading orange hue over everything in sight. Adam leant with his back against the car, staring at the ground but focusing on nothing before him. He had begun his usual internal retreat, thinking over every aspect of the operation, leaving no stone unturned and no piece of information unchecked.

'The US military are thought to be conducting research into the application of electrical currents to the head using a technique called transcranial direct-current stimulation, or tDCS for short,' Quickfall had said, sounding very authoritative on the subject. 'This type of non-invasive brain stimulation is still in an experimental stage but it has been found to cause positive brain changes in sick and healthy test subjects. This is something we believe the US Department of Defence has taken an interest in.'

'Like a shock therapy?' Adam had asked.

'Well, yes, sort of,' she had replied, clearly shifting into academic mode. 'These techniques were born out of treatments for depression or for stroke rehabilitation. It was discovered that tDCS could alter a person's response to a situation or stimulus by affecting the excitability of brain cells. Researchers then began to explore the potential benefits of tDCS in enhancing healthy brains.' Adam had been drawn in by her passion for the subject as she spoke excitedly about the research. He played with her for a while with the most technical questions he could think of, before enquiring about the technique's military application. At this point Quickfall clammed up, reminding Adam that he operated on a 'need-to-know' basis.

A cooling breeze whirled around Adam's feet and

deposited a thin film of dust over his highly polished black shoes. He refocused to the present. The light had all but disappeared whilst he'd been in his trance-like state and the fading sun felt less intense. Early evening birdsong carried over the warm Ohio air, alerting Adam to the danger of making any noise that would carry endlessly through the night. He raised the binoculars again for one last recce of the site. At this hour there was a skeleton crew of Airmen operating out of the facility. All he had to do now was get inside, take all the scientific data he could find, and get out. It all seemed simple enough.

Entering the facility had been easier than Adam had expected. His false credentials had been issued from the highest level, but Adam wasn't keen to flaunt them given that his homeland would deny all knowledge in a heartbeat. His final hurdle was the two young Airmen standing sentry on the approach to the laboratory. Adam had perfected the US Airforce salute, with its bladed hand and steep forearm, and executed it flawlessly in the direction of the two guards. His appearance, authority, and sheer audacity instantly drew the younger men to attention. He breezed past them without further acknowledgement. Three more steps to reach the key pad. Two more steps.

'Sir, may we see some ID?' said one of the men. He had a young face that looked like a once weekly shave could keep his stubble to military regulation length. The southern twang to his accent placed him from somewhere close to Louisiana, more Cajun than Creole.

'Son, I beg your pardon?' replied Adam in a subtle authentic accent that mirrored the young man's.

'May we see your ID, Sir?'

'What's your name?' asked Adam, his pulse barely rising. He was reluctant to start flashing a false identity around.

The Airman gulped hard. 'Lincoln, Sir. Tyler Lincoln,' replied the young man, who was now wishing he'd forsaken his duty in order to prevent the imminent shit-storm.

The second guard stepped forward slightly between the two men. He looked embarrassed on behalf of his mate.

'Sorry, Sir. Please proceed.'

'Thank you, son. You're just doing your job,' acknowledged Adam, before disappearing deep inside the research facility.

The Human Performance laboratory was equipped with exercise apparatus draped with high tech gadgetry for assessing physical and mental performance. Although Adam could visualise the physical exertion spent in a place like this there was little trace of blood, sweat or tears. The place was sterile and the unmistakable odour of bleach filled the air. For a brief moment he held a fleeting memory of a time spent in a university science laboratory. The image stopped him in his tracks and he allowed it to develop in his head before it petered out and then disappeared. The unsettling sense of Déjà vu came and went, displaced by the mission brief. *Get in, get out*, he reminded himself.

The lab was small and dimly lit. Everywhere was

emblazoned with the emblem of the US Defence Research Projects Agency (DRPA). Adam took his time and studied the equipment that filled the space, intrigued by the technology. His search was interrupted by a sudden movement in his peripheral vision, as a silhouetted figure arose from a swivel chair. The man's youthful face was illuminated by the strained glow of a near-by computer monitor. Adam had little time to respond to the surprise as their eyes locked on to each other's across the laboratory. The young man stood rooted to the spot, his spinal cord temporarily paralysed by a flood of fear chemicals. He wore civilian clothing and his shoulder-length hair and prickly chin confirmed to Adam that he was not a man of military discipline.

Adam kept his pistol concealed as he slowly approached the man. His hands were raised level with his broad chest, and his palms faced outwards in an open and non-threatening gesture. *Easy does it.* This would now have to be death by knife he concluded. Adam closed the space between the two of them and readied himself for a stealth kill. As he was about to make his move Adam caught a glimpse of the images showing on the man's computer screen and recognised the content as some kind of military flight simulation software. It looked like a platform for testing a pilot's response to various demands and situations. His curiosity got the better of him.

'Apologies if I startled you,' said Adam, making no attempt this time to hide his accent. The young scientist looked cautiously at Adam, who was dressed in the familiar US Air Force uniform.

'British?' he asked.

'Yes, that's correct. Special attachment,' replied Adam, 'on account of my work with brain stimulation.' The man never thought to ask why a Brit wouldn't be wearing his own national uniform and was clearly hooked on Adam's techie bait, which had seemed to pique his geekiness.

'It's late', said Adam, 'you'll need to leave shortly; unless it's something urgent you're working on?' The question hung momentarily before the trap sprang and the younger man began to stutter his first words, before quickly gathering momentum. He clearly didn't get asked much about what he did and he seemed almost excited to be given a chance to showcase his work.

'This task looks at decision making, but also tests motor skills.' He gestured toward the keyboard. 'You have to press the buttons quickly in a correct sequence. The candidates are then rated on their performance.' Adam was now close enough to slit the youth's throat. His right hand curled around the hilt of the stowed hunting knife. The blade silently left its sheath.

'What's the purpose?' asked Adam, suppressing his instinct to kill. The scientist's eyes lit-up again with excitement.

'We want to look at the transition of a task from conscious processing to unconscious processing, and whether we can accelerate this with…' The younger man paused.

'I appreciate your discretion,' said Adam with a warm smile. 'I understand if you'd rather not discuss your work now...' Reassured by Adam's confidence and openness, the man didn't hesitate in picking up where he had left off.

'Well, the results we get are amazing. By stimulating the prefrontal cortex whilst subjects undertake the task we can improve their performance by 300 per cent! We can create experts in these tasks in a fraction of the time.' Adam knew instantly that the application of this in a military environment would produce better pilots, marksmen, intelligence analysts, or any other trade, in next to no time.

'Impressive,' said Adam, swelling the man's pride and prompting continuation.

'And attention too; we can maintain high levels of attention in demanding tasks lasting over 40 minutes. By stimulating the prefrontal cortex areas responsible for attention we've been able to prevent the usual decline seen with prolonged cognitive tasks. All of this by regulating the electrical activity which is the natural way in which neurones of the brain communicate with each other. That's pretty cool.'

Adam had to agree that the application of such a basic technology gave impressive results in human function. But there was something that didn't make sense.

'Are the subjects in pain during the brain stimulation,' he asked.

'No way, man,' replied the scientist without hesitation. 'The electrical activity generates no more than a mild sensation.'

'Show me what's on your computer screen,' asked

Adam, encouraging the younger man to turn away from him momentarily. *You weren't supposed to be here tonight*, thought Adam as he closed on his target. With the man's attention fixed on his simulation game Adam changed tack and took out a syringe from his jacket pocket. He swiftly punctured the skin at the base of the man's neck with the needle and squeezed the contents of the syringe deep into his bloodstream. The synthetic opioid drug Etorphine mixed with the blood coursing through the carotid arteries on-route to the scientist's brain. Adam forced the man down into the desk chair and covered his mouth with a strong right hand. He looked straight in to the man's eyes for the full minute it took for the sedative to take effect on its victim. The younger man slipped from life to a catatonic death. To slit his throat would have left an obvious sign of intrusion and attack. This way, Adam would make the man and his research disappear, suggesting he had perhaps defected and sold his secrets to a rival. The US military research centre might then be forced to rethink its strategy and delay their ongoing work for fear of further security breaches. Adam was pleased with his method.

Leaving the body slumped in its chair Adam moved to a nearby video recording device. He tapped at a few buttons to bring the device to life. Adam watched the crisp digital video footage of a young soldier being readied for a medical procedure. The subject looked to be in his early twenties and seemed relaxed. Adhesive tape held a non-stimulating electrode to the man's left upper arm while a second electrode was being secured to the temple of his head. Adam recognised the hands extending from white lab coat cuffs as those belonging to the recently deceased man by his side. If Adam felt any remorse then he didn't show it. Instead he watched on as the sponge encased electrodes leaked a colourless fluid down the soldier's cheek. Adam guessed the sponges where soaked in salt water to increase electrical conduction. The wires terminated at a 9 volt battery, which was attended by the familiar medical technician. The young soldier didn't seem phased by what might happen next. He twitched mildly as the battery was fully connected. Adam observed the footage with interest as the man was exposed to progressively higher electrical currents. From what Adam could make out the maximum current never exceeded two milliamps and the subject appeared to be comfortable and pain-free. Once the medical attendant seemed happy with the procedure he set the soldier down to a computer-based task, similar to the one seen by Adam.

Adam watched on intrigued, as tens of scenes appeared on the screen showing images based on Middle East urban environments. Shelled and derelict apartment buildings lined crude and cratered desert roads. The soldier responded to the basic computer graphics whenever he identified well-hidden threats within the software. The soldier's observations and reaction times were impressive. Adam watched for several minutes as the test-subject remained focused and scored perfectly on the task. Not once did he appear to experience any adverse effects from the electric treatment.

Unbeknown to Adam the soldier was receiving the low-level direct current to his inferior frontal cortex; the region of the brain thought to be responsible for threat detection. Not only was the treatment increasing his response to threat but it was halving his learning time. This sort of practice would clearly yield a military advantage, by enhancing the cognitive functioning of every soldier, sailor and airman at the country's disposal. Adam understood the outcome clearly. Mistakes minimised, accuracy accentuated, and every man and woman in a combat environment displaying calm and control. The cumulative effect of such marginal gains would lead to the world's most effective and deadly military force.

Adam worked quickly gathering the paper documents around the laboratory and downloading what he could via the young scientist's login. The dead man's thumb print came in handy for overcoming some of the electronic security. Adam noted with great interest the schematics for integrating a wireless cap in to the helmets used by combat soldiers. The accompanying documents highlighted the potential of the technology to remotely monitor brain wave activity whilst delivering tailor-made electrical stimulation via tDCS electrodes. It seemed the technology had also been integrated into the helmets used by fighter-pilots. *Mind control* thought Adam to himself, *but who wouldn't want to make themselves better in combat given the choice?*

\*

Back in his usual box, Adam looked across the empty table at Grace Quickfall as she finished reading the operation report. He could see she was troubled.

'Could this produce permanent change in behaviour,' asked Adam curiously.

'That's classified,' snapped Quickfall. In truth she didn't know, and she didn't want to know. She didn't want to think about Palmer's macabre plans for the technology. As far as she was an expert in this field, even she didn't know the optimum duration and frequency of brain stimulations before adverse effects would be seen. She couldn't even be sure where the electric impulse went within the brain and how it might affect other functions. She shuddered at the thought and wondered if the Americans, like Palmer, knew or cared. Perhaps she was being over-cautious and it really was as safe as it seemed. Like most things tested on military personnel, only time would tell. Regardless, she knew she would be under pressure to help Palmer develop this technology as a weapon. Quickfall's mind began to run through the various applications in combat; an organised army charging forward like fearless ants, with sharpened senses and dulled pain responses. She shuddered again.

Quickfall was not aware of any research team, military or civilian, investigating non-invasive brain stimulation to this extent and to these ends. Whilst conducting her own PhD she had worked with a team of UK scientists who were exploring the use of tDCS in promoting learning by observation. She had later learned that the project was being funded by the

Defence Science and Research Laboratory, part of the Ministry of Defence. She recalled how this had seemed an exciting project and on reflection it had piqued her curiosity when she herself had been approached by the Secret Intelligence Service. Her role in the project had been to interpret some of the neuroscience data coming out of the study. She had had little contact at the sharp end of the experimentation. Looking back, it was now obvious that Palmer had been following her work from the shadows and he had already begun to conceive a practical application for the neuroscience. It seems, however, that he wasn't alone in his thinking. Palmer wasn't about to let his American allies beat him to the prize.

# SEVEN

The silence was punctuated by grunts of physical exertion and the clink of steel on steel. The metallic echo bounced off the mirrored walls that lined one side of the gym, which gave the illusion that the space was much bigger than it was. A thin film of condensation formed on the mirrors nearest to Adam, his body heat warming an otherwise cold room at such a late hour. He lowered himself once more beneath the heavy bar, his back pushed into the padded bench and his outstretched arms terminating in a firm grip of the 80kg load above him. He freed the bar from its resting position and lowered it to his chest, the bar bouncing momentarily before being hoisted to its start position. Adam repeated this ten times, each time the bar met his chest where the insignia of the Secret Intelligence Service was etched in white cotton on the left breast of a sweat soaked navy blue training shirt. The lactic acid began to burn across his chest and shoulders with the final few repetitions, giving Adam a mixed sensation of pain and achievement. He shelved the bar and jerked himself up into standing, where his reflection greeted him.

A few deep breaths and a gulp of a gritty protein-carbohydrate supplement drink supplied much needed oxygen and nutrients for his muscle furnaces to burn. Adam looked around the empty gym, and then back to the mirrored wall. The reflection looking back at him was his only companion in the world and for a moment Adam dwelled on the thought of his lonely existence. As hard as he tried he couldn't remember any other life. He shook the thought from his head and refocused on the last of his training session. The bar above his head had a rough grip that snagged the calloused skin on the pads of his hands. Adam relentlessly pushed out a flurry of wide-arm pull-ups until he reached failure, his blood-filled back muscles refusing to contract further. *Pain is temporary*, he told himself. This was the place Adam came to upgrade himself physically and mentally, and that, he reflected, was his motivation to exist.

The peace was short lived as the door to the gym swung open. In walked a squat-built man in his late forties, with cropped black hair that was greying at the temples.

'Bloody 'ell fella you gave me the shock of my life,' said a voice that was well known to Adam. 'But then again I might 'ave known you'd be 'ere at this 'our.' Sean Taylor was the facility's Physical Training Instructor with the physique and physical capacity to prove it. He was the proverbial brick shit-house, and his Royal Marine Commando background had given him a base fitness that rivalled Adam's, which was perhaps why Adam liked and respected the man.

'Good to see you again fella,' said Sean as he and Adam shook hands firmly. Adam gave a curt nod which he softened with smiling eyes.

'And you Sean, it's been a while.'

'Yeah well, I tend to run this place during what most people call sociable 'ours, but then you were never the sociable type!' said Taylor as he gripped Adam's right shoulder with his free hand. Adam could never be sure whether Taylor spoke with a true Cockney accent or that of popular London. He had a chest tone to his voice that projected a roughness to his character. Taylor had been the PTI responsible for delivering Adam's combat conditioning and he had been relentless in putting Adam through close-combat training. The punches could still be felt now if Adam thought long enough about them.

'So what brings you back here at this time of night?' asked Adam curiously.

'Been out for a few drinks with the lads after work and I've only gone and left my keys behind the gym desk. The missus would bloody kill me if I woke 'er!' laughed Taylor. Adam flicked him a wry smile.

'You should come out for a drink with us next time,' offered Taylor, 'the boys are all ex-military; some served with the SBS. It takes a certain character to get through their training. It's a special mind-set and I could see it in you the moment I was assigned to bring you back from the dead. I had no doubt you could pass the endurance phase of Special Forces selection - mind over matter my old son! You're a machine.'

*More than you will ever know,* thought Adam as he reflected on Quickfall's revelation.

'Any way old son, I'm off to get some kip before I

beast the new recruits in the morning. Poor bastards!'
Taylor laughed. Adam knew that even after several
pints of Guinness the night before, Sean Taylor would
still be a force to be reckoned with.

'Poor bastards,' confirmed Adam, offering Taylor his
right hand. The two men parted warmly on another
firm handshake.

Adam found himself once again looking at his own
reflection in the fogged wall-length mirror. He was tall
and lean, with a well-muscled physique that pulled at
his sweat-soaked cotton t-shirt. He stepped closer to
the mirror, focusing on the face looking back at him.
He paused to take in its features. He hadn't really paid
much attention before but in the unforgiving artificial
light he examined the lines that formed around his eyes
and across his brow. He was in good physical shape for
his age, but his face told the story of a man in his mid-
thirties with half his life behind him. His eyes showed
no sympathy for his situation. His skin was marked
with several faded scars that hinted at a violent history,
but Adam did not know its story.

'I don't remember,' he said under his breath. 'I don't
remember anything.' Adam spoke the words again as if
he was willing some emotion to stir, but the sentence,
like his expression, was cold and indifferent. There was
no pain associated with his loss, and that troubled
Adam the most.

'Nothing,' he said quietly, now looking deep into his
own eyes. A sense of duty swelled inside of him as he
refocused on the present and his commitment to SIS
and his country; yet he felt otherwise empty.

Adam headed for the shower room. It was a quarter past midnight and he was beginning to fade. His usual routine when back at the facility would be bed by one a.m. before rising at six a.m. for his morning run. This would be a hard interval session of one mile efforts at a pace exceeding six-minute miles. He didn't see the point of running any sort of distance; in his line of work if he hadn't evaded a situation within a few minutes it was game over. Hard and fast was his preferred method of operating and it had served him well over the preceding months.

As the hot water cascaded down his tired body the heat began to soften his muscles and his focus. A loose thought filled his mind and for a moment he could see the faces of two small children. Adam tried to hold the image but it evaporated into the steam that was now all around him. He leaned forward under the shower head and let the water pressure massage his aching neck and back for several minutes.

From beyond the shower cubicle Adam heard the faint sound of a door closing. His senses sparked to life and his muscles swelled again under the pressure of his quickened pulse. Leaving the shower running, he reached for his towel and stepped silently out of the open cubicle. He paused to dab the excess water that adhered to his skin. The dim light reduced his visual senses but allowed his brain to concentrate more on his hearing, which was now heightened. He rounded the dividing wall and entered the changing area. There was darkness all around, except for the moonlight that glared through one of the windows, casting his long shadow over the floor. He could sense he was not alone as he stepped cautiously around the edge of the space, his bare-feet silent against the non-slip surface. The sound of breathing in the shadows to his left stopped Adam in his tracks. The respiratory rate was high and the breathing shallow, suggesting that he was the one stalking a weaker a prey.

Suddenly and violently he lurched forward and plucked the figure from darkness, sending it hurtling into the tower of lockers. A woman's voice let out a scream of surprise and pain. She looked up, trying to orientate herself and figure out how she had come to lay dazed on the floor of the male changing room.

'It would be much safer for you to knock in future,' said Adam, standing naked over the sprawled body of a stunned Grace Quickfall. She looked up from her supine position, then suddenly back to the floor again.

'I would be grateful if you could cover up, please,' she stuttered. Adam didn't move. 'Adam, please. I can hardly have a conversation with you like this.' Adam reached for her and lifted the doctor to her feet. She landed upright, her body close to his. Her eyes were level with his broad chest. Quickfall wasn't sure whether it was the fall or his presence, but she felt giddy. She hadn't been this close to a man for some time, and she had never been this close to Adam, naked or otherwise.

'For God's sake please put some clothes on,' she said neutralising the chemistry between them. Adam turned and walked towards a neatly folded pile of clothes placed on the opposite bench. Reluctantly, Quickfall scrunched up her eyes tight to avoid looking at his naked rear. She watched with interest as he stretched a plain white t-shirt over his torso.

'Thank you,' she said.

'You're welcome,' he replied with a boyish grin covering his square jaw.

'Is this a regular place to find you at this time?' he asked. Quickfall blushed. It wasn't a typical trait of hers but the situation was far from familiar and her hormones were shaken and stirred.

'No, of course not,' she said defensively. She took a breath, and composed herself. 'I wanted to ask you a question, off record. This was the only place I could think of where I could reach you without being under surveillance.'

'Go on,' prompted Adam, intrigued as to why now after nearly twelve months of meeting in the same concrete cell his liaison officer wanted 'off-record' chats with him.

'Something's been bothering me about your report from the US research facility.' Adam listened, his silence inviting her to continue. 'You stated that you had to dispose of a research scientist that was present that night. But you didn't state how.'

'Does it matter?' asked Adam. 'Have the Americans become suspicious?'

'No,' replied Quickfall, 'it's nothing official, it's just something that's been on my mind, being a scientist in this field myself.'

He leaned in towards her.

'That's why it's my job to do the dirty work, and

yours not to. You should be careful about what questions you ask, Grace. You may not like the answers you get in return.'

'Oh,' said Quickfall, knowing full-well she would not want to hear the true extent of the outcome. 'I see. Thank you Adam'. She masked her disappointment.

There had been some small hope in her mind that Adam had let the youth run free. She felt foolish, sat there in the early hours of the morning exposing her weaknesses and intruding in Adam's world. Quickfall had gotten the confirmation she was looking for; although it was not the answer she wanted. Adam was a killing machine. Nothing more.

'You should go get a coffee,' said Adam now dressed and on his feet. 'You look tired.'

'I'm fine. I just haven't slept too well the last few nights,' said the doctor leaning forward to raise herself up from the slatted bench. By the time she had stood the man beside her had gone.

'I'll turn the shower off then shall I?' she asked rhetorically.

It was almost one a.m. by the time Quickfall reached the exit of the MI6 training facility. Her lonely footsteps clanked down the dark and otherwise empty halls shattering the eerie silence. The hairs on the back of her neck stood erect and she was suddenly gripped by fear. Her pace quickened and the staccato clack of her heels played at double time. In between her own footsteps she thought she could hear the sound of a pursuing footfall. Her heart was beating violently inside her chest.

'Dr Quickfall, is that you?' said an authoritative voice off to the left, the face obscured behind a blinding torch light. The scream was stuck in her throat and Quickfall's legs turned to jelly. The man stepped closer and lowered the torch beam.

'Sorry if I scared you doctor. It's not like you to be working so late. Is everything okay?' The security man was tall, broad, and looked ex-military based on his posture. Quickfall recognised his face and felt her fear loosen its grip.

'I'm fine thank you Alistair, although you did give me a fright! Perhaps it's best I don't work so late in future!' she joked. The security officer escorted her to the front desk, a one sided conversation passing the time it took to walk the remainder of the corridor. Quickfall felt like she might be physically sick and wondered what had spooked her so much. *Always trust your instinct*, she thought. As she passed through the safety scanners Alistair arranged a taxi for her as she had requested and wished her a safe journey home.

'You're ride will be here in five minutes,' he said from behind his station.

'Thank you,' replied Quickfall as she headed for the exit and stepped out into the warm night air.

'Shit, what was I thinking?' she muttered to herself, frustrated by the desperation she had displayed in front of Adam, and then allowing her imagination to spook her so badly. *All I need is a good night's sleep*, she convinced herself. She was lost in thought as she rounded the corner of Albert Embankment. As the car pulled alongside, her mind was busy wondering whether Adam would show her any loyalty, or whether he would report their rendezvous to Palmer. Another thought played on her mind as she reached for the door handle. If the American scientist was killed for knowing too much, could a similar fate await her at the hands of Adam? She threw herself into the back seat of the taxi.

Alone in his room, Adam lay back on his bed. His body ached and he could feel himself gradually slipping into sleep. He thought of Quickfall and their conversation. Why the questions, and why now he wondered. He had come to respect and admire her in the year that had spanned his rehabilitation and progression to active duty, but he realised he knew little about her. She was direct and could manage Adam well, even when he teased her, which was something that he did with increasing frequency. Laying there with his eyes closed he opened his mind to what might have driven Quickfall to make contact with him. She was hiding something tonight and she seemed scared. As the stream of questions flowed through his mind Adam's breathing deepened and he descended in to his reverie.

The alarm sounded and Adam stopped it before it beeped a second time. Five hours had passed in what seemed like a matter of seconds. His sleep had been peaceful and heavy and he was still laid on top of the duvet. He remembered his last thoughts of Quickfall as he swung himself over the side of the bed and spread his bare feet out against the cold smooth tiled floor. *Was she in some sort of trouble?*

In the familiar briefing room Adam sat at the desk waiting for Quickfall. In anticipation of her arrival Adam adjusted the sleeves of his fitted cotton light-blue shirt under his tailored dark navy suit jacket. The shirt's cuffs came to rest neatly at his wrists, the smart business look being in stark contrast to the various scuffs and scars on his hands. His mind dwelled for a moment on a healing wound on the back of his left hand, acquired recently in Geneva. His operations were becoming increasingly more difficult and he had found himself battling a small army of bodyguards before dispatching a crooked British banker who had been pay-rolling several British politicians. He wondered what Quickfall would have lined up for him this time. *First, I need to find out what's troubling her.*

There was a short sharp electronic beep and the door to the briefing room swung open. Adam got to his feet sharply.

'Good morning Adam, my name is Richard Palmer. I'm Director of the Special Operations Unit.'

'Sir,' acknowledged Adam with a straight back.

'It's good to meet you in person at last,' said Palmer.

'And you Sir,' lied Adam. He knew instinctively that this was the man who had been watching from the shadows. He felt like he already knew the sickly looking man standing before him.

'I'm waiting on Dr Quickfall Sir, will she be attending this morning?' asked Adam.

'No,' said Palmer flatly. 'Walk with me.'

# EIGHT

The two men strode down the short corridor in silence, Adam half a step behind Palmer, towards an open lift door where a suited man stood waiting. The two men continued into the lift and were joined by the muted and suited man whose jacket failed to conceal the Walther P99 secured in a shoulder holster. Adam estimated Palmer to stand at six foot two inches and weigh heavy at around 100 kilograms. He had a commanding presence about him and conducted himself like someone with a military background, although he looked like he'd been out of that game for some time. Palmer's trousers were heavily creased at the backs of the knees hinting at a day spent sitting either in meetings or behind a desk, and from the smell on his clothes and his ashen appearance, Adam concluded that he was a heavy smoker. The lift pinged to indicate they had ascended four floors to their destination and the doors opened allowing the three men to file out.

The atmosphere was light and airy, an architectural marvel of steel and toughened glass that was in stark contrast to the concrete that constituted the four basement floors extending below ground level. Unlike the SIS Building at Vauxhall Cross, which was generally regarded as the British Secret Intelligence Service's worst-kept secret, the Special Operations training facility was hidden in plain sight. Located also on Albert Embankment in Vauxhall, the SIS training facility was only half a kilometre east along the River Thames from the block-like façade of the SIS Building, and while one dominated the landscape like a Lego replica of an Aztec temple, the other resembled any other modern day office block. The biggest and best secret of the Special Operations Unit was not the four storeys of office and meeting space above the ground, but the four sub-terrain storeys where Adam spent much of his time either on the firing range, in one of the gyms, or in his cell-like room. In the twelve months of his life that he could recall he had certainly never been up to the fourth floor, where now he stood before Richard Palmer's office door. Adam considered the various reasons behind the change in routine and scenery. *Whatever they want from me this time, it must be important.*

The heavy oak door was dressed with an engraved brass door sign heralding Palmer's name and title of 'Director of Special Operations'. In an open space to the left of Palmer's office sat a lady behind a desk. Adam reckoned her to be in her mid-40s. She was typing furiously on a computer keyboard, whilst never taking her eyes from the monitor in front of her. The secretary's gaze broke away from the screen momentarily to acknowledge the men, and in particular her boss Richard Palmer. A faint smile broke out across her dainty jaw and she seemed both surprised and pleased to see Adam, as if he was known to her.

'We're not to be disturbed,' barked Palmer to his PA before he and Adam disappeared into the large office. The third man turned and stood guard at the door.

'Is he for my benefit?' asked Adam.

Palmer gave him a direct stare. 'Don't be silly Adam, I am fully aware of your capabilities. Unfortunately, we live in dangerous times where our enemies walk amongst us. He's there to protect me from those crazy bastards.'

'How do you know he's not a terrorist?' asked Adam. Palmer shot his guest another look that suggested he should stop asking questions.

'I trained him. Broke him down as a person and then rebuilt him through training and discipline.' Adam knew that such a technique was the backbone of any sort of military organisation, confirming his suspicions about Palmer's past.

'Do I have your trust Adam?' he continued.

'Of course, sir,' replied Adam without hesitation.

'Good.' Palmer was studying Adam's expression. 'I consider you to be this country's answer to these terrorist threats.'

Palmer gestured for him to sit, before lowering himself in to his luxury swivel chair. He leaned forward on to his desk and eyeballed Adam. The leather creaked as he shifted in his chair.

'You are the one we send in to do our dirty work Adam and you are proving to be bloody effective at your job. This is why nothing can compromise the work you do for me on behalf of this organisation and this country. Do you understand?' It wasn't really a question but Adam answered, giving Palmer the reassurance he was seeking.

'What is it you need from me Sir,' he asked. Palmer paused for a moment as he considered whether Adam was ready for the answer.

'How's your memory for detail?' he asked. There was no need for Adam to answer. Palmer had been there to see his prototype be fitted with memory enhancing brain implants and then be subjected to hours of transcranial direct-current stimulation. He spun a document across the desk and Adam brought it to a halt by placing a firm hand flat on the file's loose folder. As he lifted his hand he saw the words 'Top Secret' stamped on the folder. He looked up at Palmer. The stony expression on the face of the Director of Special Operations had changed, seriousness was now etched in to his rock-like features. Adam gave the document his full attention.

'Once you have read this document it will be destroyed. It is the only copy,' said Palmer firmly. Adam nodded, opened the file, and began to read.

## Top Secret

For some time, the British Government has been aware of a number of Russian athletes who competed at the London Olympics despite having abnormal blood results recorded in their biological passports. An independent commission headed by the former president of the World Anti-Doping Agency is due to investigate these claims after exposure by a German Broadcast.

The Russian Ministry of Sport is thought to be providing the World Anti-Doping Agency (WADA) with a list of Russian athletes having abnormal biological passport profiles prior to the London Olympic Games. While some of these athletes were sanctioned before the games, others went on to compete and win medals, contributing to Russia's fourth place finish in the medals table.

The widespread doping of Russian athletes represents a Russian state cover-up and a gross failure of the International Association of Athletics Federations (IAAF), the Russian Athletics Federation and the Russian Anti-Doping Agency to act prior to competing in, and thus sabotaging the Games.

The integrity and reputation of the London Games risks being tarnished by a joint cover-up by both the Russian state and a known British Parliamentary Minister. The sports minister Joanne Harwin-Smith is heavily suspected of exchanging information on doping tactics with Russian coaches and doctors for a guaranteed safe passage to the London Olympics. By suppressing the activities of doping controls in London and helping to process false biological passports, the sports minister now has in her possession in-depth detail on cutting-edge doping methods. These documents outline the most advanced techniques for enhancing physical and mental human function, including gains in strength, endurance, mental focus, and psychological resilience to training and competitive stress. It is anticipated that Harwin-Smith will look to sell this information for financial gain, either within the British sporting community or overseas to our competitors. Either way, for the sake of the reputation of British sport, and to maintain our competitive position in world sport, these documents must be retrieved.

Recent intelligence suggests that the doping documentation is still in Harwin-Smith's possession at her London home. Before the independent commission conducts its investigation it is considered highly important that both the documentation and the sports minister be dealt with in a definitive matter. Such action should be taken with immediate effect.

This information is not to be copied in any way or retained in hard copy by any persons.

Adam looked up from the file, his expression indifferent to the information in his possession.

'Will Dr Quickfall be controlling me on this one?'

Palmer didn't hesitate. 'That's very unlikely. She's taking some time off to consider her options.' There was a pause, then Palmer continued. 'Last night Dr Quickfall left the Office at an unusually late hour. Did she make contact with you during this time?' Adam fixed eyes with Palmer and didn't flinch in his response.

'No, Sir,' replied Adam. The two men held each other's gaze for what seemed like an eternity.

'Nothing stands in the way of the work that you do Adam. Nothing. When you return I may have some loose ends for you to tie up.' Adam took his cue to stand and thanked Palmer for his time.

'I will prepare for the mission immediately Sir'.

'Good,' said Palmer. 'As always, I can't sign off on this. Can you source the equipment you need?'

'Of course,' said Adam confidently.

'Do you understand what needs to be done with Harwin-Smith?' asked Palmer.

Adam nodded, then asked, 'and the documentation, should I destroy it?'

'No,' replied Palmer hurriedly. 'Deliver it to me personally. And it's for my eyes only, is that clear?' Adam gave a curt nod. 'Then be on your way Adam. I'm counting on you.'

Palmer swivelled in his chair to look out over the Thames and beyond to the Regency architecture of Pimlico. He considered whether Adam was fully committed to his cause but then realised that it didn't matter. If Adam failed there would eventually be others to take his place, and they would be better. Once Palmer had in his grasp the doping secrets of the Russians, alongside the transcranial experimentation by the Americans, the next generation of ADAM would be his perfect creation. A single ADAM operative was only the starting point. As he gazed out over central London Palmer began to visualise his rise to the top as Chief of the Secret Intelligence Service. With a team of elite operatives at his disposal his reach would extend anywhere and to anyone, and that included members of the UK Government. Nothing or no one was going to stand in his way.

The intercom on his desk buzzed, wrenching Palmer away from his own thoughts. He spun on his chair to answer.

'Yes Janet, what is it?' he demanded.

'I have Lee Dawson waiting to see you Sir. You requested a meeting with him.' Palmer instructed her to send the man through, and a second later there was a rap at the door. A smartly dressed man side-stepped through the opening and into Palmer's office.

'Sir, you wanted to see me?' Lee Dawson was Palmer's second in command, with an official title of 'Section Lead for Special Operations'. Palmer did not stand to greet the younger man, nor did he invite him to take a seat. Dawson didn't seem fazed. He was not a fan of Palmer's and the less time spent in his company, the better. There were many issues the two men did not agree on regarding the running of the Special Operations Unit and on many occasions the subordinate had challenged his superior's approach. In his mid-forties, Dawson had progressed rapidly within MI6; he was regarded as a career spy, joining the SIS after a short spell as an Army Officer. He held a degree in History and Economics from Oxford University, where he was first approached by MI6, and since joining the Office he had undertaken multiple overseas postings in Europe and the Middle East. He was on the fast track to the top. In contrast, Palmer hadn't joined

MI6 until he was in his forties, leaving behind a long career in the British Army. He had reached the rank of Colonel despite having no formal further or higher education. Instead he had commissioned in his mid-twenties after demonstrating strong leadership potential as a Corporal in the Grenadier Guards, which he had joined aged seventeen. His style on the battlefield had been aggressive, in conflicts such as the first Gulf War, Bosnia and Kosovo, and the same aggressiveness had seen him rise within the Secret Intelligence Service. Their experiences and approaches could therefore not have been more different and both men despised and envied the other's background. They were both men of outstanding ability in their field. One had earnt his position through education and careful mission execution. The other through force and unrelenting grit. Only one man could take the top spot within MI6 and each knew the other one had it in their sights.

'Has she talked?' asked Palmer, skipping any formalities. He was referring to Grace Quickfall, who had been on house arrest since last evening.

'No Sir, and she is not at all pleased to be held under armed guard in her own home,' answered Dawson.

'I couldn't give a toss whether she's pleased or not,' hissed Palmer, 'what the fuck was she doing in the building last night?' Dawson paused, knowing that his answer would not please his boss.

'She insists she came to pick up some personal effects that she had left behind,' he said finally, 'and she's sticking with that line.'

'Bullshit!' erupted Palmer banging his fist down hard

on the heavy desk. 'I don't buy it.'

'Sir, we have no reason to hold Dr Quickfall. We should consider letting her go and keeping a watch on her.' Palmer didn't look impressed.

'Leave it with me,' he said eventually.

'But Sir, I can handle…'

'I said leave it with me,' interrupted Palmer, his tone final. Dawson looked like he might challenge for the last word. *Fuck it,* he thought to himself, *I'll let the old bastard hang himself with this one.*

Dawson summoned his most courteous response. 'Of course Sir, as you wish.'

The SOU Director waved his right hand and dismissed his second in command.

'And Dawson, tell Dr Quickfall to be more vigilant when getting into cabs,' said Palmer with an evil smile on his face. 'Observation before action is basic training.'

Dawson's teeth were clenched tight as he left Palmer's office and stepped into the waiting area.

'Fucking prick,' he muttered to himself. Janet was looking right at him and he wondered if she'd heard his little outburst. She smiled and then raised her eyebrows, feigning disapproval.

'Good meeting, Sir?' she asked from behind her desk. Dawson strode over to her and parked himself on the corner of the desk, crumpling a pile of neatly filed papers.

'Don't ask, Janet,' he said exasperated. 'I don't know why you still work for him. Can't you get a transfer to Vauxhall?'

She gave a mock sigh; 'it pays better than most PA roles within the Company and besides, he told me that if I ever put in for a transfer he'd make sure he got me fired.' Although she was smiling at him Dawson fully believed the words.

'Well when you work for me,' he said leaning over towards her, 'I'll treat you much better.' Janet felt herself heating up.

'Janet, the man who left Palmer's office just as I arrived, who was he?' asked Dawson. The PA looked up at Dawson incredulously.

'That's Adam,' she said, 'Adam Newman'. Lee Dawson looked none the wiser; his blank expression prompting her to continue.

'He's a Special Operations Agent; call-sign 1.0,' she said in a tone that suggested it was obvious.

'Call sign 1.0? What unit is that?' asked Dawson.

'It's the pilot for Richard's new task force. It isn't live. Adam has been on a series of training exercises for the past twelve months from what I understand. I thought you'd be aware of it?' she said.

'Hmm,' sounded Dawson out loud. 'Yes, you would think I'd be aware of it, wouldn't you.' Janet felt that she'd said too much.

'Were is he now?' asked Dawson. Janet looked at the monitor in front of her and waited for a moment, her fingers dancing across her keyboard.

'He's scheduled for some range time.'

'How strange,' said Dawson, 'I was just heading there myself to let off a little steam!' Janet was now wearing a look of concern. Dawson smiled knowing that his subtle interrogation skills had worked their magic.

'Don't worry,' he said with a wink of his left eye, 'remember that you'll be working for me one day soon anyway.'

*

The firing range in the SIS training facility didn't look much different to the ones you see in most places around the world. The bare grey walls formed a dull perimeter, which belied the technology housed within. The range had static and tactical facilities with eight lanes that all had their own glass shooting booth. A digital control panel within each booth allowed the shooter to operate a turning target retrieval system, which at the press of a button sent out targets to an exact specified distance. The control panel could be programed for up to 100 training scenarios, and Adam had done all of them, several times over. As Dawson looked through the sound proofed viewing glass he could see the man of interest in the middle of an 'advancing and retreating' scenario. With his lane flashing 'tactical mode', Adam was permitted to leave his stall and move forward down the range toward the targets. He did so with exact precision and Dawson was impressed with a level of marksmanship he hadn't witnessed before. *Where did Palmer get this guy from?* he wondered.

A small group of male and female officers were leaving the range, kitted in SIS training attire and brandishing powerful assault rifles. Dawson waited in line behind them as they returned their weapons to the armoury. Collins was on duty, and he stiffened to attention when he saw Dawson, a habit of his time in the British Army. He nodded to greet the Section Lead of Special Operations.

'Sir.'

'Good morning, Collins,' said Dawson as he placed his ID card over the counter in exchange for a weapon of his choice. 'Long time no see.' The two men had often exchanged stories of their time in the army, but as Dawson had been a 'Rupert', which was British Army slang for an Officer, Collins assumed most of his action stories were bullshit.

'What can I get for you, Sir?' asked Collins. Dawson perused the array of weaponry behind the cage of the armoury as if he was choosing from a McDonalds' menu board.

'A .44 Remington Magnum please, with 24 cartridges,' he said finally.

'Right you are, Sir,' attended Collins turning quickly on his heels to conceal the huge grin taking over his face. *Who do you think you are, Clint Eastwood?!* Moments later he returned with the weapon and placed the large-bore handgun on the counter.

'Sir, one .44 Remington Magnum with 24 cartridges.' Dawson nodded, took the weapon and ammunition and made his way to the range.

'Watch out for those grizzly bears!' chuckled Collins in a low voice.

There was one armed guard patrolling the entrance

to the range. He cradled a mean looking assault rifle and wore an even meaner expression on his face. He had about as much joy in him as the devil and he gave every impression that he would send you to hell in the blink of an eye. Dawson strode past him trying not to look intimidated and stepped into the sound-proofing airlock. Not a fraction of a decibel left the range as he transitioned between the two worlds. The sound-proofing was excellent, but then it had to be in the middle of London. The combined use of concrete and air acted to absorb the acoustics of the high powered weaponry being discharged within, and the rubber berm bullet traps deadened the sound of impact and reduced bullet fragmentation. As the airlock opened to allow Dawson on to the range the taste of cold metallic air hit the back of his throat and a waft of stale gunpowder lingered in his nostrils. It was a smell instantly recognisable to any marksman and it took Dawson back to his basic military training at Sandhurst. He set himself up in a lane next to Adam, whose booth was now flashing the word 'static' above his head, meaning he was firing from within his stall.

Adam was in his element. He was now engaged in a 'spin, stop' scenario and seemed to be making easy work of it. He could sense he was being watched and he eased his focus on the lane ahead. Adam became aware of the smell of the spent rounds and he inhaled it deeply like the smoke of a cigarette. He continued to fire until he had emptied his magazine.

'Great shooting,' came the voice from the next booth. Adam tapped at the control panel that summoned the target toward him for inspection. He would be the one to determine how 'great' his shooting had been.

The target was punctured by several tightly grouped bullet holes over the central chest. Adam visualised the way in which this would have incapacitated his enemy in the field and concluded it would have killed them. The heart would have been shredded like pulled-pork. Adam finally looked across to the man in the next lane, who was also surveying the damage to the target, and acknowledged his remarks.

'Thank you,' he said. Dawson immediately picked up on the opening.

'Adam, isn't it?' he asked.

Adam placed his pistol on the counter in the booth and replied, 'that's right…Sir.' He knew Lee Dawson, as it was his habit of knowing everything and everyone, and he'd had plenty of time whilst he was rehabilitating to study the structure of the Special Operations unit.

'I'm surprised we haven't met before now, what with me being the SOU Section Lead, and you being…' Dawson left the sentence hanging, inviting Adam to fill in the blanks, but he didn't take the bait.

'I'm sure as Section Lead you'll know my role in Special Operations, Sir.'

'Well of course I'm aware of your title,' lied Dawson, 'but I'm not familiar with the nitty gritty of the role you undertake for us.'

Adam did think it strange, but then he had only just met Palmer and perhaps his work really was top secret, even to many of his superiors.

Dawson pressed on, 'and I can't believe I haven't seen you here at the range before.' Adam glanced at the Magnum in Dawson's right hand and thought to himself that there was a reason he hadn't seen the man on the range before. He looked more style than substance.

'Do you shoot often, Sir?' he asked.

'Not as much as I would like these days, Adam. There's not much danger sat behind a desk apart from the odd paper-cut.' Adam smiled.

'If that doesn't get you then heart disease will,' he replied.

'So, what work do you do for MI6?' asked Dawson. Adam didn't respond immediately as he went about checking his weapon and gathering his things together.

Finally he said, 'I'm sorry Sir, but you know that's classified, as is the work we all do.' Dawson knew he was beaten. As Section Lead he should know what Adam did and if he was cleared to know then he would be able to look it up.

'Very good Adam,' he conceded. 'I was testing you, and you passed with flying colours.' Adam made his move to leave and as he walked behind Dawson's booth he stopped suddenly.

'Did I work with you before my accident, Sir?' he asked. Dawson gave him an inquisitive look.

'Your accident?' he said as if he were trying to recall such an event. 'No I don't believe I did work with you before your accident.' Adam nodded his head to signal his goodbyes and then turned towards the exit. Both men were left with questions running through their minds.

As Adam reached the air-lock door he heard the mighty boom of the .44 calibre Magnum ring out. He turned to see the target hanging unscathed in the lane.

# NINE

Adam finished his lamb shank and knocked back his espresso before leaving the Dog and Fox public house, and headed in the general direction of the All England Lawn Tennis and Croquet Club, commonly referred to simply as 'Wimbledon'. The wind had picked up slightly and Adam buried his hands deep in to the pockets of his Harrington jacket to stop it from flapping open and revealing the pistol concealed below his left arm-pit. It was a short walk as he headed East away from Wimbledon Common before arriving at his destination; the home of Joanne Harwin-Smith, Conservative MP and long-standing Minister for Sport and Tourism.

The four bed detached house was set back from the road and surrounded almost entirely by a high wall of thick conifers. Boldly, Adam turned off the footpath and strode up the block-paved driveway, leaping up the few steps to the front door. He rapped on the door. As expected there was no answer, only the yapping of Harwin-Smith's Yorkshire terrier. Adam was not surprised to hear the dog, which was now working itself into a frenzy on the other side of the door. He had done his research on Harwin-Smith and had undertaken some reconnaissance on the house a few nights earlier. He reached back into his jacket pocket, took out a dog treat and posted it through the letter box that was to the right of the door. The treat never touched the floor as the small dog caught it in its mouth mid-air, and seemed to swallow it whole.

'Good doggy,' said Adam dryly. He slipped silently round the side of the house and left the tranquiliser to take effect on the dog. The MP's garden was well maintained, with an impeccably kept lawn that was mown in alternating stripes of a lush light and dark green. The garden extended to a reasonable size, but perhaps not what one would desire from a million-pound home. Adam smiled to himself when he spotted the imposing fountain in the middle of the lawn, a stone half-naked woman balancing on one leg whilst spurting water from a vessel in her outstretched hand. *How very upper class.*

The unlocked window of the utility room was easy to breach, and as Adam entered the house he held his breath in anticipation of the alarm system sounding off. After a few seconds only silence filled the house. He had jammed the wireless alarm system by suppressing the non-encrypted radio frequency signals between the window sensors and the control system. Jamming the signals also meant that there was no alert being pinged off to Harwin-Smith or the Police.

In the hallway, Adam found the compact Yorkshire terrier laid haphazardly across the parquet flooring. He checked the dog's pulse and seemed marginally pleased that he hadn't killed it. Adam grabbed it by the scruff of the neck and carried it in to the kitchen, which was a contrast of modern ceiling spot lights and more traditional solid-wood oak fitted units, and placed the limp dog neatly in its basket.

Alone in the centre of the breakfast bar was a slip of card inviting Harwin-Smith to a function at the Hilton hotel in West London in two days' time. Adam made a mental note of the venue and date and considered it as a possible venue for the Sports Minister's death. Stepping lightly through to the dining room, Adam followed the parquet flooring through open double doors and on to the living room, all the while scanning for signs of a secure hiding place for the MP's documents. He continued through another set of open double doors and found himself back in the hallway in full view of the glazed front door. He opened a set a white glossed louvre doors concealing an under-stairs storage area, packed with the usual rack of shoes, mountain of coats, and a vacuum cleaner. The walls seemed solid and were largely unobscured, the floor seemed firm under his feet. He dismissed the area, pushed the doors to, and made his way swiftly to the first floor where he was determined to find the hidden documents.

Before reaching the first floor landing, Adam stopped suddenly as the hum of a car engine sounded from the driveway. He turned to look back down the stairs, straining to hear the outside world over the creak of the staircase beneath his shifting weight. His pulse quickened as he heard voices; one female, one male. The only way he could get eyes on the new-arrivals would be to make his way back down stairs, and that meant passing in front of the glazed door panels. Using the worn bannister handle to take some of his bodyweight Adam leapt down the stairs, three steps at a time, until he was right before the front door. He crouched and looked out, recognising immediately the Mercedes-Benz C-class saloon belonging to Harwin-Smith. A few deep breaths steadied his racing heart rate, and with that he was able to clearly evaluate his options.

Harwin-Smith was now stood by the door to the driver's side, Bluetooth earpiece in place, and a brown leather briefcase in her left hand. She was looking over the roof of the Mercedes as the passenger stepped out, a male in his mid-forties dressed in a tailored dark grey suit. The pair shared a joke, and laughing, they turned toward the house. Adam saw the opportunity and took it, judo-rolling across the hard wooden flooring of the front hallway, keeping his body low and obscured by the UPVC panelling in the bottom half of the front door. He cleared the hallway, grabbed his brogue shoes that he'd removed on entering the house and swiftly closed himself into the utility room. He stayed low and put on his shoes, his steady hands forming tight knots in the laces as his mind formulated a plan of action. He stood upright and peered through the ajar door, eyes narrowed and focused like the lens of a camera, in time to see the Sports Minister and her male companion entering the hallway. Adam removed the SIG Sauer P230 which had been concealed under his jacket and gave a long pull on the stiff slide, setting the pistol to its double-action firing position. The gun made a slight click as he did so. He froze. If the situation came to the worst, Adam would kill Harwin-Smith, the man, and the yappy dog before turning the house upside down like a bungled burglary, which is exactly what it would become. He would be sure to make a rough job of it, leaving no trace of a professional execution.

'Where's that little rat of a dog of yours, Jo?' asked the man casually. Harwin-Smith paused as if she had just realised that her normal home-coming routine was slightly amiss.

'Good question, it's not like her to not make a fuss,' before calling, 'Harriet, Harriet.' As she walked through to the kitchen Adam's grip tightened on the contoured pistol handle. The couple were now out of sight but still within earshot.

'Harriet darling, are you ok?' asked Harwin-Smith who had by now seen the dog curled up in its basket.

'Leave her be,' said the man. 'I could do without her yapping putting me off my stride.' The pair giggled and then all went quiet.

Adam was trying to make sense of it all when finally, they stepped back into view, embracing each other and kissing passionately. Harwin-Smith threw off her shoes and led the man upstairs. Adam stepped back from the gap in the open door, piecing together the events of the last few minutes. The man was not her husband, the father to their two teenage children, and their arrival back at the house was obviously well planned – the meetings in her electronic calendar being a cover for the affair. Adam's thoughts were disturbed as the pair stopped partway up the stairs. He peered through the opening in the door.

'You go up, darling,' said Harwin-Smith withdrawing from the man slightly. He looked like a boy who was just about to be told he couldn't have any sweets. 'I'll be there in a second, I just need to put something away – you know, work *stuff.*' The man's excitement rose again and he bounded up the rest of the steps. Harwin-Smith came back to the hallway and took something from her briefcase before disappearing from Adam's line of sight. *Damn.* He craned his neck. A clicking sound came from the hallway and Adam recognised it to be the opening louvre doors at the entrance to the under-stairs cupboard. He heard a grate drag over concrete, a few electronic beeps, then more grate on concrete before the louvre doors snapped shut. Adam could not believe his luck – she had led him to the safe, which he had, to his own disappointment, previously overlooked.

Joanne Harwin-Smith rushed up to her lover and once Adam heard the bedroom door swing-to he made his way towards the under-stairs storage area. He gave a quick glance over to the dozing dog and then to his watch, which warned him that he probably had ten minutes or less to get the job done. He wondered how much time the man upstairs would take to get his job done, and perhaps ten minutes was a luxury Adam did not have.

He knelt to the floor, peeled back a loose carpet, lifted a metal cover and exposed the safe which was secured in the concrete floor. Adam took a small bottle of fluid from his jacket pocket and sprayed a fine mist of it over the key panel. After a few seconds he shone an eerie light over the dried liquid and found dense fingerprint marks over four of the keys on the panel. He quickly computed that the correct code would be one of a possible 256 combinations of the four well-used digits. Adam withdrew a small electronic device from his jacket pocket and punched in the four digits and instantly received a list of all 256 possible combinations. He then used the device to cross-reference all the possible combinations with any significant numbers from Harwin-Smith's file, including all contact numbers, addresses, ID references and of course all the dates of births of family members. Within seconds the small device matched 11 combinations of the four-numbered sequence. After the seventh attempt Adam smiled to himself. 'So much for national security,' he uttered under his breath. The noise upstairs seemed to be reaching a climax as Adam gently pushed the louvre doors closed. Another glance toward the sleeping dog and within a minute Adam was clear of the house and back on the main street heading towards Wimbledon Underground Station. *I'll see you at the Hilton West Hotel in a few days,* thought Adam as he strode down the road.

*

The Hilton West hotel was the venue for a sports charity dinner themed around the hosting of the Rugby World Cup in England. It was a black tie event and was attended by numerous sporting legends, past and present, as well as honoured guests from various grass-roots clubs and charities affiliated to the sport of rugby. Maxim Nevzlin could have passed for a rugby player as he approached the entrance to the hotel.

'Good evening Sir,' said the Doorman as he greeted the tall, sturdy man in front of him. 'May I see your ticket?' Nevzlin reached a massive hand into the inner pocket of his dinner jacket.

'Of course,' he replied in a subtle Russian accent. He produced his ticket, along with a confident smile, and passed through without hindrance to the hotel foyer where he took a glass of champagne from a passing waitress before blending in to the scene of dinner jackets. Minutes later the sports minister arrived and was immediately engulfed by a swarm of do-gooders all vying for her endorsement of their various projects and events.

The evening was pleasant enough, providing a lavish four-course meal and a popular line-up of mostly high profile speakers, including the sports minister herself who was largely predictable and dreary. After the meal came the usual networking opportunities, with many of the evening's guests fighting to raise the awareness of the work they did. Harwin-Smith was starting to flag and so she made her way to the bar.

'Large glass of pinot grigio please,' she said, taking the opportunity to ease herself up on to the barstool and rest her blistered feet. The waiter was in his mid-twenties and was smartly dressed whilst still maintaining the arrogance of youth with his tussled hair and his loose off-centre tie. He returned with Harwin-

Smith's wine and placed it down in front of her.

'Allow me,' said a voice to her left, the Russian intonation clearly audible. Harwin-Smith turned quickly, unable to hide her anxiety. The powerful looking man sitting next to her met her eye and smiled, but Harwin-Smith knew this wasn't going to be a networking conversation or a chat-up.

'That's really very kind of you to offer, but there is no need…' The sentence became redundant as Maxim Nevzlin pushed his money towards the bartender, who dutifully accepted.

'Keep the change,' said the Russian, to avoid the young barman returning and disturbing their conversation. The youth smiled gratefully as he accepted the large tip, and left the pair alone. Harwin-Smith's heart sank as if it had turned to solid lead and for a moment there was silence between the pair. The Russian did not take his eyes off her for second, his large frame making her feel uncomfortable. She broke the silence.

'What do you want?'

The big man leaned in.

'We are aware of an impending situation related to Russia's participation in the London Olympic Games. We would like our information to be returned…' Nevzlin paused '…for safe-keeping.'

'Fuck you,' hissed Harwin-Smith, 'we had a deal and I upheld my end of the bargain. It's not my fault that some bloody journalist has been digging around.' Nevzlin could see straight through her bolshie attitude as he leaned in further, so close now that she could feel the heat of his breath. His tone was deadly serious.

'My intention is to leave with those documents, and if you cooperate your death will be less painful,' stated Nevzlin. He got up and walked away casually.

Harwin-Smith downed her large white wine in almost one gulp, the glass shaking in her hand. The bar tender appeared instantly, keen to make more easy money, but Harwin-Smith waved him away with her free hand. Making her way back across the floor she quickly made her excuses to several notable figures and then disappeared up to her room.

The hotel room was a fusion of trendy interior design and chic furniture, all of which went un-noticed by Harwin-Smith as she entered, her mind preoccupied. The Russian's imposing features were burnt onto her retinas and she couldn't shake his image, or his words – *'your death will be less painful'*. A hot panicky feeling came over her and she rushed straight for the door leading out of her room and on to a small terrace. She flung the door open and a blast of the cool night air engulfed her. She gasped. Staring blankly over the lights of London she considered her limited options.

'You don't look so well,' said a soft voice from the shadows of her room. Harwin-Smith swivelled on her heels to find a tall lean silhouette standing in the doorway. His face was in darkness. She could not detect any trace of Russian in his tone, and for that she was momentarily grateful.

'Who the hell are you?' demanded the sports minister, 'and what do you want?'

Adam stepped forward allowing the moonlight to

illuminate his features. He continued to the edge of the balcony and placed both hands on the railings, and looked out over the city.

'You've been a very naughty girl, Joanne. We know about your dealings with the Russians, and I'm here to offer you a way out.'

'Who's *we*?' demanded Harwin-Smith. 'You don't know anything; you have no proof.'

Adam turned to look at her.

'I have the documents. It's over.'

Harwin-Smith pushed on in her defiance.

'I don't know what you're talking about, what documents?!'

'You are wasting your time,' said Adam, now inches from her. He could smell the alcohol on her breath. 'I took them from your home, from a safe under your stairs, using the code 1904.' Harwin-Smith's jaw dropped open in disbelief and she struggled to make a response. Her eyes rapidly scanned the man's face, looking for sympathy but finding only emptiness in his eye sockets. Adam leaned forward for the kill, 'I know about your affair too,' he whispered.

It was all too much for Harwin-Smith, her head was light and her stomach lurched.

'What's the way out?' she begged, her face looking up at Adam in desperation. Adam held her eyes for a moment.

'Jump,' he said, gesturing with a nod of his head towards the city streets below.

'What?' said Harwin-Smith staggering backwards, 'but, but...' No other words would come. She was bewildered. Overcome with fear and panic her mind was a frenzy of white noise.

'Jump,' said Adam more forcefully. 'Because if you don't I will kill you, and then I'll destroy your memory by leaking your affair and your involvement with the Russians.' He took a step towards her and continued, 'think of your children...' but Adam was unable to finish his sentence as she struck him hard across his face with an open right hand. He made no attempt to stop her.

'You bastard!' she yelled, 'don't you dare bring my family into this.'

Adam felt her pain and anguish; it overcame him for the briefest moment and he faltered in his task. For the first time he thought about the consequences of his actions. But a second later he knew it didn't matter.

He heard the scream from the street below and looked over the edge of the balcony to see Harwin-Smith's body lying awkwardly before horrified bystanders. Adam staggered backwards, his mouth suddenly dry and his legs weak. A thousand thoughts came at him all at once and he couldn't hold on to any one of them. He shook his head to dislodge the torrent of words and images and willed himself back into the present.

It took Adam a moment to regain his focus. He had been taken completely unaware by the surge of empathy for the woman's predicament, and he was totally unprepared for the unfamiliar feelings that had stirred suddenly within him. He felt disarmed. Realising the need to leave the scene as quickly and as calmly as possible he exited the hotel room, making sure to wipe down the few things that he had touched. He hadn't placed a single finger on Harwin-Smith and she had jumped of her own accord, albeit with some encouragement, and so he had no need to worry about being linked to the body.

Adam stood in the doorway and gave a quick pull on his shirt and suit sleeves, checked his Raymond Weil Chronograph watch, and straightened his tie. A rush of cold air blew in through the open balcony door and chilled the back of his neck, causing the tiny hairs to become erect. It carried with it the screams and gathering chatter from the streets below. It was time to move. He stepped into the hallway, closing the room door softly behind him, and as he did so he saw a broad-shouldered man in a tuxedo walking towards him. The two men fixed eyes. Instantly, they recognised that they were both players in the same game.

# TEN

The encounter lasted a matter of seconds, but in that brief moment the two smartly dressed men were able to form accurate conclusions about each other; their intent, their training, and their capabilities. Neither man made a move, instead they stood motionless about 20 meters apart. At this distance both men would easily hit their target with a round from a pistol, and so it would come down to a Western style quick-draw to decide the victor. But Adam hesitated, several conflicting thoughts crossing paths in his mind. He considered stepping back in to Harwin-Smith's room. Then he realised it was now a crime scene and in the next few minutes it would be swarming with hotel staff and Police. His opponent seemed to read his mind and for a fraction of a second his eyes flitted between Adam and Harwin-Smith's room door. Still neither man moved. Adam's arms felt like lead weights and he recognised that his chances of winning a quick-draw, should his opponent gesture, were now slim. The consequences of losing played on his mind. He felt nauseous.

The sound of approaching sirens was beginning to fill the night air and the reverberations crept under the room door behind Adam. The noise rapped on his ear drums and plucked him from his day-dream. Adam gave the man one final glance, the cold merciless look in his eyes were like a reflection of his own. He bowed his head and turned to walk away. Adam didn't look back and as he heard the man's footsteps behind him he fought hard to resist the urge to break out in to a run. Thirty metres ahead he could see the entrance to the stairwell and wondered if he could get there before several bullets tore into his head and back. The negative thoughts grew rapidly and swamped his mind, fuelled by an uncontrollable and unfamiliar emotion. *Fear.*

Adam rounded the corner of the corridor and burst through the doors leading to the stairs, instantly breaking into a sprint. His pulse was racing and he gasped for air. Panic and an overwhelming loss of self-control fuelled his spiral descent. His palms were sweaty and his stomach ached. Adam listened anxiously for the noise of the door swinging open two flights above him but it never came. He didn't look up and he didn't stop until he reached the ground floor, stumbling as he cleared most of the last flight in one leap. His leather soled black dress shoes slapped hard on the floor and he skidded slightly trying to turn his vertical momentum into a horizontal thrust of effort. He entered the foyer to a sea of pandemonium where he was instantly swept along as people piled out of the venue to see the corpse in the road. Adam found himself deposited on the pavement by the tide of rubber-neckers, but while they all filed right to get a glimpse of the morbid incident Adam staggered away to the left of the building where he started to be violently and uncontrollably sick.

Eleven floors above the unfolding chaos, Maxim Nevzlin had let Adam go in pursuit of his primary target, Joanne Harwin-Smith. Using a skeleton key card he had taken from the reception desk he entered the room swiftly, his pistol raised in his right hand. The room was in darkness, the only light coming through the open doors which led out on to the balcony.

Nevzlin sensed instantly that the scene was amiss, but there was no sign of a struggle as everything lay undisturbed. He noted Harwin-Smith's clutch-bag and key card by the TV as he stepped past the bed towards the doors which hung open and as he discretely looked over the edge of the balcony terrace he could see the gathering crowds below. Nevzlin leaned back so as not to reveal himself as people on the streets looked up and speculated where the dead woman had jumped from. He surmised instantly that the man in the corridor had beaten him to the job. Harwin-Smith was dead on the eve of a British political shit-storm and that didn't seem like a coincidence to the Russian. *He has the documents*, thought Nevzlin leaving the room as he had entered it, swiftly and silently.

The corridor was still empty by the time he reached the lift and he summoned for it. The doors glided open and Nevzlin stepped in undetected as the first of the eleventh floor residents started to peer out of their rooms. It was easy for him to slip out of the building amid the chaos, the few police officers on the scene unable to stem the haemorrhage of guests on to the street.

'Please go back in to the hotel and let the emergency services do their jobs,' requested a PCSO in vain before changing tack, 'keep to the left in an orderly fashion.' As Nevzlin stepped out in to the night air he surveyed the scene of people awash with the glow of blue flashing lights.

'Excuse me?' he said to the Doorman who didn't know whether he was coming or going, 'I don't suppose you've seen my friend, a tall lean gentleman with blue eyes and dark hair?'

'Sorry Sir' replied the dazed Concierge, 'I can't say that I remember seeing a gentleman of that description, but then I've probably seen a hundred faces in the last few minutes.' Maxim Nevzlin smiled calmly at the man.

'Indeed. Thank you for your time,' and with that he left the Doorman seconds before he was approached by a couple of Police Officers taking witness statements.

Adam jumped at the sound of his phone ringing. He cursed to himself, then answered.

'Hello?'

'Adam, it's Palmer. What the hell's going on? I'm getting reports about the Sports Minister decorating the streets of London. Do we have a problem?' Adam took a few deep breaths and composed himself.

'No Sir. Objective achieved. I have what we needed and the situation is resolved.' Adam almost sounded like his old self.

'Any witnesses?' asked Palmer.

'No Sir, but...' Adam hesitated.

'But what?' demanded Palmer.

'There was a man. Professional. He was on the scene shortly after the incident.'

There was a pause on the line. 'I knew they would send *him*. Find him Adam and take him down. I want the body.' Adam felt his stomach churn again at the thought of engaging the larger man.

'Yes sir,' he confirmed down the phone.

Before he hung up, Palmer said one last thing; 'Be careful Adam. Tonight you will meet your match.' The line went dead.

The garden square offered Adam a feeling of security; the trees stood tall and silent like sentries around the perimeter of the open space. He had never really stopped to appreciate the natural world around him and suddenly in that moment he felt out of touch with its law and order. But now he got it. He had been ordered to take down a man who he felt was bigger and better. Adam felt like he was the prey, not the predator. Nature would surely assert itself tonight and Adam would find his place in the circle of life. He paced around, his steps unusually noisy and awkward but he couldn't hear it over his heavy breathing.

'Come on man, get it together. This guy is no different to the rest. I can do it,' he willed of himself. But Adam didn't believe the words like he used to, and they conflicted with his bodily sensations. A thick fog of doubt hung over him, and Adam wondered if he was experiencing some sort of post-traumatic stress disorder, from the numerous killings he had notched up; or perhaps from his accident. Yes, maybe that was it, he thought. The accident that he couldn't remember. Maybe it was so horrific that his mind had blocked it out, but now it was coming back to haunt him, to finish what should have happened over a year ago. *Fuck it*, he thought. *Either I'll kill him, or I'll die trying*. His pulse quickened again, but this time it was for all the right reasons. Adam checked his SIG Sauer P230, holstered it, and stepped out of his sanctuary and back in to the urban jungle.

Nevzlin was sat behind the wheel of a black Porsche 911, his black dinner jacket fading into the leather seat under the dim street lights. He had pulled into the side of the road and watched as Adam left the square and began walking towards him. The Russian patted his left chest and felt the bulk of the holstered PSS silent pistol beneath his jacket. He reached across to the glove box, flicked it open and took out a MR-443 Grach pistol with a full seventeen round magazine.

Whether it was instinct or the iconic look of the car Adam couldn't be sure, but something caused him to focus on the idling Porsche up ahead. As Adam came to a stop under a sickly orange street light the Russian reacted and stepped out of the car, weapon levelled. Adam was like a rabbit caught in headlights as he lurched to his left, and then to his right. In a blind panic he ran out in to the road. A small car screeched to a stop but the friction of rubber on road wasn't enough to fall short of Adam and he turned at the very last minute to take the brunt of the impact on his right thigh. He reeled backwards through the air, feeling weightless for a fraction of a second before hitting the tarmac hard, his head ricocheting off the road surface.

Stunned and in a state of shock the driver and her passenger got out of the car.

'Oh my god, oh my god, are you ok?' asked the woman frantically. She and her passenger were stood over the unconscious body laid out in the road. The abandoned car obscured Nevzlin's view of Adam, and already a few people had gathered on the periphery of the scene. He slid back behind the wheel of the Porsche, and watched and waited in anticipation.

'What do we do?' said the driver to her passenger, both of whom were shaking with panic.

'Oh shit, I don't know. First Aid or something. Is he alive?' replied the passenger incoherently.

Adam was semi-aware of the voices around him but he was somewhere deep in his mind. He could see a woman but couldn't make out her face. She seemed to be reaching out for him, calling to him, but her voice was muted. Adam wondered if he was dead, and whether it had been the impact from the car or a well-aimed bullet from the predator that had done the damage. The vision of the woman remained before him, her face blurred. In his mind he tried to step towards her but his legs were weak and he couldn't move. The woman reached out again, this time she was closer but he still couldn't make out her face. She had two children by her side but as hard as he tried he couldn't see their faces either.

'Who are you?' was the question he tried to scream but it fell silently out of his mouth. He willed himself forward but he was bound to the spot. The noise of the outside world was getting louder and he could feel hands on his body, shaking him. Adam tried to fight it but consciousness was seeping into his inner world. He looked one last time to the faceless woman in his mind, and with all his might he strained to hear her over the noise of the living world. It was faint, but he heard it; 'Come back to us.'

The small crowd fragmented as the man in the road gasped, opened his eyes and tried to get to his feet. His eyes were wild and several of the onlookers screamed in surprise and terror. Adam pushed his way through the thin congregation and craned to see over to where he had last spotted the Porsche. *Had that been a dream too*, he wondered. Adam leapt up on the bonnet of the small Mazda, and then on to its roof. Up ahead he saw the Porsche and he slid down the back of the small car, a splinter of pain driving up his right leg as hit the ground. He ignored it and began running towards Nevzlin as if he were possessed. The Porsche swung backwards out of its space, the wheels skidding as it shifted to forward drive and then raced towards Adam who was centred in its main beam. At the last second Adam flung himself to the right and as he slid over the bonnet of a parked car he drew his pistol and fired off two rounds through the passenger window of the Porsche. Nevzlin wasn't able to level his weapon in time as one of the rounds buried itself in his left shoulder. He screamed out, more in frustration than pain, as his opponent drew first blood. Despite the hit to his shoulder Nevzlin knocked the Porsche in to reverse then loosed off a couple of rounds from the Grach pistol out through the shattered window and in to thin air. Adam had disappeared behind the line of parked cars but as the Porsche screamed backwards down the road he popped up and squeezed the trigger of his Sig twice more, another round landing on target and nicking the fleshy part of the Russian's muscle bound neck.

'Fuck!' he yelled in his native tongue, as he alternated between the hand brake and accelerator to turn the car in the road. A black plume of tyre smoke engulfed the car as the vehicle swung around, before Nevzlin slammed down his right foot and fired the Porsche down the street.

Adam stepped out into the middle of the road and glanced the one hundred yards behind him to the small group of onlookers. Some had fled the scene, others had taken cover behind the parked cars. He could make out a couple of people on their mobile phones, and he knew that a Police firearms unit would be only minutes away. Adam broke out into a run, hindered by the damage from the car's impact. The reinforced skeletal frame of his right leg had prevented any major fractures but the intervening soft tissues had been pummelled and it took several seconds for him to shake off the 'dead-leg' feeling.

As he ran down the street Adam could see many of the house lights flickering into life. He surveyed the choice of parked motors available to him, all of a high calibre given the fashionable London location. He passed several varying models of Mercedes and BMW before one car caught his eye. Adam stopped by the Jaguar XE S and patted himself in search of his phone.

Under the glow of the street lights the row of parked cars all appeared monochrome, a phenomenon caused by the narrow wavelength given off by the sodium bulbs used commonly in street lamps. He keyed in his phone's passcode and brought up the secure application section, a facility that very few MI6 agents had the privilege of using. Within seconds he had located what he needed and after typing in the car's make, model and year the phone emitted a small beep that stirred the Jaguar from its slumber. The keyless security and ignition were instantly overridden, allowing Adam to slide behind the wheel of the idling beast.

The streets of London where relatively quiet in the midnight hour, except for the SCO19 armed response vehicle that had just raced past Adam. He was impressed by the speed at which British uniformed services could respond to a threat, even if he was that threat. Nevzlin had about a minute head start on Adam and he could not be sure of the direction he had taken through the Capital. He used the car's Bluetooth to patch his phone through to the Special Operations control team back at the Office.

'Call sign 1.0 requesting a secure line,' he said firmly.

'Secure line confirmed 1.0, how can we help?' came the reply immediately.

'I'm looking for a Black Porsche 911, last seen heading north on St Anns Road.' He gave the car's registration number from memory and waited a few seconds as the team used the City's network of cameras to locate the vehicle. Hiding in a city such as London was near on impossible these days and he was confident that the Russian would soon be found. Adam didn't need to give his own location or direction, he knew they could track him as they always had, a concept which all of a sudden he began to question. His thinking, though, was quickly interrupted.

'Target located 1.0, maintain your current course. The vehicle was last seen about a mile and half ahead of you and appears to be keeping to the speed limits.'

'Can you send through the map and GPS?' asked Adam.

'Already done 1.0,' said the voice at the other end of the line as the map flashed up on his mobile. Adam sent the image through to the car's eight inch sat-nav screen, studied it for a few seconds, and then jammed down the accelerator in pursuit.

In the few moments available to him Adam contemplated the events of the evening. He couldn't make sense of it all; the emotion, the panic, the uncertainty of it. What he did know was that he was fired up for the fight ahead. The vision that had come to him whilst he was unconscious had seemed so real, as if it were a part of him; or part of his past. He would get the job done tonight and then go in search of the answers he needed.

Adam looked up from the sat-nav to see the Porsche at the traffic lights ahead of him. He slowed to a roll. There was no other car between Nevzlin's and his own and he willed the lights to change before he got too close to the car in front. Suddenly the Porsche revved its engine and jumped the red light, tearing away from Adam with its 370 brake horse power. The Jaguar immediately responded and gave chase, the element of surprise now lost. The power of the Jaguar excited Adam as his bodyweight sank back into the leather seat, and a surge of adrenaline coursed through his veins. The emotion he was experiencing could be a double-edged sword, a weapon he could use to his advantage.

The two cars raced through the empty streets of west London. Adam managed to catch up to the Porsche by thrashing the supercharged V6 engine which roared under the Jag's bonnet. He swung out to the right and used the oncoming lane to get alongside Nevzlin. By keeping just short of being parallel with the Russian, Adam was able to sit in his opponent's blind spot as he lined up another shot. Nevzlin anticipated the shot and lurched his car to the right, knocking Adam off target and causing the rounds to go astray. The Jaguar buffeted the kerb. Adam repositioned himself in Nevzlin's blind spot, confident that the next shot would be the only one he needed. Looking down the integrated sight of his Sig Sauer P230 Adam focused on the back of the Russian's head and exhaled as his finger feathered the trigger. He was about to apply the final gentle squeeze when in his peripheral vision Adam saw two drunken women stagger out in to the road. Nevzlin saw them a second later as they stepped in to his path. He gunned the accelerator and readied himself for the impact, hoping that the two bodies would fly over the car rather than under it and slow his progress.

Instinctively, Adam banked left and rammed the Porsche hard, sending it up on to the kerb. He pulled sharply to the right on his steering wheel, swerving the car and missing the terrified teenage girls by only a few feet. Adam fought desperately with the car to bring it back under his control but the speed and momentum of the car spun it sideways and it flipped into the air. The Jaguar somersaulted and tumbled from roof to wheels and back to roof again before skidding to a halt over several meters. Fighting hard to resist the violent forces acting on him, Adam's body went rigid. There was nothing he could do now but wait and see where and how he ended up. Glass shattered all around him and the fragments hailed down on his bare face and hands, stabbing and slashing at the flesh. The sound of breaking glass and crumpling metal instantly triggered a series of painful flashbacks and Adam felt like he was about to die for the second time in his life. Then it all went quiet, and black.

It was the soft click of leather on tarmac that roused him. Adam hung upside down in the wreckage of the Jaguar, a pool of his blood merging with the Italian Racing Red paintwork of the car's twisted frame. He fumbled weakly to unclip the seatbelt that was suspending him but he couldn't orientate himself. The sound of the shoes got louder and Adam could see the legs that they belonged to approaching him. The noise stopped and the man squatted, revealing an evil smile drawn across his thick face.

His accent was strong; 'whoever you are, you are good. But I was *made* to be better.' The man sneered as he jutted his pistol through the open window frame. Two muffled shots sounded out. Blood splattered against Adam's face and the Russian slumped forwards.

As the body fell away to the side, Adam could see that it was quickly surrounded by several pairs of black boots, all laced tightly over trouser ends.

Before he passed out Adam saw Richard Palmer kneel to peer into the car.

'You made a right cock-up of that.'

# ELEVEN

Adam opened his left eye. It felt dry and coarse as if it had been sand-blasted. He closed it again, the heavy lid scraping over the scorched eye ball, before opening it again and repeating the cycle a few more times to spread a thin film of lubricating fluid over the orbit. His vision was blurred and lacked any sense of depth. He quickly realised that his right eye was still closed but as he willed it to open the pressure of the blood around it forced it shut. The ceiling above him was white and flawless, like freshly fallen snow. A ceiling strip-light off to his left emitted a natural white light that ordinarily would feel like daylight, but it burned Adam's left retina and he forced himself to look away.

'*Where am I?*' he asked himself. The scent of disinfectant swirled through his air passages, lodging in his nose and sterilising his sense of smell. He cleared his throat and tried to speak but a dry rasp fell out of him.

'Hello sleepy head,' came a voice from his right. He was blind-sided and he couldn't make out the face. As the figure moved around the foot of the bed to his left-hand side his vision was hardly improved, the white light creating a silhouette and his now teary left eye refracting the light around its head to create a halo.

'How are you feeling?' said the voice again. He blinked and tried to focus, a tear rolling down his cheek. The nurse was young, probably late twenties, and attractive thought Adam.

'Where am I?' he croaked. Realising his throat was dry the woman reached towards his bedside table and poured him a glass of water from a plastic jug which was topped with a green plastic lid. The water glugged into the beaker and the noise of it made Adam realise how thirsty he was. The nurse took hold of a small control panel which was attached to the bed with a white coiled wire and used it to raise Adam gently in to a long-sitting position.

'Thanks,' he said briefly before the beaker and a drinking straw were placed at his cracked lips. Now upright, with his thirst quenched Adam was able to focus on the nurse more clearly. His first impressions had been right, she was very attractive.

Setting the beaker down on the bed-side table the nurse turned to Adam and smiled.

'My name's Claudia,' she said. Adam knew this, having already seen her name badge, which was pinned to her crisp uniform just above her left breast, but he played along.

'Nice to meet you, Claudia,' he said pausing to let his dry mouth recover before continuing, 'where am I?'

'You're in the Thornbridge Hospital, London. An independent hospital. You've been here for two days now, drifting in and out of consciousness.' She scanned his face; 'you still look very weak, but much better than you did. You lost a lot of blood and needed several transfusions.'

'Well, it must have done the trick. I feel ready to leave.' Adam tried to lean forward in an attempt to get out of bed but his head thundered and his chest felt crushed as if he were at depth under water. Claudia lunged forward to steady him, her hands were warm and soft and the scent of her aroused something inside of him. She lowered him gently back against the bed.

Easy, easy; we don't need any heroics in here thank you!' He got the message loud and clear. Adam was surprised to feel so physically weak and helpless.

'We don't want to be using the paddles on you again,' said Claudia, interrupting his thoughts.

'Paddles?' asked Adam curiously.

'The defibrillator,' she explained, 'your heart stopped twice because of your low blood volume and we had to shock you back into a normal heart rhythm. The second time was a bit touch-and-go and it took three rounds of defibrillation to start you back up again!'

Adam's eyes widened, his eyebrows arching skywards. His head lolled to the right as he took in the news of being electrocuted back to life, and for the first time he looked down the ward. Including his own bed, there were eight beds in total with his being the only one occupied. He rolled his head back to the left, using the comfort of the bed to take the strain from his neck.

'Where are all the other patients?' he asked. Claudia smiled at him.

'There are none. You have the whole ward to yourself. It's been rented privately, which is the beauty of using a facility such as this.'

'And you?' asked Adam, 'do you work for the hospital?'

Her smile broadened. 'Yes, and you have me all to yourself.'

They exchanged pleasantries for a few moments, Adam's easy charm now in full flow.

'You look different with your eye open,' said Claudia, 'very steely; determined. I wonder how you'll look with both working.' Adam wasn't sure how to respond, so he just smiled. 'That's better,' she continued, 'you don't look so intense now.' He couldn't be sure but if he didn't know better Adam thought she was giving him the come-on. After the roller-coaster of events in the last few days he had yet to get to grips with the barrage of emotions he had experienced, but this one, a feeling of warmth and playfulness, he could get used to.

'Do you want to talk about your accident?' asked the nurse.

Suddenly Adam tensed, 'what accident?' Claudia detected the brevity in his tone and apologised.

'I'm sorry,' she said, 'I didn't mean to pry, I was just interested in how you...' Her words petered out. Adam realised that she had not been referring to the accident that had left him void of memory and identity.

'No, I'm sorry,' he said. 'I didn't mean to sound short with you. I'm not really able to talk about the circumstances.'

'Oh, a *secret* agent,' said Claudia in jest. She gently squeezed his arm and he felt himself stir.

'That's right. I could tell you,' he teased, 'but...'

Claudia interrupted, 'you'd have to kill me?' They

both laughed at the old line.

'Something like that,' he said. There was a slight pause in the conversation as they enjoyed the laughter, and then Claudia asked a question that hit Adam like a bullet to the heart.

'So who is Adam the secret agent really?' Adam's mind imploded in on itself. He stared into a space beyond the nurse as the question rattled around his empty head, pretending he hadn't heard the question.

After more light hearted conversation over a surprisingly enjoyable hospital meal Adam convinced the nurse he was now feeling tired and could do with a rest. He watched Claudia as she turned and strode down the ward, her soft-soled shoes squeaking slightly on the spotless hospital floor. His eyes came to rest at her shapely calf muscles, formed by the slight heel on her shoe, and then his gaze wondered upwards to appreciate the way in which her uniform pulled at her body in all the right places. She turned briefly to check on him and Adam could feel a boyish grin cracking out over his face. *Bloody hell man, pull yourself together.*

When she was out of sight Adam slid himself over the edge of the bed and slowly lowered his heavy legs to the floor. It felt slick and cool, and the sensation of pressure through his feet seemed alien for a few seconds. He kept his weight back over his arms fearing that his legs would give out, but they didn't. Eventually he stood upright, his full weight balanced precariously over his feet, his toes clawing at the floor as if to get a better grip of it. He took a few steps forwards and winced as a jolt of pain shot up his right thigh, but after a few more steps it had gone and Adam felt nothing other than the strain of using stiff muscles. He performed a quick body check. Legs OK, pelvis, ribs and spine OK. The neck was a little stiff, probably from two days of bed-rest, probably from some degree of whiplash.

Adam thought back to the car crash – the twisted wreckage, the sound of glass and metal disintegrating around him. He shuddered as he visualised himself trapped in a vehicle, its shell and innards crushed and contorted. There was no inner city backdrop though in his mind; instead he was surrounded by open fields with only the light of the moon cast over him. The night was cold, and he longed to be home…with his family.

Adam let out a groan and dropped to his knees, suddenly sapped of all strength by the fragment of memory. He fought to hold on to it, as painful as it was, but it danced around him and then it was gone.

Sat in the middle of the vacant hospital ward Adam felt utterly alone and depleted, his body throbbing and his head pounding. He was certain there was more to him; all the clues were there and he could feel it at his core. His mind turned over the question asked by Claudia, '*who was he really?*' No answer offered itself. The cold floor steadily began to drain Adam of his body heat and eventually caused a shiver to run through him. A survival instinct kicked in and alerted some well-trained part of his brain to acknowledge the sensation and respond to it. He heaved himself upward, restarting the methodical process of checking that his injured body could safely take the strain.

The second attempt at standing seemed no better than the first. When Adam finally steadied himself his gaze came to rest on the nurses' computer station in the middle of the ward, momentarily abandoned, screen unlocked, and the NHS access card still planted in the keyboard. *Sloppy security*, thought Adam, but his conscience wasn't about to kick in now and stop him from seizing this moment. He gritted his teeth and commanded his legs to move forwards, progressing from a painful shuffle to a purposeful stride by the time he reached the PC. The opportunity to delve into some part of his past, his medical *history,* had presented itself and he was now wrestling desperately with his physical and emotional pain to capitalise on it. He threw himself into the wheeled office chair and it spun to bring him level with the keyboard whilst jarring his neck in the process. Adam blocked the hurt from his mind.

'Focus,' he muttered. He jabbed at the space bar and the machine hummed to life. He clicked at one of the many tabs that lay across the top of the screen and a search facility flicked to full-page. 'Patient ID' read one of the options, 'Date of Birth' read another; Adam paused and wondered whether the birth date he had memorised since his accident was actually synchronised with his actual biological clock. 'Surname, first name' read the next line. *That's more like it.*

Claudia's voice echoed from a distant corridor signalling to Adam that tea-break was over. He could hear the faint squeaking of her shoes.

'Come on, come on,' he said hurriedly, willing the PC to return his details faster. One hit flashed up for the name Adam Newman. The date of birth matched the one he called his own, but there was no NHS number, and very little else recorded. Adam's heart sank. There were three scans listed that dated back over the last few days. Nothing from his previous accident. Adam glanced over the recent scans - an X-ray of his right upper and lower leg, an X-ray of his eye sockets, and a CT scan of his head. He paused and craned to listen beyond the ward. The squeak had stopped, and he could hear Claudia's voice along with one other, making small talk. Adam turned his attention back to the computer and clicked on the scans in turn. His mouth hung open. There were no images attached, only a typed report outlining the main findings, in white text on black background. The X-ray reports of his legs stated succinctly 'no bony or joint abnormality seen'. *How could that be,* thought Adam. Quickfall had explained to him the augmentation to his skeleton following his accident. He had witnessed the additional power for himself on several occasions.

'Why no mention of the implants?' he asked himself. Wasting no time, he hovered the mouse icon over the CT scan of his head and punched at the keyboard, hoping to see images of greyscale brain slices against a black backdrop. Nothing. The report read, 'No mass, haemorrhage or hydrocephalus. No established major vessel vascular infarct. No fracture demonstrated. Conclusion: Normal study.' There was not a single mention of the non-biological additions to his brain.

The supposed 'neurotech' that enhanced his cognition, information processing, and knowledge bank. Was he so 'top secret' that even his scan results were being doctored?

The automatic door to the ward swung open. Adam lay motionless in his bed, except for the rise and fall of his ribcage, his breathing rapid and deep from the sprint across the bay. He rolled his head slightly and saw that Claudia wasn't alone, but his vision over any distance lacked focus and he struggled to make out her companion.

'I found you a visitor out in the corridor,' she said smiling. Palmer's charmless outlook seemed to be wasted on her.

'How are you Adam?' he asked.

'On the mend Sir, thank you.' Adam spat out the words in-between stifled breaths. Claudia winked at Adam before turning to leave the two men to their conversation. The polite exchange was short lived.

'You're lucky to be alive Adam. You left one hell of a bloody mess out there. I had to shovel some bullshit to cover your tracks.' Adam looked disappointed with himself, his own critique of the failure stinging more than Palmer's words.

'I had the shot but then the girls…' Adam stopped himself but Palmer's ears had already tuned in to the words.

'Yes, tell me about the girls Adam.' His tone was pushy. Adam recounted how they had stepped out in front of the Porsche, causing him to respond in a split-second and throwing his car into an uncontrollable aerobatic display. Palmer reacted, his short fuse burning like a straw-fire.

'You mean to tell me that you passed up a kill-shot on a key target because he was about to run-down a couple of pissed-up tarts?' His lips were pursed, his head shaking from side to side in solemn disapproval. His mouth looked like he was about to push out an expletive, but then he seemed to step back from the edge of his fury. 'No matter. I had a team on stand-by to take care of the immediate aftermath, and the rest was all paperwork.'

'And the Big Man?' asked Adam, 'Russian?'

'Yes' replied Palmer. 'FSB. Or at least he used to be, but Maxim Nevzlin has been on my radar for some time. He seems to have a special affinity for targeted killing.' Targeted killing was a legal power given to the FSB, Russia's Federal Security Service and re-embodiment of the former KGB, to engage in selective assassination of terrorism suspects overseas on orders from the president.

'Let me guess, they wanted the Sports Minister's documents returned to the Motherland for safekeeping?' asked Adam. Palmer nodded in affirmation but offered no further information. 'You said on the phone that I had met my match in Nevzlin. What did you mean?' Palmer looked straight at Adam, his expression impenetrable, a silence settling between the two men with Palmer in no apparent rush to fill it. After what seemed like an age he opened his mouth to speak, but before the first word could spill out of his ashen jowls his phone started to ring loudly.

Palmer turned away from Adam, offering no apology as he slipped the black iPhone to his ear. As he stared straight through Palmer's back, Adam began to mull over his question to the Head of Special Operations; *'what was so special about the Russian?'* He was likely known to Palmer as a feared assassin who had perhaps carried out previous targeted kills on British soil in the interests of their Head of State. Unlike British intelligence the FSB, or the Federal Security Service of the Russian Federation, was a military service, like the armed forces. It was under the control of an army general, a model of operation which seemed to echo Palmer's ambitions for the Special Operations unit of MI6. But what if Maxim Nevzlin was known to Palmer for different reasons? Did the FSB have their own highly trained field operative who had come back from the dead with life-saving, skill-enhancing technology? Perhaps Nevzlin had never even been half dead, perhaps he volunteered for such experimentation. The question hung in Adam's thoughts, suddenly illuminating the darkest recesses of his mind like an intense sun burning off the hazy morning mist.

The phone line connected.

'Palmer here,' he said.

'Richard, it's Mr Kishore. Can you speak?' The voice was tinged with an Indian accent. Palmer walked away from Adam.

'Yes, go on,' he gestured. Raj Kishore had introduced himself as Mister by the virtue of his qualification and experience as a surgeon. Once a reputable orthopaedic and spinal surgeon in a large city teaching hospital, Kishore was less employable these days after gaining himself a name as a maverick in the field of integrating technology in orthopaedic implants. He considered himself a pioneer, and perhaps in many ways he was, but the old establishment of British medicine wasn't ready for his ideas and some of his practices had led to law-suits and heavy financial settlements. Kishore couldn't see how medicine would move forward without taking a few risks. It was this very attitude that put him on a path to work for Palmer, and supposedly the British Government, under the Official Secrets Act. It was Kishore's vision and expertise that turned Alex Black from a pile of shattered bone and shredded soft tissue to the deadly and seemingly indestructible Adam Newman. All of which had been orchestrated by Richard Palmer in his attempt to get a jump on the enemies of British interests, and in doing so catapult himself to the top of the Secret Intelligence Service.

'What do you have?' snapped Palmer, 'and keep it brief.'

Adam watched from his bed, but with Palmer's back turned to him there was no way he could even lip-read the conversation.

'Your man from the East,' started Kishore, 'I've given him the once over and it is all rather unimpressive. Very little to be learned from the experience.'

'Very little, or nothing?' pressed Palmer.

'Well there was one clever thing to be found – a minute device implanted alongside his pituitary gland nestled in his brain. From what I can gather it measured and regulated the release of gonadotrophic hormones…'

Palmer broke in, 'English please.'

'Yes, of course,' acknowledged Kishore. 'So, the device appears to have ultimately controlled testosterone production in the testes, allowing for continuous or intermittent higher levels.' Kishore sounded pleased with himself and very enthusiastic about the whole thing.

'And what would be the advantage of this?' asked Palmer, yet to be impressed by the science.

'Well, there would be higher levels of the hormone for muscle production and recovery from trauma, but one could also give higher surges for aggression during conflict situations.' Palmer started to nod in approval as the conversation had settled to his level of understanding and application – how could it make a man a better killing machine? 'Also,' continued the surgeon, 'you could regulate sexual desire and function, allowing your man to stay focused on the task in hand and avoid distraction, or even seduction.' Palmer was impressed.

'Anything else?' he asked.

'No,' said Kishore, 'everything else about him seemed to be the effect of doping, intense physical and psychological training, and a good dose of brain-washing I should think. How's my man?' asked Kishore referring to Adam.

'Hmm,' groaned Palmer. 'It's all gone well to date. Seems robust enough physically but I'm having doubts about his psychological function.' As he spoke Palmer found himself standing in front of the nurses' computer station. He noted that the screen was unlocked and that Claudia's access card was docked in the keyboard slot. He glanced over his right shoulder to Adam, then continued his conversation into the phone. 'Could the brain implant be failing?'

'It was always a risk,' replied Kishore. 'The man we brought in to the team for the neurosurgery was working to the very limits of his profession. This stuff has never been tried before, let alone tested. It could be disrupted by a trauma to the head or even his own thoughts and memories could remodel the neurons around it.' Palmer thought for a moment.

'What about a surge of electricity through the body?' he asked, 'like having the heart restarted with a defibrillator?' There was a pause on the line, then Kishore answered.

'In such a case, you would have a major problem on your hands.'

Adam watched as Palmer slipped the phone back into the inner pocket of his jacket and retraced his path back along the ward. Claudia was fussing around the bed and had left some pills in a small paper case on the bedside table. She was refilling Adam's glass of water as Palmer arrived.

'How soon can you be operational?' he said. Adam was about to speak when Claudia interjected.

'At least two weeks to recover from his injuries, possibly three.' Palmer ignored her. She looked to Adam for support and noticed that the boyish grin had been wiped clean off his face.

'When do you need me for, Sir?' he asked.

'Three days,' said Palmer, 'that should give you enough time to convalesce and recuperate your strength for what I have in mind.' He waved the nurse away with his hand before he divulged anything further. Claudia didn't move and attempted to reiterate her professional opinion. Palmer wasn't interested and he was clearly starting to lose patience with the girl. Adam intervened.

'Claudia, it's fine. I look much worse than I feel and I heal pretty quickly. Please, give us a moment.' His voice was calm and reassuring, but she was still not happy with the proposed timescale.

'Fine,' she said tersely and walked away with her arms folded tight below her breasts. Once she was out of ear-shot the two men picked up their conversation.

'What's the assignment?' asked Adam, his tone now serious.

'Do you remember I mentioned a loose end that I needed tying up?' asked Palmer. Adam nodded as he recalled the conversation. 'Well I need you to pay Dr Quickfall a visit.' Adam's blood ran cold as he listened to the rest of the brief. Palmer was scanning his face throughout for a reaction to the order. 'Is that clear Adam?' he asked, the words piercing Adam's newly formed conscience. Adam gave the Head of Special Operations a direct look.

'Yes Sir.'

'Call me when it's done,' said Palmer who turned to leave, and then hesitated. 'Did you find anything of interest on the computer?' he asked. Adam's face didn't even twitch, his expression impenetrable.

'Computer, Sir?'

Palmer let out a jet of air through his nostrils and rolled his eyes skywards before dismissing himself from the conversation.

As soon as he had left the hospital ward Palmer pulled the phone from his pocket once more. He scrolled through the phone book until he found the name he was looking for. *Smithy.* He punched at the name bar with his thick index finger and the call connected. It rang a few times before being answered.

'Dick, how's things?' asked the gravelly voice.

'Smithy,' replied Palmer, 'we need to meet for a drink. It's time for me to call in a favour.' The voice on the other end of the line turned business-like.

'Usual place?' he asked.

'Usual place,' replied Palmer.

# TWELVE

Palmer walked along the Kings Road, Chelsea, allowing himself a rare opportunity to fill his lungs with fresh air and not the rancid smoke he abused them with. He had taken the District line of the London Underground to Sloane Square tube station and had chosen to walk the distance to his destination rather than jump in a cab. The last of the day's light felt warm on his face, and cast alternating bands of orange on the road, interspersed by long-drawn shadows from adjacent buildings. The sun was low at this time of day and he wore a pair of black Ray-bans, shielding his cold eyes from the intense light. For the first time in a long time Richard Palmer felt a sensation close to relaxation. From a few hundred yards away he could make out the Victorian frontage of the Coopers Arms public house. It was a familiar sight to Palmer and as he approached it he was flooded with memories of times past; drinking, socialising and being more human. More recently, however, it had become a regular meeting place when his old friend was working out of the Duke of York Barracks in London. Palmer reached the pub's heavy doors and heaved one back with his shoulder.

'Palmer, you old bastard, good to see you again,' said the thick-set man rising from his chair. 'I've got you a beer in.' Palmer almost cracked a smile.

'Smithy,' he said, 'hope it's not a half, you tight arse!' The two men shook hands firmly before Palmer broke away to lift the pint glass to his parched mouth. What the bloody hell's happened to this place?' he asked.

Smithy chuckled and shook his head, 'it's called the future mate; you should get with it.' They both looked around at the contemporary décor that was starkly juxtaposed with the traditional Victorian features.

'Delectable wine menu?' said Palmer reading the chalked words scribed on a slate board behind the bar. 'Bollocks. At least they've still got some decent beers on tap.'

Smithy chuckled again.

'You don't change, do you?' Peter Smith was almost fifty years of age with greying temples and a battle-sculpted physique. He had all but lost the colloquial dialect of his descent from the mining communities of Nottinghamshire, whilst retaining an earthy sort of quality about him. His time in the military had brought him into contact with all manner of people at all levels of society and unlike Palmer he had become sociably adaptable and gradually more refined in his ways.

The two men spent a few minutes catching up on events since their last rendezvous, with the conversation mostly based around their shared military links. Peter Smith held the British Army rank of Major and for several years had been the Officer Commanding, or OC in military parlance, of UK Special Forces E-squadron. As the head of one of British Special Forces' most shadowy units he had overseen many clandestine operations, often in conjunction with the SIS and his oldest friend Richard Palmer.

'How's The Wing?' asked Palmer, referring to the time when E-Squadron had operated as the Revolutionary Warfare Wing.

'Good,' said Smithy. 'Recruitment is healthy. And recent operations have been successful.'

'Still taking from the SBS?' asked Palmer.

'Of course we are,' replied Smithy. 'They're a tough breed, but then *you* know that.' Smithy's words conjured up images that still haunted Palmer. He hadn't failed at many things in his life but not getting in to the Special Boat Service in his younger years still hurt. The training had been brutal and although he'd scraped through the physical phase of the selection process it had been the specialist training in the water that had finished him. The fear and panic of never knowing when the next gasp of fresh air would come had broken him; quite ironic as he checked how many cigarettes he had left in his packet.

'Crazy bastards,' confirmed Palmer, trying to ease his own disappointment. 'And what about your boyfriend at the bar?' he asked. Smithy shot a glance over Palmer's right shoulder to his watch-man sitting on a tall stool at the bar, and then looked back to his old friend, fixing eyes with him.

'You don't miss a bloody trick do you?' said Peter Smith. Even with his back turned to the man sat at the bar, Palmer was able to recall the man's features, his clothing, and the 'tell-tale' signs. Smithy looked at him incredulously, his head gently shaking from side to side.

'That's why I'm a spook, and you're a squaddie,' said Palmer.

Gary Roberts was perched at the bar sipping his pint of London Stout and pretending to read from a lowbrow tabloid newspaper. He was oblivious to the conversation behind him despite his best efforts to listen in. He had been tasked with two things that evening; the first had been to blend in with his surroundings, and the second had been as look-out for any potential threats to his new boss. He was half-way to failure.

'Was he that obvious?' asked Smithy. Palmer shot him a stare over the top of his pint glass.

'I am the Head of SOU, Pete,' he emphasised, 'perhaps it wasn't the fairest of tests.'

'He's newly recruited to the Increment,' said Smithy, again referring to a former incarnation of the secretive E-Squadron. 'I thought I'd give him a trial run against the best MI6 operative alive today.' Palmer didn't look flattered.

'SAS?' he asked knowingly.

'Yeah, but not long since. He was on the endurance phase last winter when that recruit died of hypothermia.' Palmer nodded as he recalled the incident, which had once again brought the Special Forces selection process under public scrutiny. He had an opinion on the usefulness of civilian interference in military conduct but on this rare occasion he decided to keep his own counsel.

'He's served about 15 months in the Regiment,'

continued Smithy, 'but already has a kill to his name and he's not shy about getting his hands dirty.'

'Sounds perfect for The Wing then,' replied Palmer. 'Get his details over to The Office and we'll vet him.' All those seconded to E-Squadron, whether from the SAS, SBS, or the Special Reconnaissance Regiment (SRR) were vetted first by SIS. Every aspect of their past; their education, social media footprint, employment, family, and choice of friends where ruthlessly scrutinised by British Intelligence to rule out any potential threat to security. Gary Roberts would be no exception, especially as he had little experience in British Special Forces; confirmed kill or not.

'He might come in useful for your next operation,' continued Palmer as he fixed his gaze on his friend. Smithy's smile tightened and his jaw tensed. Palmer was finally getting down to business.

Conversation between the two men paused momentarily as the waiter set down two plates of hot food. Peter Smith inspected his Lincolnshire sausages with mash, crispy leeks, and onion gravy and looked rather pleased with himself.

'I'm starving,' he said while looking across to Palmer who seemed to be less impressed with his beer-battered cod and chips. 'So that's what pea puree looks like,' he said disapprovingly. Smithy smiled smugly to himself before taking down a massive gulp from his second pint, which had been brought to their table moments earlier.

'You've had worse!' he said encouragingly as he cast his mind back to their squaddie days of forcing down cold ration packs whilst on hard-routine. Palmer seemed to know instinctively the times that his old friend was referring to, a bond forged through the sharing of miserable times during their army days together. Those days were now long gone and both men were much wiser and, of course, older. Out of the two of them Peter Smith was ageing better despite the physically punishing schedule he set himself, and although he was a little younger than Palmer he had also not subjected himself to near chain-smoking and the modern day stress of riding a desk. Smithy's job was both demanding and stressful but when the pressure was on he was able to vent his adrenaline surge physically, while Palmer just stoked his blood pressure and furred up the insides of his arteries. Now, sat there in that Chelsea pub, the two men could not have looked more different despite their shared beginnings. As a British Army Major, Smithy had doubly earned his status after firstly following Palmer's lead and commissioning from a NCO rank and then again by establishing himself in the British military elite – the Special Air Service. But part of him always wondered if he'd have made it this far without Palmer's lofty position in the SIS creating a few opportunities for him along the way. He knew that's how his friend and mentor liked it; always a favour in hand despite the numerous times the debt had been repaid.

Palmer heaped the white fish up on his fork before shovelling it into his mouth without so much as a care of how he might have looked to others in the pub. He started where he had left off minutes earlier, only this time forcing his words out through a bolus of partially digested fish and chips.

'So, this favour I need.'

Smithy responded professionally. 'When E Squadron is not tasking for the UK Directorate of Special Forces you know we're at the disposable of you and the SIS.' Palmer nodded approvingly as he swallowed down another mouthful of food. It was true, E Squadron's role was to carry out clandestine operations for Britain's foreign intelligence service, where intelligence officers were active throughout the world. Often operating in hostile regions the MI6 agents would require Special Forces escorts and Smithy's squadron of elite operatives were specially trained and selected to work with MI6.

'The Increment has done me many favours in the past Smithy and for that I'm grateful,' continued Palmer. 'This one's a deep-black, operating on the fringe of the General Support Branch.' He was referring to the operational link between UK Special Forces and MI6, the most deniable relationship in the eyes of the British Government. The full extent to which these two organisations worked together was highly secretive but the two men who sat casually enjoying a catch up over a beer would be able to recount every last detail of that partnership.

'What can I say?' conceded Smithy finally, knowing that he could not say no to the Director of MI6's Special Operations Unit. 'Discretion is our middle name. But we're not as shadowy as we were back in the Increment days. You've got Libya to thank for that.' He was referring to the 2011 NATO mission against the Gaddafi regime in Libya. It had been the first time that the elite group known as E Squadron had been mentioned in the national media.

'What a balls-up that was,' confirmed Palmer. 'And who got your boys out of that shit-hole?' he persisted. Smithy conceded again.

'Yeah, yeah, and don't I know it. I owe you.' He paused, still clearly riled by the whole incident. 'We didn't think the bloody locals would mistake us for Libyan forces and detain us.'

'Well they did,' countered Palmer, 'along with some of my best intelligence officers. Anyway, I got them all released didn't I?' It was true. Palmer had instigated a diplomatic maelstrom that had swiftly, but publicly, ensured the release of the E squadron team. And it was for this reason that Peter Smith would eternally be in Richard Palmer's pocket when it came to the use of his elite clandestine unit.

'I knew we should have used camels instead of a Chinook helicopter,' said Smithy dryly. The two men laughed and clanked the glasses of their second pint.

'So what exactly is the job?' asked Smithy, still smiling from his joke.

The smile was wiped clean off his face with Palmer's reply. 'It's an assassination. On home soil.'

He leaned in, now deadly serious. 'Ok, I'll put my best man on it.'

'No' said Palmer, 'it's going to take more than one man. I need a team; of your best operatives.' Peter Smith looked offended by the request, although he wasn't quite sure whether or not Palmer was pulling his leg.

'A whole team for one hit – piss off. You're talking about the best of the best here, Dick. My guys are ruthless, and deadly.'

Palmer matched his seriousness.

'I'm fully aware of E Squadron's capabilities,' he said, 'your ranks feature some of the toughest and nastiest SAS and SBS operatives around, but this target; he's the most advanced field agent I've ever trained,' then he paused and lowered his voice. 'The best I've ever *created*.' Smithy stopped chewing and looked at Palmer with an expression of confusion. 'Understand this Pete, I created my own task force – a one man army. And he was the best I'd ever seen.' Smithy still didn't look convinced and was not happy to have a single SIS operative equated to his killer force.

'Why the past tense?' he asked. 'What's happened to him, and why the hit?'

'He has a weakness,' replied Palmer, 'and it's not his technical ability or his physical or mental toughness.' Smithy pressed Palmer for the target's 'Achilles heel', wanting to know every advantage over his enemy.

'What's his weakness?' he asked.

Palmer paused. 'He has a conscience. We tried hard to suppress it, using all the usual training, psychological techniques and even some new technological applications,' said Palmer trying not to give away any detail. 'But despite it all, with everything he had to offer us, this one weakness grew like a cancer inside him, until...' Palmer didn't finish the sentence. He hadn't really given it much thought until now but as he attempted to justify his position to Smithy, and to himself, he realised that he felt betrayed by Adam. His first born of Project Adam now seemed destined to walk another path and there was nothing his creator could do about it. He had to die.

'I'm not sure that having a conscience is a weakness,' said Smithy.

Palmer shot him a cold stare.

'Just kill him.'

# THIRTEEN

Against best medical advice Adam had discharged himself from hospital the day before and in truth he was glad to see the back of the place. He'd quickly discovered that he wasn't one for sitting around waiting to heal. His body had stiffening and his mind had softened. The only thing he missed about his stay there was Claudia, mostly for her looks if he was being honest with himself, but also she had been the first person he could remember feeling connected to in some way. He had enjoyed her humour, and the attention he had received from her. He had found it difficult to turn her down when she had asked him out for a drink. Adam had blamed work and travel commitments for preventing him taking up her offer of a drink, and probably more, but deep down he had another reason. He felt committed to something or someone else, but he couldn't quite pin down what or who the feeling was based on. He hoped today's rendezvous would shed more light on his past, but it would also involve him saying goodbye to part of his present life.

After spending the night back at the SOU building he had slept well, waking refreshed and feeling part way to his self. He started the day with a treadmill run but his right leg throbbed as he pounded out the first kilometre. By two kilometres it was all over, the cramp and spasms burning deep in his thigh. Perhaps Claudia had been right to protest his early return to work. When he returned to his room Adam caught sight of himself in the full length mirror hanging on the wall. It was like looking at someone else's reflection. His usual attire was business-like, but on impulse he made his way to Oxford Street and made quick work of assembling a new wardrobe. By the time he'd finished he looked like he'd just stepped out of a fashion catalogue. Adam executed his new look with ease and he wondered what Claudia would think now if he turned up after her hospital shift in his tapered black denim, red knitted polo shirt and grey wool blazer.

Finally, Adam reached his destination in central London, and was surprised at the state of it. Riddled with litter, and generally a bit run down it was not the standard of living he had expected of his target. He shrugged it off, and after reaching the Victorian town house he was looking for he bounded up the few steps to the front door. The house had been converted to flats and so had the obligatory intercom by the external door, and as expected few of the buttons on the panel were assigned flat numbers. Except for one. Adam smiled to himself and jabbed his right index figure against the labelled button, not even bothering to check the number. *Only Quickfall would keep such exact standards,* he thought to himself. Thirty seconds passed without an answer to his call. He pressed again, this time stepping back a few paces to get a line of sight to a window up and to his left. He had done his usual reconnaissance and knew that this window looked in to Grace's living room. The curtain twitched slightly, hardly at all but enough for Adam to see. He gave a discreet wave in the direction of the window. Seconds later the intercom buzzed and the front door clicked. Adam pushed it open and entered in to the shared hallway and staircase. *What a dump,* he thought, wondering what a woman of such high standards saw in the place. Then he remembered the SIS pay scales, which were far less than most people expected them to be, and in conjunction with Quickfall's time in education and research he figured it would amount to a shit-hole like this.

Adam cleared the stair case quickly and quietly, two steps at a time until he was at the door to the flat. It was already open, slightly ajar with no chain fixed across the gap. Adam still knocked before he entered. There was no reply, only the faint background noise of a string symphony emanating from a BBC radio channel.

'Hello?' he said tentatively. Still no answer. Adam drew his pistol, a compact Sig Sauer P228, from beneath his blazer and levelled it ahead of him. He kept it close to his body with his elbows flexed and tucked tight. Operating in a confined space like this was a compromise between having the weapon extended and aimed and giving the game away by jutting it out ahead of your position. As he glided down the hallway to the living room his sense of smell was hit by the sweet scent of mature lilies. Rossini's symphony was reaching its climax over the airwaves, which seemed in time with Adam's rising pulse rate. He didn't expect this sort of behaviour from Quickfall and he wondered what scene might lie ahead of him. He questioned whether it had been Quickfall at the window; perhaps Palmer had sent someone else to dispose of her and to create a trap that would draw him in. His heart rate was approaching maximum. He raised his pistol slightly and stepped swiftly into the door way, dropping to one knee and a stable firing position.

Grace didn't flinch. She just sat there on the sofa looking gaunt and devoid of care. She looked awful; a massive departure from her usual business dress and polished exterior. As she sat there in the middle of her two seater sofa flanked by excessively large amethyst cushions, only her eyes moved and they seemed to roll listlessly in Adam's direction. He got to his feet and cleared the room of any third party. Only when he was satisfied there was no immediate threat to himself did he lower his weapon, although as Quickfall observed, he didn't re-holster his pistol. At first he just looked at her from a distance, with a weary expression that you'd use on a stray dog that looked badly treated but that you couldn't be sure wouldn't bite you.

Without even looking at him Grace spoke first. 'What took you so long?' Adam squatted and came to rest on the backs of his heels, poised on the balls of his feet and with the pistol rested over his right thigh. He continued to study her. She looked up at him and their eyes met. 'You look awful,' she said, referring to the bruising around his face and the purple - green swelling that seemed to have engulfed his right eyeball.

'I was going to say the same about you,' replied Adam. Her gaze fell away.

'Just do what you came to do Adam. I'm tired. I've died a thousand times already inside.'

Adam straightened and stepped forward, towering above her with the pistol muzzle inches from her forehead. He angled it slightly over her temple. He respected her enough to make it quick. The trigger met the pressure from his index finger, equal and opposite for the briefest moment. The pistol fell to his side. Grace remained upright, her eyes still locked on his. He needed answers, and killing Quickfall would leave him no further on with recovering his past. He opened his mouth to speak but before he could say a word she leaped at him, eyes wide and arms flailing.

'You fucking monster,' she yelled, 'just do it, just kill me and get it over with.'

With the pistol in his right hand, he fended her off easily enough with just his left hand but she was relentless and seemed possessed, or crazed.

'Do it. Fucking do it! I can't take it anymore,' she screamed, thumping her balled hands down on him. Adam wasn't sure what to do; his usual methods of silencing someone would have been a bit overkill and there was a large part of him, or rather all of him, that didn't want to harm her.

Finally, she stopped screaming and flailing. She broke down on the spot and flung her arms around Adam's wide shoulders. She had completely lost it, her apathy and fatigue dispelled to reveal the basic emotion of fear. Grace Quickfall sobbed uncontrollably, her face buried into Adam's chest so much so that he could feel his skin getting wet as the tears soaked through his shirt. He brought up his free left arm and placed it around her upper back. It felt surprisingly natural and as he held her close he could feel himself soften. He closed his eyes and rested his head against hers.

'I knew they'd send you one day,' she said between the sobs. 'I thought I was ready to die but I'm not. I'm terrified.' She wailed on some more. Adam let her get it out of her system, and maintained the embrace as her body shook gently in his arms. He didn't know what to say but he figured he was better saying nothing.

The crying eventually subsided and a quiet descended on the pair of them. They both seemed aware of their bodily contact with each other and their senses were heightened to the other's breathing pattern. Grace slid her arms up over Adam's shoulders and ran her hands gently up the back of his neck and into his hair. He seemed responsive to it. She withdrew from him slightly, maintaining chest contact but arching her head and neck enough to make eye contact with him. Adam's steely eyes were intense, his pupils wide like black holes in space, their gravity pulling Quickfall inescapably towards them. He touched her face gently. She opened her mouth slightly and leaned in. Their lips were inches apart, then at the last moment she dropped her head bringing Adam's kiss to meet her forehead.

'What's wrong?' he whispered.

'I have wanted this for so long,' she said with sorrow in her voice, 'but I can't do it.'

Adam used both of his hands to cup her face and direct it towards his. He didn't speak but his eyes questioned her. She brought her own hands up over his, pulling them free of her face and kissing them softly before letting them fall away.

'I think you're married,' she said.

Adam staggered backwards and patted his torso with both hands, convinced Quickfall had seduced him to obtain his pistol and shoot him through the heart with it.

'Tell me,' he said, 'tell me what you know?' He didn't seem to question the truth of her statement. Deep down he knew it was true. It sounded right, congruent with some buried belief about himself. 'What else do you know?' he demanded. His tone was now firm. Quickfall stepped backwards but it wasn't quick enough to avoid his iron-grip as he took her by both upper arms and clamped them down against her sides to prevent her from breaking free.

'I don't know,' she started, but Adam didn't seem convinced and squeezed hard on her arms. 'Adam please you're hurting me.' But Adam's eyes were glazed over, his focus now internal like he was watching a replay of a life inside his head. His eyes flicked back to the present moment, and to the woman in his grip who was wincing with pain.

'Tell me,' he shouted. Quickfall didn't have time to think about the consequences of her actions as she blurted out the only other fact she knew to be true about him; 'your name,' she said, 'your name is Alex Black.'

It was as if she had unleashed a barrage of heavy blows to his head and stomach, like a far-fetched fight scene from a boxing movie. He felt disoriented and sick all at the same time. The name *Alex Black* rattled around painfully in his head and tore through his fogged brain. Quickfall could do nothing but watch as he drifted backwards aimlessly, and then dropped to one knee gripping his temples between his flattened palms. She was pleased to be free of his grip and began to rub at her own arms to distract from the pain in them. Adam wrestled with the thousand images that flooded his memory, all partial and disordered. He saw what he thought might be his parents, an aging couple that seemed to look and posture themselves like him; his childhood, a wife, and…his own children. A girl and a boy, he thought.

He got to his feet, taking two long strides to reach Quickfall.

'Tell me more!' he yelled, but she was shaking her head; she was spent. The strike came hard and fast and it almost took her off her feet. She managed to recover her footing but she was stunned and couldn't compute what had just happened. He caught up to her and before she could utter a word his left hand grabbed her face, his fingers pressing hard in to the fleshy parts between her cheek bones and jaw bones. She tried to scream out but the shape of her mouth was distorted and the little sound that she managed was deflected backwards by Adam's palm that spanned the fingers and thumb gripping either side of her face. He pulled his pistol up under her chin. It hurt badly, but not as much it could do and she began to cry at the thought of being back on the end of a loaded gun.

'Who the hell am I?' he demanded, his eyes wide and wild.

The question hung in the air. The man stood before her was almost unrecognisable; erratic, and emotional. His shoulders were low and rounded giving him a deflated appearance. Quickfall pondered the question, her educated brain computing the possibilities before her. She took a chance.

'Alex,' she said, 'it's Alex isn't it?' The man's eyes stopped shifting from left to right and fixed on her. He seemed to be responding to the name. Buried deep in the man's mind was another personality that had been suppressed by a mixture of trauma, science and psychology, but was now erupting with violent consequences. Grace knew this, and she wished to God that she hadn't revealed this identity, but the damage was already done. Her only hope was to use every ounce of her psychology training to talk him down and negotiate her own safety. The major problem being that she was unsure of which identity she was talking to, and if it was Alex and not Adam then she had no common ground on which to build rapport. She knew nothing about the man.

'Tell me more,' he yelled. Sweat was running over his face and neck, soaking his shirt. He waved the pistol around freely and intermittently jabbed it in her direction.

Before commencing her research career in neuropsychology she had worked with personality disorders and had become skilled at psychiatric diagnosis. Quickfall guessed that her aggressor was showing elements of identity fragmentation, a sign of Dissociative Identity Disorder. Once referred to as a multiple personality disorder the condition had been relabelled to reflect the improved understanding of two or more distinct identities existing in an individual. It was a controversial diagnosis at the best of times, she had come to learn, but in this instance she could see one man wrestling with his two identities; one of which she had helped create.

'I don't know much more,' said Dr Quickfall truthfully, holding her shaking hands in front of her with palms forward facing. The man lunged at her.

'You're fucking lying,' he said, thrusting the Sig in her face, his own hands shaking as much as hers. She knew her situation was critical. Alex Black, the man now wielding the gun, was unpredictable and therefore very dangerous. Adam on the other hand was deadly in a predictable sort of way.

'Please, please. I will tell you what I know if you lower the gun. I can't think straight with that in my face.' She had to buy herself time. Although her psychological background had allowed her to diagnose the personality disorder, simply knowing the diagnosis was going to do little to treat it. She had to try something before the frenzied gun man blew her head off. 'Your name is Alex Black – I know that much. And your age, and a few other medical facts about you.' She paused to let that register with him. 'But you have to believe me, I've tried researching you using all the resources I had available. It's like you never existed. I don't know what Palmer did but I can't find records of your birth or death, marriage or medical history. There are no available news reports of any accidents around the time you came to us. You're a ghost. He made you vanish.' The man's head was thick with pain.

'Why?' he asked.

'To create Adam,' came the reply almost instantly.

The man stood back and lowered the weapon by his right trouser pocket. He looked exhausted. With eyes like a lost child he looked across to her.

'Please,' he said, gesturing to her to continue. She had found a way in, and as long he stayed in a rationale state she had a chance. She searched her own memory for anything she could find on Dissociate Identity Disorder, and remembered that the only way to treat the splintering of identity was to integrate the memory and consciousness of Alex Black and Adam Newman into a single identity. Ordinarily this would involve long-term psychotherapy to deconstruct and then reunite the different personalities. But time was not a luxury available to her, and not knowing which of his personality states was his primary identity meant it could all go very wrong very quickly.

Quickfall moved slowly over to a small round wooden table in the corner of the living room and helped herself to the red wine bottle that was half corked in the centre of the table top. She took a long large gulp from the well-used glass that had been next to the bottle, and felt her nerves settle slightly. She had to get her head in the game. If she couldn't untangle this psychological disaster quickly then they were both fucked.

'I'm going to tell you what I know about you after your accident,' she said calmly. The man just nodded. He had joined her at the table and had the gun rested on the table top, pointed in Grace's direction and with his finger gently feathering the trigger. 'You were given the name Adam Newman, and that was all I knew you as for a while. I was recruited to SIS a few months prior to working with you because of work that I had done with brain injured subjects. I helped them learn and rediscover memories at a faster rate using novel technologies and methods. And from what I initially understood about the project, that was what I was doing with you.'

'What project?' asked the man.

'Project Adam,' she replied, 'the project which gave you your name and your new identity.'

'Why Adam?' he asked again.

'Palmer once joked that it was an acronym for Accidently Damaged and Modified' said Quickfall with a childish smile forming in the corner of her mouth, before instantly realising the inappropriateness of her remark. She blushed the colour of her wine and pushed the glass away wondering whether its contents had gone to her head. 'But it had a deeper meaning,' she continued and began to paraphrase the Holy Book; 'in the Biblical sense, in Genesis, Adam is made from the earth which is one part of his identity, but he is taken from it and estrangement from the earth. His curse represents humankind's divided identity of being earthly yet separated from nature.' She couldn't bear to look him in the eyes but he could see the tear form and begin to find its path down her cheek. 'That's what we did,' she said, 'we estranged you from nature, from your true identity. You weren't reborn, you were stolen.' Her shoulders began shaking and more tears raced down her hollowed face. 'I'm so sorry Adam, I didn't know what I was getting in to. I would never...' she broke down and left the sentence to drown in her emotion.

Adam moved over to the living room window and stared vacantly out on to the street below. The well-pressed floral curtains in the foreground were starkly contrasted with the filth and waste that blew along the pavements. He admired Quickfall's defiance in maintaining her standards amongst such dreariness. It had been less than an hour earlier that he had looked up from that street and seen the slight disturbance of the curtain by which he was now stood. In that time his world had been turned upside down, and so he noted, had Quickfall's. Palmer and his macabre project had a lot to answer for.

The ambient classical music had been replaced by a faint sobbing, that was occasionally punctuated by sniffling noises or a deep sigh. He looked back over his shoulder to see Quickfall slumped over the small table. She looked completely shattered. Adam resumed his observation of the street below, where ordinary people seemed to be going about their daily routine. Some walked with a purposeful pace, perhaps cutting across the City and not wanting to dwell in such a downtrodden part of it. Others looked like they belonged here, their faces grey and miserable like the concrete under their dragging feet. *Do I really want to go back to this life?* considered Adam. He thought about what he knew of his former self, Alex Black, married with kids, a steady job and most likely a mortgage. He sighed. But then he contemplated the alternative of running back to Palmer and executing more of his dirty work until eventually he met his own nasty end. Karma was inescapable in his work and his sins would come back around if he played the game long enough. He tried hard to think about what his life was like as Alex but the scene was riddled with holes, and his life story seemed out of order and context. Like trying to recall a dream he could see the people in his life but not their features clearly. Instead their faces were substituted with those of people he knew in his current life, as Adam Newman. His mind and memory where mangled. Strangely though he felt OK. Before breaking down, Quickfall had worked her professional magic and somehow fused the disparate identities of Adam and Alex.

'Who am I?' he asked himself in a low whisper, flicking his focus to the glass in front of him to see a faint reflection.

'Adam,' came the soft voice from behind him.

Grace Quickfall was standing behind him, a broken smile on her tired face. She repeated her answer to his question.

'Adam. That's who you are. I would recognise you anywhere.' Whilst he had stood with his back to her she had glanced across at his silhouette formed by the light of the window and she had known instantly who the primary identity was. His stature, his control, his calm presence. She wanted to tell him that she loved him. 'Here,' she said holding out the Sig pistol in her hand. Adam took it from her and without thinking checked it over.

'They say that in the UK nearly 80% of female murder victims are killed by someone they know.' By now her tears had dried up and she had nothing left to give. Adam gave a knowing nod and raised the loaded weapon. His words were full of sorrow.

'Good bye Grace.'

# FOURTEEN

A light rain had started to fall from the wisps of grey overhead. The best of the day was long gone, obscured by the congregating cloud that seemed to promise worse was yet to come. Adam noted to himself that it was unusually dark given the time of day and the unexpected cold wind forced him to flick up his collar and fasten his jacket. He picked up his pace as he headed in the direction of Hackney centre. Adam held the mobile phone close to his head using a cupped hand to keep out the worst of the rain. The line connected and he felt his sodden heart begin to weigh heavy as he thought about the previous few hours. There was an answer at the other end but no voice. Adam spoke into the void.

'It's done,' he said without any sign of emotion.

'Excellent work,' came the reply finally. Even with the ambient tapping of the rain there was no mistaking the rasp of the heavy smoker, a slight rattle to his chest. 'I've been thinking,' he continued, 'you should take a few days to recuperate further. I have a place on the Heritage Coast, Sussex; you should go there. Take as long as you need.' Adam was surprised by Palmer's offer but he didn't refuse it. After the day he'd had he needed some time away from the SOU, and this sounded as good an opportunity as any. The wide open spaces appealed to him and he accepted the offer and the idea of solitude. He listened on as Palmer gave him instructions.

'There's a key box,' he said. Adam noted the code and then the address and committed them both to memory. 'You've been a great help,' said the voice finally before hanging up. Neither man had used a name or given any specific detail of the job in-hand. The conversation had been easy and non-descript, as was the way on an open line. Adam slid the slender Samsung phone into his inner jacket pocket to avoid the wet.

The break would do him good. There was just one visit he had to make first.

Palmer had barely ended one call before dialling the next. As he waited for the dial tone to start up he contemplated Adam's actions. He hadn't been sure whether Adam would go through with it but once again he had delivered on his word. Palmer had not known a more reliable and accomplished killer, yet whenever he thought of Adam he did so with a sense of disappointment. Ever since Palmer had collected the near-corpse from Dr Kenneth Baker he had viewed Alex Black as a make-shift candidate, barely adequate for the expectations of his long-awaited project. Adam could do no right, and this suited Palmer as it would make disposing of him much easier. He began to contemplate the ultimate perfection he could achieve with future attempts at Project ADAM. For a few seconds Palmer found himself looking straight ahead into dead space, away with his thoughts. When the phone finally connected it jolted him back to the present.

'Dickie. You have news?'

'It's on,' said Palmer. 'Give it a day or two at the latest. Enough time for him to relax his guard but not long enough to recover his strength. Location as discussed.'

'Roger that,' acknowledged Peter Smith. The line went dead. Palmer kicked back in his leather office chair and swivelled round to admire the view over the Thames. A grin spread across his face, revealing his tarnished yellow teeth. Everything was back under his control and by the end of the week he could start planning for Adam's successor. Given all that he had learnt from this experience, and added to the information obtained from the Russians and Americans, Adam 2.0 would be a force to be reckoned with. Palmer would be unstoppable.

Adam reached the internet café on Hackney Road and hurried in to escape the weather. The precipitation had been mostly light but given the distance he had walked it had left him feeling damp and uncomfortable. The internet café was a grim looking little place, made all the more gloomy by the fogged windows caused by moisture in the air, most of which was now steaming from Adam's body. The place was as cheap as chips and from the look on the face of the woman serving him the fee did not cover hospitality. He made sure to get his change and not appear flash, but at £2.50 for an hour's internet use *and* a cup of something resembling coffee he felt like he was taking the piss by accepting money back from a fiver. Leaving any sort of tip in a place like this would have given the woman at the counter good reason to pay attention to him, attention that he could do without. He took his money and seated himself alone in a dingy corner. As he waited for the PC to load up, which it seemed to be doing quickly in all fairness to the place, he thought back to his time at Quickfall's flat. Her wireless internet had been running yet he didn't seem to be able to update his memory like before. When she had revealed *that* name; 'Alex Black', he had hoped that some internet source would provide vital information to spark a memory. Nothing had materialised from the ether, but then Quickfall had said it was like he had never existed.

Adam trawled his rutted organic memory whilst simultaneously punching keyword combinations into the search bar that had now appeared on the monitor before him. All initial entries returned thousands of responses which meant nothing to him. He continued to sift through the deluge of information. After 20 minutes of guesswork and Boolean logic a search return caught his eye. He wasn't sure why at first but the article on cross-country running inter-club championships seemed vaguely meaningful. He followed his instinct and the link. His fingers scrambled hurriedly over the keyboard as each successive search seemed to drip-feed buzzwords that were leading him in the direction of a tangible past. A note popped up in the bottom right of the monitor to warn him of the ten minutes of paid internet he had left. He had no intention of paying for further access, not least because he didn't want the near-cadaver at the desk remembering his face but also a small crowd was gathering and it seemed people were keen to take his seat. He wondered if it was the bad coffee or the crap décor that pulled in the punters. With minutes to go he found what he was looking for. He had followed a partial address referred to on a snippet of some social media, and combined with a property search website and Google maps street view he found himself staring at an image of a house. Adam's hands recoiled from the keyboard as if the keys were hot to the touch. He stared at the image, eyes wide in shock. His head began to thud again in the same way it had done when he heard his true name for the first-time. The vision on the screen before him forced dormant synapses in his brain to explode into action and reconnect with mothballed memories.

Stepping out on to Hackney Road Adam felt like the blanket of grey sky had intensified its threat, and the dreariness he felt within seemed continuous with the veil of precipitate all around him. He no longer cared about the rain as he headed towards the tube station, his focus was internalised as he reflected on the meaning of the day's events. Had he really been Alex Black, teenage cross-country runner and owner of a life other than killing for Queen and Country? He now believed it beyond doubt. He was a logical man but even if he wasn't the evidence was overwhelming; a man back from the dead, void of memory and driven only to serve a master. He was definitely more than the sum of these things and it seemed that only a visit to the Tunbridge Wells address, and specifically to a red-brick detached house, would answer his questions.

Adam was so wrapped up in his inner world that he didn't notice the black Ford Mondeo ease out of a store's loading bay opposite the internet café. It still didn't draw his attention when it rolled into a bus lane, all of which would have waved red flags in his mind on any other day.

'Target on the move,' said a plain looking man down his radio, 'heading south towards Bethnal Green.'

'Roger that,' crackled the reply from the earpiece. The driver continued to watch his man from behind tinted glass.

'Target appears to be moving to the underground station. Shall I pursue on foot?' There was a delay in the response as the recipient weighed up the options.

'Negative. We have the onward destination. Stand down.' The Mondeo man affirmed the message swiftly and professionally using standard military procedures for radio communication, 'Wilco. Out.' He looked pleased to be heading back to base for a decent meal and a good brew. His work for the day, like much of that in the Special Forces had involved hanging around for hours on end whilst remaining able to respond to any situation at a second's notice.

Peter Smith put down his radio on the desk top. At Palmer's request he had put surveillance on Adam in case he had refused the offer of a stay on the Sussex coastline. Following Adam's multiple encounters with a defibrillator whilst hospitalised, Palmer's worst fears had been confirmed. Not only was his protégé now potentially capable of free thought, emotion and recalling long-term memories he was also now largely untraceable. The neurotech implant had provided two methods of locating Adam's position anywhere on the planet. Like most smartphones, the device combined a GPS Global Navigation Satellite System with Wi-Fi positioning systems. The use of Wi-Fi had been incorporated to overcome the poor performance of GPS in indoor environments. Both of these methods had been incapacitated by the surge of electricity from the life-saving defibrillator. Unbeknown to its host, and Palmer, the intense electrical activity had caused the neuro-technology to fuse with Adam's own neural networks. The artificial synapse with his own brain cells was now running on the electrochemical power source provided by the nerve cells themselves. Adam had been freed of the restraints of the technology yet he was still benefitting from some of its applications. He just didn't know it yet.

As Smithy stood there in the briefing room at the Duke of York Barracks he was confident he had made the right decision in calling off the pursuit of his target. Palmer had confirmed to him that Adam intended to be at the coastal cottage and so he didn't see the point of wasting resources in observing him into the following day. *What was he likely to do in this time?* thought the Army Major to himself.

'All eyes on me,' snapped the order from the front of the small room. It was windowless and featured age-old military insignia and history on its walls. There was a slight fustiness to the room, a smell of wood, and old kit, which seemed to be an obligatory characteristic of British Army barracks. Eight men fell silent and turned to face their address. E-Squadron was one of the most shadowy of all British Special Forces units. The eight operatives had been hand-picked by Peter Smith based on their prior work with the Secret Intelligence Service, all except one who was 'riding along' on his first mission.

'Gentlemen, you are being tasked with the assassination of a British citizen,' said Smith as he jabbed his index finger toward an enlarged head-and-shoulders photograph of Adam. The end of his finger tapped against the mobile whiteboard to which the photo was tacked and the sound seemed to emphasise his message. 'He is believed to pose a potential terrorist threat. He is therefore to be terminated on sight. We do not want to take him alive.' The men nodded in acknowledgement and Peter Smith continued, feeling encouraged by their engagement. 'He is an SIS operative and he is highly skilled.' Smith looked serious.

'Who's got the job?' asked a voice from the middle row of chairs. It was Joseph James, a former Royal Marine Commando who now sported a homeless look. He stroked at his beard while he waited for the answer.

'All of you,' replied Smith.

A scoff broke the lull, the Geordie accent of John Ryan clearly driving home the point, 'for one man?! Who the fuck is he, Rambo?' Laughter broke out around the briefing room before settling into outbursts of disapproval.

'Is he taking the piss?' muttered the ride-along recruit, 'I could take that guy down myself.' The two men sitting either side of him shot each other a look which acknowledged that the new guy's face didn't fit in their unit, but that they were more than happy to remodel it for him if his bullshit continued. Gary 'Gaz' Roberts was too arrogant and deluded to pick up on the not-so-subtle hint, but fortunately for him he didn't have the intellectual capacity to follow it up with anything else. Smith let his men vent their opinions, for what they were worth, before exercising his leadership, military-style. The team of elite soldiers fell quiet again and listened as he briefed them on everything he knew about their target; which was everything that had been relayed to him by Palmer. Their briefing did not extend to Adam's full capabilities or operational activity, all of which was classified and known only in full by Richard Palmer himself. The lack of true fore-warning meant that the clandestine band of Special Forces men were never going to be fully fore-armed. This was not a situation that troubled Palmer.

The sun had fallen below the horizon by the time Adam got back to the Special Operations building. His eyes were stinging with a mixture of tiredness and acid rain from the city skies. He slumped onto his bed, pleased to be resting his aching limbs. He was still covered in bruises from his encounter with Maxim Nevzlin and his body felt soft and weak. It was his mind that felt most fragile though and this was Adam's main concern. The throbs in his head were getting worse and his focus was deteriorating. He knew he needed to get himself together. Whatever Alex Black had been, it was now part of Adam, and vice versa. He could not separate the two facets of his being. But what he needed now was to be the best of both men. Quickfall had helped him greatly with this, using her specialist skills and knowledge to integrate the identities, and despite the pock-marked memories he felt strangely comfortable with who he was then and who he was now.

Adam's train of thought steamed ahead of him and he found himself mulling over Quickfall's life. Talented, genuine and naturally very beautiful, she had had it all. Project Adam had been her only downfall, recruited by Palmer she had been pulled so far into his dark world that she never stood a chance of making it back out alive. There was a bitter-sweet feeling to her exit from Palmer's sick game thought Adam, and it had been the least he could do for her. The thought of Palmer and his wilting influence caused the hairs to stand erect on the back of his neck. He instinctively reached for his Sig and started checking the chamber and magazine. When he was happy with its state of readiness he placed the weapon on his bedside cabinet and threw his legs round onto the bed. A wave of weariness washed over him and then the only sensation he seemed aware of was his thudding heart, strong and efficient, beginning to slow and count him down to a state of sleep.

Tomorrow would reveal who or what was waiting for him in the place he used to call home.

# FIFTEEN

Like an orchestrated firework display the fragmented images in his mind collided into one larger and much clearer picture. The small gravel driveway leading to the red brick house with its blue painted front door were framed in Adam's memory like an old photograph. A spasm of guilt pinched at his gut as Adam rolled the Audi R8 to a halt by the kerb and sat in contemplative silence.

The faint ticking of the cooling engine flickered in his ears, stepping in time with his thudding heartbeat. His own vehicle was in stark contrast to the average looking family hatchback sitting on the drive. Plain and predictable.

Adam's palms were sweaty and the moisture greased his tight grip on the steering wheel. Adam recognised the bodily sensations of the fight or flight response, and for a brief moment he was tempted to turn the key in the ignition and get out of there. But the urge to stay was too great. Who was beyond the blue door and what life had he left behind. It was time to find out the answers to the questions that had been gnawing at him.

Placing his pistol in the glove compartment Adam felt strangely naked without the sidearm. Compared with all of the hell holes he had been to, this was one place he wouldn't need to be armed, yet he felt more vulnerable than he ever had done.

The front garden looked in need of some attention with its over-hanging hedges and weed-filled borders. He reckoned that at some point in the recent past they would have been well tended. Adam tentatively stepped on to the driveway, the gravel crunching and sliding beneath his heavy feet; another familiar sensation. *Home.* His pulse rate punched into a higher gear. He was close now and the sense of déjà vu felt overwhelming. *Maybe this sleeping dog should be left to lie.*

Standing before the front door Adam studied the weathered paint covering its exterior. Small cracks ran through it like a network of blood vessels and as he brushed his hand gently over it the fragile blue skin fractured under his touch. The light pressure caused chips of paint to flake and fall to the floor, and Adam wondered whether he might be able to glimpse the life behind it. The door was solid wood and windowless. There would be no way of him seeing the approaching figure on the other side. Adam's pulse raced again at the thought of who might open the door to this forgotten world. He hovered a trembling finger over the doorbell. The brass was fogged and dirty. Mindlessly he jabbed his finger forwards and the faint internal chime of the bell alerted him to his actions. All he could now was wait.

\*

The car door slammed shut and the noise of it snapped

Adam out of his trance. *What the hell just happened?* He tried the words again in his head and this time they tumbled over his quivering lips. 'What the hell just happened?' His frustration echoed around the inside of the car, the waves of sound crashing in his ears. Then he fell silent. Had he just dreamt that last thirty minutes? Thirty minutes of trying to explain himself to a mute woman who just stood there, stony faced except for the solitary tear that had finally come to rest in the corner of her eye. He yelled again and thumped the steering wheel. That's when he saw her; the woman, his wife Amy, tears cascading down the contours of her taught face. She was slumped by the corner of the open front door, the blue door that had promised so much behind it. Her slender arms were wrapped around herself, a feeble embrace providing little self-comfort. Adam couldn't bear to look at her. The last half hour had been anything but a dream.

Adam gunned the engine of the car and secreted his pistol into its holster. The Audi swung violently into the road, the wheels spinning furiously before gaining traction on the tarmac. Adam's thoughts were scattered about his head and he couldn't bring a single one of them to his attention. Anger, frustration, despair and sorrow created an emotional soup within him, and it was at boiling point. He wanted Palmer dead, and he wanted his wife and family back, but he couldn't figure out how he could achieve any of it. Adam pointed the Audi in the direction of the Sussex coast and set himself to autopilot. Much of his brain power was diverted to reliving the scene from moments earlier.

Amy had just stared at the man in front of her. She said nothing. She moved nothing. She was looking straight through the ghost of her husband. Adam had instantly recognised Amy's features and had fallen in love with her all over again. But she didn't seem to know or care.

He was back in the moment again.

'Amy?' said Adam tentatively, carefully testing the flash of memory. Her stare was impenetrable and for a second he was convinced he had mistaken her for a trick of the mind. She didn't flinch when he mouthed her name. The lack of recognition was killing him as he stood there on the doorstep.

'Amy, can I come in?' he asked. 'We need to talk.' The silence hung between them for what seemed like several minutes and just as Adam was about to start backing away she nodded her head and stepped to one side. Adam glided past her like the ghost that he was.

Framed photos lined the walls of the hallway providing Adam with a time-line of his children's development. He was pleased to see how young they still were, their innocent faces suggesting there was still time in their formative years for him to find a way back in to their memories. Their faces looked so joyful and full of life. Adam forced a broken smile. He would never have walked away from something so precious.

'They're beautiful,' he said, surprising himself with the words. Amy didn't respond.

The décor looked new. Images of family life were dotted around the house, encased in shiny white wood or plastic, and formed pieces of a puzzle to a life before the one he had now. From beneath the glass each photo was an experience for him to relive all over again. The two of them continued on to the lounge, Adam leading and instinctively knowing the way. He took a seat on one of the sofas. The woman didn't sit, but stood opposite him staring incredulously at the man sat before her.

Momentarily back behind the wheel of the car, Adam attended to the high rev noise from the engine. He was half-way to the Sussex coast and couldn't recall a single feature of the route he had travelled to this point. He cursed, knowing he should never have allowed such nonsense. He had lost focus and the lack of mental and emotional discipline had led to this mistake. *Shit.* His actions had compromised the safety of Amy and the kids, and as soon as he had realised his error Adam had walked out on his former life again without a word. He could not have looked more heartless if he had tried, but when he left Amy broken hearted for the second time Adam was doing it for her own good. The more she knew, the more danger she was in. Palmer was never going to let him walk away from the SOU, and with Amy involved there would be more leverage on him to stay. He had no choice but to take hold of his senses, get out of there, and end his business with Palmer once and for all. But even with Palmer out of the equation Adam wondered whether he could revive the man in the photographs. Could he bring Alex Black back from the dead?

*I will come home, or I'll die trying.*

# SIXTEEN

Splinters of sunlight illuminated the side of Adam's face. He opened his eyes briefly and waited a few seconds for it to register where he was. After what seemed like an eternity he remembered he was at the cottage, and he recalled arriving in the dark and fumbling with the coded key box. He allowed his heavy eyes to close as he turned his back on the morning rays.

The cottage was situated high on the ridge, surrounded by the springy turf of chalk grasslands which fell away rapidly to reveal the stony Sussex coast line. As much as Palmer had made out this was his place to offer, it was in fact an asset of the British Government; officially a safe house, but more commonly a staff perk. Adam finally rolled out of bed after 9 a.m., a leisurely lie-in by normal standards but to Adam it was half way through the day. He didn't care though, nor did he feel guilty. He owed it to himself to get his mind and body back on track. He had some serious decisions to make, and when he confronted Palmer he needed to bring his A-game.

The kettle began to whistle as it sat steaming on top of the flaming stove. Adam immersed himself in the sounds and the smells. Everything seemed intensified a million times over. The sound of birdsong filled his ears and the smell of smoked bacon diffused around the kitchen as it crackled and crisped in the heavy pan. He restocked the cafetiere and finally poured himself another black coffee. The steam rose from the mug, finding its way through the heavy cold air that hung in the kitchen. Adam took his mug through to the lounge and threw another log in to the crackling open fire. He watched the flames leap up in excitement and engulf the wood, and as he stared vacantly into the display of red and orange he took a long gulp on his fresh brew. The caffeine got to work quickly and he was ready for the day ahead. He walked back through to the kitchen ready to enjoy the rest of his breakfast. It was amazing what sleep and good food could do for the body and mind. After the last few days of riding an emotional roller-coaster he was beginning to find his feet on more stable ground. By the table in the kitchen hung a large mirror framed by drift wood. It added light and depth to the cosy kitchen area. Adam caught sight of himself in it and shuffled lazily across the quarry tiled floor. The man looking back at him was barely recognisable. Rugged and boyish, with a stupid lop-sided grin spread across his face. The smile ruffled up the three-day beard he had mindlessly acquired, and the laughter lines creasing his upper face opened up his steely eyes to reveal a crystal blue that mirrored the water lapping at the coast-line. He looked human, and he felt it too. The combination of sorrow and joy, hurt and elation, which swirled around the pit of his stomach signified he was no longer Adam Newman. Well, not entirely.

It was supposed to be a walk along the beach but the minute Adam had put on shorts and trainers he had subconsciously committed himself to something more vigorous. The sea mist was beginning to burn off as the mid-morning sun simmered beyond it. Soon it would be fully exposed but until then Adam started a steady jog to raise his body temperature. The scene was perfect. Bracing sea air flowed over him, creating a steady resistance to his increasing running speed. The wet sand and shingle compacted under Adam's feet and provided a firm enough platform to propel him forward. He felt incredible. Exposed to the elements he realised this was the basis for his existence, to push himself to his limits at every opportunity, and this was not an opportunity to be wasted. He moved up a gear and his stride opened up. Adam's breathing was deep and rapid but he didn't care, nor did he care about the dull tension building in his right thigh. He felt free. The frothy water's fringe occasionally washed over Adam's feet, the icy chill striking up his senses. Combined with the view, towering chalk cliffs to one side and on the other a blue expanse of water that at some indistinct point became sky, there was no place he would rather be. He began to picture what life would be like here with his family, with Amy and the kids, all running around enticing the tide to catch their dancing feet. He smiled so widely he felt his face begin to ache.

As he headed west along the coast he could see a figure ahead, hugging the line between sea and beach. From this distance he could just about make out she was a runner, he couldn't be one hundred percent certain but there was just that impression of the way someone's body might move when running as opposed to walking. Regardless of who or what was ahead, it was a target, something to chase, and Adam welcomed the challenge. He put down the hammer down and kicked-on in pursuit.

By the time he reached his prey they were within a few hundred meters of the Seven Sisters Country Park. He had read in a leaflet back at the cottage that the country park offered some of the finest scenery in the whole of the UK, and as he closed in behind his fellow runner he found himself enjoying the view. He eased his pace as he came up alongside her, mission accomplished.

'Hi,' he said. The woman seemed startled and veered to her left, her feet splashing into the lapping waves. 'I'm sorry,' said Adam smiling, 'I didn't mean to scare you.' The woman smiled back and put up her hand to gesture she was ok.

'No problem,' she gasped. She was early- to mid-thirties, attractive and with a body that told of her regular fitness regime. Her cheeks glowed from a combination of the cold air and the physical effort. Adam thought he probably looked the same, especially after the pace he had held for the last ten minutes. 'You took me by surprise. I wasn't expecting anyone to catch up to me.' Adam apologised again, and after a few minutes they'd reached the country park. The woman stopped and began to stretch. Adam stopped too and walked off the lactic acid that was still stinging his leg muscles. He noted a sign mounted on a wooden stake;

it read 'Take nothing but pictures, leave nothing but footprints, kill nothing but time.' Adam smiled at the sentiment. In his line of work the motto might have read 'take pictures of everything, leave no footprints, kill anyone who stands in your way.' He turned to look back at his footprints, signs of his recent past, but they had all but disappeared, dissolved in the sea. Adam contemplated the analogy.

'Are you running back along the beach,' asked the woman. Adam nodded, struggling to find his own breathless voice.

'Yes,' he said finally, 'do you mind if I run with you?'

The woman looked unsure; 'depends on whether you plan on keeping to your usual pace.' He held up his hands in surrender and the two of them laughed.

'My name's Sarah.'

'Adam,' he replied, and wiped his right hand against his shorts before offering it to her.

She shook it; 'nice to meet you Adam, I think.' He sensed she was wary of him. They started their run back alongside the massive white cliffs that illuminated their route along the coast. The sun's warmth had now penetrated the earlier haze, and the glistening towers of chalk-stone reflected the gentle heat down on to the two runners.

'It's beautiful isn't it?' said Sarah.

Adam nodded in agreement, 'sure is. Do you live locally?'

'No. I'm visiting family. What about you?'

Adam paused for a second, then said casually between breaths, 'No, unfortunately not. I'm on holiday for a few days.' His mind flitted to Amy and the children and what life together might be like. Allowing the image to fade Adam fell in step with Sarah's pace and the two of them enjoyed each other's company for the few miles back along the shore-line.

It took them less than a quarter of an hour to cover the distance and Adam enjoyed every minute of it, using it as an opportunity to exercise his charm. Like the running it seemed to come naturally to him but he guessed both skill sets were the result of years of training, with much of the groundwork put in during his life as Alex. Finally, they reached the point for Adam to ascend the cliffs to the cottage. He began to slow. His pulse settled almost instantly as the muscular chambers of his heart ejected massive volumes of oxygenated blood around his system.

'Good pace. Thank you for your company,' he said. Sarah kept her legs ticking over by running on the spot. She looked light on her feet as she floated on her tip-toes and shifted her weight from leg to leg. Adam was now practicing the skill of keeping eye contact whilst ignoring other distracting features.

'You're welcome,' she said, before continuing, 'are you staying alone up there?' Adam was momentarily lost for a response, not wanting to read too much into the question. She must have read his mind. 'Oh, I'm sorry, I thought maybe…well, it doesn't matter.' Adam pondered his response some more. He thought about asking her back for a coffee, but that was just too predictable and potentially misleading.

'I'm quite busy today,' he lied after an awkward

pause. Sarah looked at him with a mischievous smile, still pushing her agenda.

'I expect you're married?' It was a statement but she had given it a hopeful inflection at the end.

'Yeah, I'm married.' It sounded weird for him to say the words, but they felt right.

'Oh well, can't blame a girl for trying.' She drew out the opportunity while she walked backwards over the shingle beach, away from Adam but still facing him and holding his gaze. He smiled and gave a look that said, *thanks but no thanks.* He was kicking himself inside. What had he been missing over the last two years? As Sarah turned and restarted her run Adam was left there wondering what had just happened. He felt excited and aroused, but more than that he felt alive. He watched Sarah disappear along the slither of beach as he climbed the cliff steps. She turned and he thought he could see her smiling. A massive grin spread across his face for the umpteenth time that day. *Cold shower for you mate,* he told himself.

Once Sarah Turner was out of sight she slowed her pace and slipped the slender mobile phone from the zip pocket of her running tights. She punched in a number from memory and the line connected after a few rings.

'Yes?' said the man's voice at the other end.

The woman spoke in veiled speech; 'He's home alone.'

'Excellent,' said the man, 'did you get to see the layout of the cottage?'

'No,' replied Sarah flatly. There was a pause on the

line and Sarah took this to signify disappointment.

'Very well, enjoy the rest of your run.' The line went dead.

Before slipping the phone back into her pocket she tapped at the screen until she found her music play-list and retrieved the ear phones that were pushed deep in the pocket of her tights. She plugged herself in to the upbeat tunes and within minutes had increased her running speed to that rivalling an Olympic middle-distance athlete. She didn't know what had pissed her off the most; being turned-down by Adam, or failing on her objective to recce the internal layout of his accommodation.

Danny Grant stared at the disconnected mobile phone in his hand and pondered the latest intelligence. He held the rank of sergeant, a position he had earned through tenacity and aggression during his time in 22 SAS, with much of his service in E squadron.

'Gather round everyone.' His tone was firm, which reflected his authority as 2IC, or second in command, on the present operation.

'Latest intel confirms the target is in-situ at the cottage. He is also confirmed to be alone. We don't know whether or not he is armed but we must assume that he is. His weapon of choice is a pistol, and it's likely to be a Sig P226 or the more concealed P228. We don't know about ammunition, but if the intel is accurate then one magazine is all that is needed to see all of you incapacitated or killed.' Banter bubbled up from the ranks, with a few of the men sneering at the idea. 'I'm fucking serious boys,' said Grant more sternly. The scene was tense. A couple of the men were exchanging glances, wondering what had rattled his cage.

'Looks like he's feeling the pressure,' muttered John Ryan.

'I don't know what the problem is,' replied Joseph James in a stage whisper, 'all this drama to kill one man in his sleep.' Danny Grant couldn't make out the words but the noise coming from the two men seemed enough to light his fuse. It didn't burn for long.

'Will you two shut-the-fuck-up?!' he commanded.

Message received. Ryan looked like an angry teenager who'd just got a bollocking from the head teacher in front of his class mates. James tried to cover his embarrassment with a smug grin.

After about another ten minutes the briefing ended, with Grant adopting a more fatherly approach; 'Complacency kills. Assume he's every bit as good as you and you'll do fine.' The team respected Grant; he'd proven himself time and time again and was a rock-solid character. If there was shit going-down he was the man you wanted leading you through it. Once he'd finished relaying the new intelligence and the mission details low-level chatter broke out amongst the men. Gary Roberts was frothing at the mouth with excitement but was mostly ignored by his peers. His face didn't seem to fit anywhere in UK Special forces, and it had crossed the mind of more than a few in the unit that if he didn't make it here then he'd end up dead or returned to unit, wherever that was. His endless stories made it hard to know fact from fiction.

The eight man unit had now got a few hours to finish getting their kit together and then resting up. They were to strike in the early hours of the morning, when their target was most vulnerable. If all went to plan he wouldn't even wake and the job would go down smoothly. The general feeling was that the job *would* go to plan.

With weapon selection and zeroing done, it was just a case of throwing together tactical clothing and body armour. Most of the cell had opted for the close quarter battle, or CQB, C8 Carbine. It was a shortened version of the Special Air Service's standard assault rifle, making it ideal for room clearing. As Sarah Turner had not been able to establish in which room of the cottage Adam would be sleeping, the adapted rifle seemed an obvious choice, although a few of the guys had thrown in an MP5 sub machine gun for good measure. Each member of the team would also be equipped with a handgun, either a Sig Sauer P226 or a Browning Hi Power, some Flash-bang stun grenades, and even a few combat knives. The latter being a lesser preference of the British Special Forces.

With everything ready and with time to kill a couple of the guys sloped off for a brew.

'So what's the background on this guy?' asked John Ryan.

'Not a lot mate, other than he's SIS, well trained, and experienced. And he seems to have Smithy and Grant spooked,' offered Les Cooper, another strong member of the eight-man elite.

'Ex-Regiment?' persisted Ryan. The guys who were

gathered round enjoying their hot tea all shook their heads.

'Fuck knows,' said Joseph James finally. Nobody seemed to have the answer.

'He was on the endurance phase with me,' said a voice finally. All heads turned to Gary Roberts who was part-way through dunking a bourbon biscuit in his brew. In an attempt to draw out the tension he scolded the ends of his fingers and the biscuit disappeared in to the mug's murky contents. 'Fuck!'

The guys all laughed and began to turn back to their own conversion.

Roberts tried to recover the conversation and the biscuit, 'Seriously. He turned up out of the blue and passed the bloody drag. Then he disappeared on the back of a four-tonner and I never saw him after that. I assumed he'd been binned.' Looks were exchanged.

'Bollocks,' said John Ryan. Laughter broke out again.

'I bet he beat you over the course, didn't he?' asked James, arching one eyebrow to the heavens inquisitively.

'No fucking way,' lied Roberts. Then it dawned on him; what if the target recognised him during the planned contact? Roberts felt the sting of a potential exposure.

*Adam Newman was a loose-end that needed tying up for good.*

# SEVENTEEN

The thin film of perspiration on his skin was beginning to dry in the early afternoon sun as Adam stopped to stretch his cooling muscles. With his left arm leant against the stone barn adjacent to the cottage he reached back for his right ankle with his free arm and pulled on his bent leg to strain the front of his thigh. There was a dull gnawing ache where the car had struck him a few weeks earlier. Bathed in the sun's warmth Adam closed his eyes and allowed his mind to drift back to the encounter. He relived the fear and bewilderment that had consumed him that night. The lack of control, the self-doubt, and the disappointment of not completing the mission without Palmer having to intervene. The defeat had left a bitter taste in his mouth. Adam's right quadriceps muscles began to burn under the stretch and the sensation burst into his day dream, transporting him instantly back to the present. Perhaps another day or two of recovery would do him good he concluded.

After a short stretching routine Adam walked off the stiffness in his legs, using the time to explore the cottage's surroundings. Set on open grasslands the cottage had perhaps belonged to a farm in its former life, with a barn that looked like it would have housed machinery of some kind, and the remains of another form of outbuilding beyond that. The two buildings that were left standing, the cottage and the barn, were made of thick stone and topped with red pan-tile roofs. They were fed by a single track of about 500 metres in length that finally joined a slightly larger country lane leading on to the nearest patch of civilisation. The picturesque scene, sea air, and the sound of waves crashing at the foot of the cliffs was beginning to heal Adam's mind, more so than he had thought possible. He contemplated later walking the mile and half to check out the local pub.

He circled the cottage and barn, passing his Audi that was parked up between the two buildings and checked his 'tell-tales' planted at the front and back door. Simple yet effective. He could see that the two fine twigs remained upright at the base of the front and rear door, and the leaf between the door and frame was just how he had left it. There was no obvious sign of entry to the cottage in his absence. Finally, he stopped by the kitchen window and checked the gas cylinders for signs of tamper. Once he had put his mind at ease he entered the kitchen via the rear door, filled the kettle and set it boiling atop the gas stove. *There was nothing like a good brew after a hard run.*

A hot shower followed the tea and Adam was thankful for the instant hot water offered by the cottage's combi-boiler. As basic as the cottage was it had clearly had a few updates over the years. There were obviously standards for SIS hideaways and Adam made the most of it as the water washed away his tension and the physical and psychological pain of the last few weeks. He found himself thinking about his morning run partner, Sarah. Adam's heart rate quickened when he pictured her. Had he read the signs properly or was there more to her? He pondered the question for a moment and then let it go when he couldn't unite his professional paranoia and his recently rediscovered sex drive. He thought of Amy; she was more beautiful than he could have imagined and he hoped it was not too late for him to be part of her life again. He hungered for a physical connection with her. Adam stepped out of the shower and traipsed through to the kitchen covered only by a towel tucked around his waist, poured himself another brew from the pot, and found himself on autopilot, dialling Amy's home phone number from his mobile. He knew the number by heart, courtesy of Alex's memory. Despite the intermittent signal at the cottage the line connected quickly, but after a few rings Adam came to his senses and killed the call.

Amy had been left shattered by the reappearance of her dead husband, and had packed the kids off to her parents for a few days. In her current state she was barely able to look after herself, never mind two helpless dependents. Her tears had finally dried up but the air around her felt so scarce that she thought she might suffocate. She welcomed the peace of death and suicide had relentlessly crossed her mind. To lose her husband once had been agony, but to lose him a second time had forever torn apart the healing wound in her heart. Pacing their family home, she even wondered if she was going mad. Had she even seen him at all, or was the whole thing a dream, or nightmare? Then her phone rang, the shock and dread suspending the beating of her heart. It rang twice, then stopped, and the blood in her fragile body started to pump once more.     Was that him? The number unknown, like so many things in her life now.  And like the identity of the caller, she may never know the answers.

*What the fuck was I thinking?* Adam was breaking all the protocols and he cursed Alex Black's emotional spontaneity.   Operational security was page one, paragraph one of the training manual and he had already compromised it by visiting Amy, and now he felt compelled to call her too.

'Get a grip man,' he urged himself out loud. The less Amy knew of him the safer she was and the less he thought about her and the kids the more he could hold out if things didn't go to plan with Palmer.  As it stood at the moment, some part of Adam or Alex was on track to jeopardise the whole thing.  As if to emphasise the point Adam's mobile phone beeped harshly at him. He looked down to see an exclamation mark where the battery symbol should have been. He took the hint and connected the phone up to a power supply. Pangs of hunger told Adam he was in need of a recharge himself.   He kicked up the stove again and stirred through five scrambled eggs in butter and milk until they were golden yellow in colour and fluffy in texture. The smell intensified the pains in his stomach as Adam tipped the contents of the pan on to two slices of buttered wholemeal toast. He made light work of emptying the plate, which satiated his hunger, but could not suppress the sensations of nervousness in his gut.

The TV in the lounge had nothing of interest to offer as Adam flicked disapprovingly through the channels. Somehow the box was receiving a variety of free-view channels that mostly screened old war movies, reruns of American Sit-Coms, or car shows with over-bearing presenters. Unimpressed, Adam turned the TV off and tossed the remote control on to the sofa. Amy was still on his mind and he felt like he needed to off-load his thoughts and feelings. It wasn't a forgone conclusion that he would ever see her again if Palmer didn't like what he had to tell him, and there was little chance of him successfully relocating his family in secret. Besides, what life would that be for Amy and the kids? Sure he could survive the secretive existence but it was too much to ask of anyone else to indulge his fantasy. That's even if they'd take him back after walking out a second time. He fended off the barrage of negative thoughts and started a search of the cottage for pen and paper. A tall pine dresser flanked the wall of the lounge and seemed a good place to start in his quest for writing materials. The lower cupboards held a few random board games and a haphazard tower of dated CDs. A quick flick through the CDs revealed a collection of free-with-this-weeks-newspaper compilations; mostly soundtracks of films long forgotten or orchestral covers of popular music. A classical radio station's 'best of' album took his fancy and he mooched over to the CD player, powered it up and fed it the disc. After a few seconds of hopeful whirring the disc took and the first hint of Rachmaninov's Piano Concerto No.2 filled the space around Adam. His mind instantly tuned in to the smooth sound and his brain-waves shifted to a different frequency.

His search continued back at the dresser as Adam rooted through the three pine drawers. His finds were a mix of useful and random items. Several boxes of matches had already proven useful in starting up the open fire that now crackled and smoked across from Adam. Its heat was slowly filling the lounge, replacing the sun's gentle warmth that now was bowing out for the early evening, its blood-red hue barely breaking the smoke that billowed from the chimney of the cottage. Further inspection of the drawers revealed a screw driver, an almost empty roll of duct-tape, some loose change, a few leaflets on local attractions, and finally, a pen. Adam checked the pen was working by scribbling on the back of a used envelope that lay on the kitchen side, and after a walk through the rest of the cottage for paper he decided the used envelope would be his best option. He sat at the kitchen table and unfolded the envelope to increase the surface area on which to dump his most intimate thoughts.

Mozart's Clarinet Concerto soothed Adam's restless mind, allowing him to connect with a million things he wanted desperately to tell Amy, but in reality all of which would risk her safety. He stared at the empty sheet in front of him as the tracks on the CD played out to themselves. An hour later Adam had managed several lines to Amy, starting with an apology and ending with his hopes for the future and how much she and the kids meant to him. The middle part of the story involving him becoming a trained assassin working on behalf of a high-ranking rogue MI6 officer never made it on to paper. What she didn't know couldn't hurt her, or so the theory went. Adam straightened up his stiff neck and back and began to realise how much the falling temperature had drained him of his body heat. Leaving the letter where it was on the kitchen table, Adam promised himself he would come back to it later and add something of substance to his story. The thought prompted him to consider his whole experience of Project Adam in one quick summarisation; would anyone ever believe his far-fetched story, and could this tale penned by Palmer be easily deleted with the press of a button, or a trigger in the right hands. Adam knew it was only a matter of time before he would face such a threat. The question was when, and who?

By now the lounge had reached a snug temperature as the open fire faded to white-embers. Adam gently placed a few more chunks of dried wood in the grate and felt the heat instantly kick up and snap at his hand. The closeness left his face feeling dry and tight for a few moments. The CD was reaching its close, with two tracks left to play. Adam slumped on the sofa, pulled the throw over him and closed his eyes. The classical music seemed to spark bursts of colour behind his closed eye-lids, dancing in time to the slow but powerful thump of his heartbeat. His legs ached with the day's activity and a wave of tiredness washed over him. Whatever the final track of the album was, Adam never heard it. Sleep came swiftly and peacefully to him as he lay there in the warmth emanating from the glowing fire.

\*

The eight-man team had waited for dark to fall before piling four-up in two black Range Rovers. It was just after twenty-two hundred hours when they departed Chelsea for their 70-mile drive south to the Sussex Coast. At this time of night they would make the journey easily in under two hours, but were only an hour in before John Ryan started his best impression of a small boy on a family trip.

'Any chance of a loo stop?' he insisted.

'For fuck's sake,' replied Tom Dale, the driver of Range Rover One. 'This is what happens when you drink five brews an hour before we set off.'

'Sorry mate,' replied Ryan, 'but I really do need a piss.'

'I wouldn't mind a Mars bar,' added Joe James. Dale rolled his eyes, wondering how he'd ended up with dumb and dumber in his vehicle.

'I'll call it through to Danny, but if it were up to me Johnno you'd go the rest of the way with wet trousers,' said the front passenger Les Cooper as he pulled out his mobile phone and swiped at Danny Grant's name. The call connected and Cooper relayed Range Rover One's conversation. Tom Dale thought he saw Range

Rover Two swerve slightly in his rear view mirror in time with the raised voice on the other end of the phone.

Cooper disconnected the call; 'he's not a happy bunny,' he said, 'but he's giving us five minutes at Crawley services, which is the next junction.'

Ryan breathed a sigh of relief before turning to his buddy, 'you couldn't get me a brew and a Double Decker whilst you're getting that Mars bar mate?' The inside of Range Rover One was instantly filled with laughter, while a deadly silence filled the second vehicle.

No one disembarked Range Rover Two as both vehicles idled in the far corner of the car park at Crawley services. Riding with 2IC Danny Grant and hearing him vent his frustration with the big kids in the other vehicle had encouraged them to suppress any desires of a Big Mac and fries. Instead they kept eyes on Range Rover One. Despite the fact that Dale had stayed behind the wheel and all weapons were secured in the metal storage container fixed in the boot of the 4x4, it was less than desirable to be stationary in such a public place. Grant cursed again when he saw James, Ryan, and Cooper all swagger back with a disposable hot drinks cup in their hands. Chris Kime, a squat and sturdy member of the kill squad, leaned forward between the two front seats to get a better look at his patrol members.

'The selfish bastards,' he said. 'They could have picked up a drink for all of us.' Jeers of agreement sounded out from the final two team members, Gaz

Roberts and Aaron Bishop.

From Crawley services both vehicles got back on to the M23 and continued south with an estimated time of arrival of just after zero hundred hours. Although he didn't let on, Grant had been pleased to waste a little time in order to hit their target in the midnight hour, but also to break the tension that had been building in both vehicles since leaving London. They continued on to the A23 and skirted the westerly edge of High Weald, an expanse of green land that bridged Kent, Sussex and Surrey. It was a designated Area of Outstanding Natural Beauty, although at this time of night it was just a sea of black. Still, it captured the imagination of the men riding through it in their Range Rovers, as quiet fell over them and a few of the guys strained to peer out through the window and imagine the medieval landscape of wooded, rolling hills studded with sandstone outcrops and ancient route-ways. Soon they had left behind the 1500 square kilometre heart of South East England and were now only thirty minutes from the action. A professional silence had overcome both vehicles as they began to switch on to the task at hand.

The shrill noise of the mobile phone yanked Adam from his sleep. He had been dreaming of his children and it took him several seconds to figure out where he was in the here-and-now. The lounge of the cottage had fallen into darkness, the only light coming from the screen of his ringing mobile phone and the faint glow at the bottom of the fire grate. Still dazed from his deep sleep Adam stumbled forward and managed to reach his phone before it connected to voice mail. He barely had time to glance at the screen, but it displayed a mobile number that he didn't recognise. He cleared his throat.

'Hello.'

There was a brief pause at the other end before a female voice sounded. 'Alex?' Adam was thrown further into a post-slumber confusion. He could only think of one person who would call him by his true name.

'Amy?' said Adam, his heart feeling like it was at the back of his throat.

'No, my dear, it's not Amy. Let's just say it's an old friend.' His head was in a spin, and once again he had put Amy at risk by offering her name to the caller. Who the fuck knew this number, and more importantly, who knew about his former identity. There was anger in his voice now.

'Who is this?' he demanded.

'Alex, my name is Elisa Wakefield. We first met several years ago.' The voice waited for some sign of recognition but Adam could not place the mature female tone. He tried hard to match the name with something stored deep in his brain.

'I was fairly certain you couldn't remember me,' she continued, 'either that or you really were quite excellent at concealing the fact when you walked past me a few months ago.'

Adam was getting tired of the guessing game already, 'when did we meet recently, and how did you know me before that?' he snapped. By now Adam had found the lamp on the lounge sideboard and as he leaned forward to flick the switch the intense light bleached his vision.

'So it is true. You have no memory of your former life, although I note you haven't denied being Alex Black.'

'Maybe I'm just humouring an old lady,' replied Adam. 'You still haven't answered my question,' he pressed.

'Of course. Alex, or Adam, or whatever you are calling yourself these days, as I have already stated my name is Elisa Wakefield. You passed me in the hall of the SOU building several weeks ago, and although I played down the encounter you did the best impression of a stranger I have ever seen. I almost convinced myself you must have been someone else, but I have a memory for faces and knew I couldn't have made a mistake. So I did a bit of digging,' she paused for few seconds, 'but that's always difficult where Richard Palmer is concerned. Lucky for you I'm not a lady who gives up easily.'

Adam paced around the cottage and found himself mindlessly in the kitchen, walking around in the dark, the only light being the cold shade of the moon through the windows. He recalled the moment she was talking about; he had passed a few people in the corridor on his way to Palmer's office in the SIS training facility. She had been with a male colleague but neither face had stood out to him. He tried to picture the woman on the other end of the phone, approaching the age of sixty he seemed to remember, with red hair that maintained its vibrancy despite the years, and attractive but aged features that affirmed a life-time of working for MI6. Despite all the detail, he could not place the woman in a time before this. Wakefield seemed to read his mind.

'You don't know me from before that do you Alex?' Adam shook his head, leaving a silence on the phone. 'You were in your final year of university and had applied to do an additional year of teacher-training,' she started. 'I tried to recruit you to the Service dear boy, but you were adamant about becoming a teacher.' Her revelation almost knocked Adam off his feet. 'It was such a waste Alex; the technicalities of espionage came naturally to you. You were born to be a field operative; a man who enjoyed isolation, confident in decision making, and ruthless in achieving your goals. These traits can't be taught, and you possessed most of what was required for our trade. After University, Her Majesty's Government could have made so much more of you.' Adam could hardly believe his ears, but as hard as he tried to deny it the vague image of his younger self started to form in his mind.

'Why are you telling me this now?' asked Adam.

'Oh come on my dear, do you really want to live out your days ignorant to the truth?' replied Elisa. Adam gritted his teeth at the frustration of not knowing more about his own life.

'Ok. So why did you pick me out at University?' asked Adam.

'It was one of your tutor's that forwarded your details to me; an old colleague and friend of mine who was always on the lookout for the right material. From then on I spent some time observing you and checking out your background. When I was satisfied with what I saw, I finally approached you.' Adam had wandered back through to the lounge and rested himself on the edge of the sofa. His chest felt tight and a cold sweat formed on his forehead and neck. A clearer image of the experience began to materialise from the fog of his mind.

'I remember,' he said finally. He repeated the revelation for good measure. 'You approached me on campus and asked what plans I had for my future. I said I wanted to teach and you laughed at the idea.' She laughed again down the phone, fifteen years later.

'But you still took the tests Alex, didn't you, despite all the talk of teaching. The mental agility tests and the role play. You scored so well, but then declined to come for interview. We were most disappointed. No one ever turns *us* down.'

'Well I did,' said Adam standing his ground. 'Don't take it personally.'

Wakefield didn't respond to the inflammatory remark. She was a professional woman with a full career behind her and Adam didn't doubt for one minute that she hadn't seen and done everything a career in SIS promised.

'In my opinion dear boy, you were consumed by fear, and that was why you opted for a life more ordinary.' She seemed to touch a nerve and Adam reacted.

'There's nothing ordinary about investing everything you have in your children, your marriage, and a worthwhile career.'

'Well, I guess I will have to take your word for that Alex, or Adam, or whatever you think you are called, but Motherhood wasn't my calling. However, regardless of what you say now I could see it in you back then; the fear.' Adam seemed to be reliving that part of his life all over again in his head.

'No, I was never afraid of failing,' he said firmly. Wakefield laughed down the phone again.

'I don't doubt that darling; I'm talking about a fear of success. I could see it in you; you were scared because of the weight you gave it, the weight you placed on what it would mean to be a successful field operative. You were afraid you might like it, that you'd be good at it.' Adam was stunned into silence and couldn't find any defence against her words. 'Since we passed each other recently I've gone to great lengths to find out what you were doing in SIS and how we'd finally managed to recruit you. And although I don't know the full extent of how you came to be I have managed to find evidence of your recent activities, and it seems I was right all those years ago; you have excelled in this game.'

'That wasn't me doing those things,' he snapped, 'it was Adam.'

'Nonsense,' came the reply instantly. 'Do you think Palmer has the capacity to change someone that radically? What Palmer doesn't yet realise is that he didn't make you, he just found you. The rest was all you.' Adam was standing again and pacing furiously around the lounge.

'Are you saying I killed all of those people and did all of those things?'

The answer to all of his questions was short. 'Yes.'

Adam's mind refused to accept it.

'If you're implying I wanted part of this then you are insane. I was robbed of my life.'

'Alex, don't be so naive, it doesn't suit you. Although I do not in any way agree with Palmer's methods. It is plain to see that you were nothing more than a brain-dead pile of broken bones. He didn't steal your life; a road traffic accident did that. Call it bad luck, or fate; but that's the bottom line. Palmer offered your corpse another chance at life, and I have to say that you have made the most of that second chance.' She had him on the ropes. 'I knew you would be well-suited to the paramilitary side of the job, the close quarter and unarmed training. It was inevitable that you would cross paths with the Increment, I just didn't think for one minute that you'd be up *against* them.'

Adam was no stranger to the work and reputation of the elite killing unit. His blood ran cold.

# EIGHTEEN

His first reaction had been to kill the lights in the cottage. Surrounded by the pitch black Adam had continued to heed Elisa Wakefield's chilling warning as he pulled together a few vital pieces of kit. Her last piece of dialogue had echoed in the darkness. 'The attack is imminent Alex. I can't tell you how I came by the information, but my sources are trusted.' The heads-up could not have come a minute too soon as two sets of head lights bounced up and down on the distant country lane. Then, about 500 meters from the cottage the illuminated beams had suddenly vanished.

'Why are you helping me?' asked Adam, his tone urgent.

The line went quiet for a brief moment.

'My time in this game is nearly over, Alex. This is the right thing to do. I hate that bastard Palmer, and if I couldn't have you then he certainly doesn't deserve you.'

The call disconnected and Adam visualised the wily older woman disembowelling the second hand phone she'd acquired and destroying the pay-as-you-go SIM card rendering it untraceable. He took the SIM card from his phone and tossed it on to the dying fire, then threw his phone down on the sofa in case they were able to trace him. The plan was to tab west towards Newhaven where he could pick up transport back to London. He needed to meet with Palmer and get the message across by any means necessary; he wanted out of this game. Adam laced up his boots, pulled on his Harrington jacket to conceal the pistol tucked in his waist band, and disappeared in to the night.

Adam's night vision would take a while to adapt but he knew enough of his surroundings to make it across to the barn and then out towards the woodland to the north west of the cottage. He moved silently and swiftly making the most of the several minute head start that he had been gifted. Once again Amy came to mind and seemed to drive him onward. Then he stopped in his tracks rooted to the ground.

'Shit,' he cursed. The realisation made his stomach lurch and he felt the urge to balk. 'The letter,' he hissed. Everything had happened so fast and whilst trying to process Wakefield's revelations and prepare for the imminent E-Squadron assault he had forgotten about the scrap of paper on the kitchen table. His words would provide a bread crumb trail back to his family that would give the Special Forces group the leverage they needed to bring him out of hiding. There was only one option.

The night was murky dark; low level cloud skimmed the skies above Adam, providing him with thick cover. He knew the capabilities of his enemy and didn't doubt for one second that they would each be equipped with night vision goggles. Adam hugged the stone wall that ran towards the cottage, keeping his head low and out of sight, the bend in his knees causing lactic acid to build and burn in his quadriceps muscles. His heart was thumping in his chest and he wondered whether the armed force could hear it over the night air. He was a few metres from the cottage now, at its rear aspect and facing towards the kitchen window. The cloud cover broke for a fraction of a second to reveal the bottles of gas beneath the kitchen window, in a formation that reminded him of bowling pins. To reach the cottage from here Adam would need to move across open ground, bridging the few meters where the stone wall ended and the external wall of the cottage rear began. It wasn't far but if the elite unit was on top of him it might as well be a mile that he needed to cover. He checked his pistol again for all the good it was going to do him, held his breath and exploded in a low sprint. His back slammed hard into the textured wall, every proud feature of the weathered stone imprinted itself on his back. Adam fought to recover his breath from a combination of the sprint and coming to rest against the cottage and winding himself. He steadied his breathing and without any real thought reached across for the first of the three gas bottles. The chain binding the three cylinders was just long enough to allow Adam to hoist one on its side and rest it down across the heads of the other two. It came to rest with a gentle clink. Adam recoiled backwards slightly and squinted into the blackness, pistol raised and ready to defend his position. Nothing moved ahead. He let out a tense sigh whilst slowly easing the stiff metal flow-control knob on each of the gas bottles. As if feeling

Adam's tension they each eased out a low gasp of butane. The smell began to gently filter in to Adam's nostrils before he turned and disappeared in the direction of the kitchen door.

The door was closed but not locked, just as he'd left it minutes earlier. Now against all instincts he was re-entering the kill zone. He tried to shake the doubt from his head but realistically he would be out-gunned by a team of Britain's finest soldiers who were expert in close-quarter battle. Adam reached up tentatively from his crouched position for the door handle that was situated above his head. When gently opened Adam knew the door would let out its usual creak, the stiff hinges straining under the load of the heavy door. If Palmer's men were already inside the cottage the noise would draw some very unwanted attention. Forcing the door quickly open allowed the thick wooden frame to swing freely away from Adam, the rapid momentum easing the pressure on the croaking hinges. Adam tugged back on the handle before the door moved out of his reach, yanking him forwards in to the kitchen. He rolled across the cold quarry-tiled floor and came up against the pine table that was situated in the middle of the kitchen. With his pistol levelled, he listened in between his breaths, stifling his out-breath and clipping his in-breath to extend his listening time. He was in luck. The cottage seemed empty. Adam reached up with a searching hand and fanned it across the table's surface. The envelope jumped free of the surface momentarily as his first pass wafted a stream of air under it. He felt the free end stroke up against the back of his fingers as it fell back towards the table. Adam nipped the paper between his fingers and pulled his hand gently back beneath the table. He breathed a sigh of relief and folded the paper several times into a small tight square before stuffing it deep into his jacket pocket. He could not have let this advantage fall into his enemy's hands. He motioned toward the kitchen door, then froze. The whispers carried like song over the night air, and the sound rooted Adam to the spot. They were close, somewhere beyond the kitchen door but on the opposite side of the cottage from which Adam had approached it. In the darkness Adam listened. There was no going back the way he had come.

Moving softly over the tiles Adam positioned himself up on one knee by the kitchen window, where only seconds earlier he had been on the other side of the glass. He eased the window open, so slowly that any sound from the wooden frame seemed to be swallowed in on itself. Adam detected the faint smell of gas as the cold night air slithered under the slight crack in the open window. He doubled back on himself towards the open living space beyond the kitchen, but not before turning a few of the gas hob rings to a low-level hiss, like a snake that was stalking its prey in the tranquillity of an open grassland. A shadowed body flitted past the kitchen window. They must have been all around him now. He had less than a minute to make his move.

As Adam recalled, the dresser by the wall of the lounge had three wooden drawers across its middle.

Blindly he reached for the middle drawer, almost perfectly judging the location of the knob. He grasped it on the second attempt, slid out the drawer and took out the contents that he knew from memory where there. Much of it he discarded, but two items he held firm. They were his lifeline. One roll of duct tape and a box of Swan Vesta matches that Adam had used earlier in the day to bring the fire back to life. He wondered for a moment why the duct tape was there, but he didn't care, he was just very grateful in that moment that it was. He scuttled over to the front hall and crouched before the external door. If they kicked it open now it was game over. He got to work tearing away the strike strip of the match box and secured it in place on the wall by the front door. The duct tape tore easily and Adam was confident it would hold. He tore one final strip from the roll and positioned three matches against the door, overhanging with enough length to brush the adjacent wall with its mounted striker.

With the heads of the matches resting just before the strike strip he taped them in place and turned to run. He bounced wildly off the walls of the hallway squinting to see furniture immediately ahead of him. He caught his left shin against a small side table, and he stumbled before regaining his footing. The sound of his heavy steps reverberated over the wooden floor and Adam was sure it would carry out into the night. There was nothing he could do now, only push on and hope that he had the few more precious seconds that he needed. Now at the top of the stairway leading down to the cellar Adam was face to face with one of the few mod-cons of the cottage, a wall-mounted combi boiler. He fumbled desperately in the pitch black and identified the gas pipework that fuelled it. Just a few more seconds was all that he needed. He raised his right boot and kicked hard at the pipes. They clanked but held fast. He gave a second wild kick at the boiler's underside and this time the fuel supply cracked and hissed violently. Adam threw himself down the stone steps with not a single second to spare.

'Delta three in position,' came the voice in the team's ears as Joseph James and John Ryan steadied themselves by the kitchen door at the rear of the house. The words kicked off a cascade of recognition.

'Delta two by the bedroom window.'

'Delta one at the front door.'

'Delta four in covering position.'

The two-man units were stationed at what would be the key entry and exit points of the cottage. Anything leaving now would be shredded by a coordinated hail of gun-fire.

'Go, Go, Go,' went the command as James and Ryan moved swiftly and aggressively into the kitchen. The smell was instantly recognisable to both men as the butane gas filled their senses. John Ryan opened his mouth to command the three other Delta teams to stand down but not a single word escaped him before the powerful Les Cooper kicked with all his might at the front door.

The house seemed to take in a deep growling breath before it screamed out with intense heat and anger.

The blast blew out all the windows and showered glass over Delta-two who were posted by Adam's bedroom. The two men rolled on the grassy floor, deaf and disorientated, their backs smouldering. Both men grabbed frantically at their PVS-7 night vision goggles to limit the white-out to their vision from the intense explosion of light. There was fire everywhere and a ball of orange rolled up in to the night sky, casting a glow over what remained of the cottage below. From his cover position by Adam's car Gaz Roberts recoiled, his out-turned hand shielding his eyes from the intense heat and light.

'Get the fuck down you moron,' cried Tom Dale from his side, a strong hand gripping at Gaz and pulling him back down to a position of cover. 'Are you trying to get us both killed...' the question was punctuated by a double-tap from Adam's Sig pistol. Dale slumped forward over Roberts' legs, sending him further in to a frenzy of panic and hysteria. A gush of blood seeped over Gaz's thighs and he wondered if he'd pissed himself in fright, as the dampness covered his crotch. Adam stood over the gibbering man who writhed on the floor beneath the weight of his dead comrade. He levelled his pistol at Roberts.

'Do you want to die tonight?' asked Adam. Gaz shook his head emphatically. 'Then I suggest you leave here, and tell your boss it's over. I want out. Nobody else needs to die.' Gaz looked through Adam's legs to the two smouldering corpses by the front door, looking and smelling like a pair of pork joints. He looked back at Adam and nodded.

'Ok, ok, I'm going.' The man kicked himself free of the corpse across his legs, stumbled to his feet, and disappeared into the darkness.

Two shots rang out above the background of crackling and fizzing, and Adam fell to the ground. He rolled towards the cover of his near-by vehicle, with each turn of his body pressing down hard on the entry wound in his left thigh. He grimaced and cursed the pain and his stupidity. From beneath the Audi he could see two men staggering towards him, unable to maintain a straight line. Delta-two had just about recovered themselves and were advancing on Adam; two sets of boots incoherently slipping and sliding on the scorched earth. With his arms held out straight ahead, Adam aimed his pistol and fired. He loosed off two rounds; the first thudded into the ground, the second shot landing on target. It connected with Chris Kime's right boot, tearing open the leather and sending up a spray of red liquid amid exploding flesh and bone. One half of Delta Two hit the ground like a well-controlled tower block demolition, his body crumpling down on itself. As Kime's body hit the deck Adam squeezed the trigger twice more, sending two rounds thumping into the fallen man's chest. Adam rolled round to catch sight of the second assailant but the boots had disappeared. He craned to see beyond the rear wheels but there was no sign of the other half of Delta Two.

Adam dragged himself to a sitting position against the Audi. He checked his weapon and aimed it at the back of the car, fully expecting an armed figure to burst round the corner any second. Nothing. After a few tense seconds Adam pulled himself to standing and moved towards the rear of the car using the vehicle's wheels to shield himself from a similar fate to the recently deceased E-squadron man. Warm blood was beginning to congeal at his left thigh, the soaked denim of his jeans sticking to Adam's leg and the forming clot. He winced with pain as he equalled his bodyweight over both legs. Cautiously Adam glanced around the car, barely exposing his head but it was more than enough to draw a burst of fire. The flurry of 9mm rounds chewed-up the rear of the Audi R8, narrowly missing Adam as he slid backwards, his left leg refusing to take the sudden load. Sergeant Danny Grant, the hit squad's leader, was holed up in the old coal bunker where only minutes earlier Adam had emerged from the cottage's cellar, unscathed by the fierce blast above him. Without a proper recce of the place, and with a lack of intel from Sarah Turner, the team had overlooked this vital entry and exit point. Now Grant was dug in with his Heckler and Koch fully automatic MP5 sub machine gun, a reliable and easy to control weapon that was trained on Adam's only means of escape; his car. With a bullet tearing through his thigh he had no chance of escaping on foot. It was the car or nothing.

Adam peered over the vehicle, this time weapon aimed and intent on putting down a few cover rounds. Grant seemed to read his mind and instantly put down his own fire which ripped at the car's metal like the jagged teeth of a shoal of ravenous piranha fish. The rear wheel on the driver's side had absorbed several stray rounds and was blowing out its gaseous contents. Adam felt a stab of pain in his right shoulder, followed by the trickle of warm sticky liquid down his right arm and chest.

'Fuck, fuck, fuck!' blasted Adam. Reaching across with his left hand he could feel the hole where the 9mm round had ripped open the flesh just above his right collar bone. The bullet had narrowly missed the apex of his lung. He was still in the game, although his right arm that held his pistol now felt like a lead weight. Another hail of bullets spewed from the MP5 and all Adam could do was tense his body and hope for the best. He glanced across from behind the car and could see the old barn metres from him. Maybe he could make the distance; then come at Grant from the other side of the barn.

The sky was still cast in an orange hue and there would be no cover of darkness for this move. It was going to rely on speed and surprise. Adam kicked down on his left leg to test that it would take his weight. The pain electrified his spine but the leg did not give out. Three, two, one. The sub machine gun roared and rounds kicked-up the earth beneath Adam's feet. Above the thumping of the MP5 an ear-splitting crack sounded out, followed by creaking and then a heavy rumble. Adam felt the ground shake and then a fresh wave of heat took him off his feet. He lay in the cool dewy grass unable to move, his senses completely scrambled. Adam waited for the final punch of the machine gun, but it didn't come. He rolled on to his left side and pointed his pistol in Danny Grant's direction. All that was there was a pile of smouldering stone and burning roof timbers. The near-side wall of the cottage had finally yielded to the blast and the intense heat, collapsing in on itself, and on the kill squad's 2IC.

Adam's shoulder and thigh felt stiff as the adrenaline rush began to leave him. Using all of his remaining strength he dragged himself towards the Audi and slumped behind the wheel. He reached under the passenger seat for the spare keys and commended himself on maintaining some state of readiness. Through the pain he pushed down the clutch, punched first gear and gunned the car down the long driveway. The punctured rear tyre spun on the gravel before creating friction with the road. Adam shifted quickly through the gears and struggled to keep the steering wheel tight as the car's power caused it to lurch from side to side. Further up the track he reached the two black Range Rovers abandoned by the Special Forces patrol. Adam pulled the Audi over, limped over to the first of the vehicles and tried at the door handles. Unsurprisingly they didn't give. He checked the tops of each of the tyres in the hope of finding a set of keys. Nothing. He tried the second vehicle, half-heartedly tugging the driver's door. It gave a faint click and opened. Adam couldn't believe his luck, and was even more surprised to find the keys in the ignition. The pain from his thigh and shoulder were thumping at his brain. Struggling back to the Audi he took out his Sig and shot out the R8's two front tyres. Both spewed out the pressurised air. He emptied the remaining rounds into the locked Range Rover's tyres. Mindlessly he threw the pistol on to the front passenger seat of the remaining Range Rover, turned the engine into life and started back down the track. Ahead he could see the dotted orange street lights of the nearest village and his tense muscles began to soften. He could barely believe he had made it out alive.

The cold serrated blade of the combat knife against the soft flesh of Adam's neck came milliseconds before he saw Roberts' reflection in his rear-view mirror.

'Don't even think about a hard stop you Bastard, or I swear I'll slice straight through your neck and cut your fucking head off.' Adam didn't doubt it. The blade's pressure was such that he could feel his pulse against it.

'What do you want?' asked Adam calmly.

'You. Dead,' snapped Roberts. 'But not like this. Pull over.' He used the pressure of the knife to emphasise his command. The Range Rover banked gently to the left and came to rest slowly on the grass verge. Gaz leaned forwards from the rear of the vehicle and grabbed at Adam's pistol. The serrated blade bit into Adam's neck and brought a line of dark blood to the surface of the wound.

'Out, you fucker,' ordered Roberts. As Adam forced himself painfully out the door his assailant moved behind him like a shadow. The knife was still trained on Adam's neck as the two men stood facing each other.

In the distant background the cottage was beginning to burn itself out and the only light was that of the

4x4's head lights bathing the rutted track. Roberts slid the commando knife up and over Adam's chin and then suddenly slashed at his face. Adam lurched backwards and managed to take the depth out of the cut as the blade broke the skin beneath his right eye. He continued to fall as his heels caught in the lumpy verge and Adam hit the ground hard. Roberts towered above him as Adam lay on his back, barely able to lift the weight of his own head. The lost blood had taken with it the oxygen-carrying cells needed to maintain his energy levels. He felt weak and breathless.

'Do you know me?' asked Roberts. Adam held his gaze.

'Yes, I know you,' he replied slowly. 'You killed an innocent man during Special Forces selection.' Roberts' blood began to heat and his face contorted in anger.

'Fuck you,' he hissed. 'You don't know anything.' Adam knew he'd hit a nerve.

'I know you killed him because you didn't have the ability to get through on your own merit.' Roberts kicked hard at Adam's left thigh causing him to let out a low growl. He sucked up the pain and continued. 'You don't have what it takes to soldier in the SAS; you're weak. You let your comrades die tonight to save yourself.' Roberts was raging. He pulled Adam's Sig from his belt, aimed and squeezed hard on the trigger.

'Die you bastard, die.' The weapon clicked, void of rounds.

Adam started to his feet.

'You can't even tell the weight of an empty weapon,' he spat.

Robert's lunged forward to strike Adam with the pistol but Adam gripped at his wrist with his right hand. Roberts was unable to move in the vice-like grip and even though he thumped down on Adam's wounded shoulder he could not free himself. Adam looked him square in the eyes then gave a sharp sideways thrust with his right arm. The ligaments in Roberts' wrist tensed instantly and then snapped. The crack was loud but Gaz Roberts' screams were louder. He looked like he might pass out but the fear of death seemed to give him a second wind and he came back at Adam with the blade in his left hand. Adam parried the swipe, shifted his bodyweight back on to his right leg and then exploded forward at his opponent with a precise right hook. As his weight moved forward to his left leg it buckled under the pain of the gun-shot wound but the punch had already connected with Roberts' jaw. It seemed to flex at the joint before passing the force of the blow to the head, spinning it sharply on his neck. There was an almighty crack and Roberts fell on the spot, arms and legs twitching. Then his body went still.

Adam didn't bother to check for a pulse. There was only one outcome of a strike like that. He eased himself up behind the wheel of the Range Rover and strained painfully to fasten his seatbelt. There was unfinished business at Vauxhall, and he needed to get there fast.

# NINETEEN

The staccato thump of tyre on cats-eyes sounded out like machine gun fire and jolted Adam back in to consciousness. A burst of harsh expletives hailed from his right, punctuated by the piercing sound of car horn which shrilled the night air. Adam watched from behind the tinted window as a fellow road user gestured obscenities with his hand, before dropping a few gears and accelerating into the distant dual carriageway. He had crossed the reflective studs that separated his inside lane from one in which the severely pissed-off BMW driver was using to overtake. At the speed he was doing a collision would have probably killed both of them and perhaps a few more unsuspecting road users. He tried to mouth a belated apology to the disappearing BMW but no words fell out. His desiccated lips and mouth couldn't form any useful shape to articulate the remorse he felt for falling asleep at the wheel. Adam forced the Range Rover toward the hard shoulder and slowed to a halt amidst the broken glass and blown-out tyres. Another car horn chorus provided the soundtrack for his rash decision making. *Fuck you*, thought Adam less apologetically as he watched the red lights fade away in to the night. *Fuck you.*

Searing heat ran through his body as Adam contorted himself to search the 4x4 for drinkable fluids. The best he could do was drain three disposable hot drink cups of the residue left in the bottom; a sickly mix of tea and coffee with congealed sugar forming a syrup in the bottom. Adam felt like he had struck gold when he finally came across a quarter full 500ml bottle of mineral water. The liquid was warm and tasted of its plastic surround but to Adam's parched palate it could have come straight from the promised French Alps. The contents of the bottle were not enough to satisfy his thirst or to restock the vital fluids that had been lost from his circulation. His vision was narrow and blurred around the edges. A basic survival instinct urged him to keep moving if he was to live. He straightened himself up in the driver's seat and pushed the Range Rover into first gear before spinning it out of the gravelled hard-shoulder and back into the race for life. The few quid that was stowed in the central arm rest would be enough to buy him food and water. All he had to do was get there before it was too late.

The Golden Arches sign was immediately visible as Adam pulled off the A23 by the westerly edge of Croydon. Only a place with a drive-through would serve him in his current state, and as he waited in line the red glow from the brake lights in front illuminated Adam enough to inspect his face in the rear-view mirror. He fixed his hair the best he could, fighting with the tangled mane that was matted with congealed blood. He wiped at his face to remove the dirt, sweat and smoke residue but all he did was smudge it further until it covered his face like camouflage cream. Adam patted his damp finger gently around the deep red line left by Roberts' blade but it was held by the thinnest of clots and a new film of blood gathered before trickling down his neck. He cursed as he pulled alongside the harassed teenager peering out from behind her booth.

'Can I take your order please?' she said in a polite voice that was starkly contrasted by her nonchalant body language. Adam lowered the blackened window of the driver's door, just enough to make himself heard.

'I'll have a Coke please; large, no ice.'

'Anything else?' asked the girl, not bothering to look up at her customer. Adam checked the loose change by his side.

'Yes. What desserts do you have?' The uniformed teen looked up for the first time, the expression on her face was one of disbelief that caused her taught forehead to fold into a series of deep lines. Adam slumped back into the shadows of the car. What planet had this guy just arrived from? She obliged his ignorance and spent a few seconds reeling off the menu. Adam ordered some sort of ice cream whose name started with 'Mc', and an apple pie that resembled a sausage roll. The change just about covered it and Adam was pleased that the equally nonchalant teenager at the pick-up window didn't give him a second look.

He quickly found a parking space given the early morning hour and reduced the apple pie to crumbs within a matter of seconds, ignoring what damage the molten-hot contents could do to his mouth. It didn't take long for the extra glucose to reach his starved cells

241

and start taking effect. The fluids that were slowly filtering from his swollen stomach began to re-pressurise his circulatory system, shunting blood through small blood vessels that permeated his brain. Almost at once Adam's tunnel-vision opened up and the colour returned to his hollowed cheeks. He rested back in the driver's seat, feeling almost human again, while using his improved brain function to figure-out his next move. The three-litre diesel beast idled beneath him as Adam tapped at the console buttons below the in-built satellite navigation display screen. He went to work tapping at the touch-screen display until he found the 'phone' option. Adam scrolled through the call history. Peter Smith was high on the recent call list, a name that Adam instantly recognised from his training and contact with the UK's military elite, confirming that the kill order had come from the top. Adam pondered the intimate relationship between the SIS and the British Special Forces Officer. He dialled up another number from memory.

The line rang briefly, allowing Adam a few precious breaths of fresh oxygen, before connecting. The voice on the other end was tentative.

'Yes?' He obviously knew the caller ID, thought Adam, which further confirmed his suspicions.

He leaned forward in his seat, causing the Oxford leather to creak beneath him; 'it's over,' rasped Adam. There was no reaction, only silence, but Adam could picture Richard Palmer shifting in his swivel chair studying his hand for the trump card.

'It's over!' mouthed Adam with more intent, his face

now so close to the console that his breath fogged the screen. He coughed slightly after the effort of leaning forward and a tang of metal filled his mouth before the blood formed at the corner of his lips. Adam suppressed the cough and forced the blood back inside him. He was going to need every last drop.

'Adam,' said the voice finally, 'I don't know what you mean.'

'Cut the bullshit Palmer,' spat Adam as a spray of red liquid covered the dashboard. 'They're all dead and their blood is on your hands. I didn't want anyone else to get hurt but you…' he broke off, 'you don't give a shit how many good men die for your personal gain!'

Adam's blood pressure was building despite the dangerously low amount of fluid in his system. His heart was pumping harder with each word. He rested back in the seat of the SUV and composed himself.

'We need to meet,' he said finally. Palmer scoffed at the notion.

'I hardly think so, Adam. You're tired and emotional, and that makes you a danger to me. You sound like you've lost the plot with these insane accusations. I'll send a team out to meet with you. Turn yourself in and we'll do this properly.' His voice was convincing and Adam didn't doubt for a second that Palmer believed his own fiction.

'If you don't meet me in one hour I'll turn myself over to Jim Stevens, and I'll spill everything. I wonder what he'll find with a few x-rays.'

Palmer laughed again into the phone, but this time it was forced and shaky. Sir Jim Stevens was the Chief of the Secret Intelligence Service, a fierce and intelligent man who had seen every aspect of MI6 in his long career. He would almost certainly entertain Adam's story and scan results.

'One hour,' agreed Palmer, 'Battersea Park?'

'No,' replied Adam, 'let's bring it home. I'll see you on Vauxhall Bridge,' and with that he killed the line.

The little blood left within him felt like it was pooling in his arms and legs, weighing heavy with every attempt to move his limbs. The gasps of air brought faint wisps of life to him, but Adam was intelligent enough to know that his existence was ebbing out of him at a faster rate. The inside of the Range Rover felt warm and comfortable and for a moment he contemplated sleeping out his remaining hours in the sanctuary of his leather surroundings. It wasn't an effort to close his eyes and they fell shut easily under their own weight. Amy seemed to already be waiting there in the darkness for him. All he had to do was reach out for her and finally he could be laid to rest. The rise and fall of his chest slowed and the faint throb of his pulse beat out a distant background rhythm for his mind to follow. Physical pain began to melt away, draining from him with every drop of blood that left his open wounds. Darkness was all around. Peace was right in front of him and the effort required to fight it seemed monumental.

The rap on the window was hard and curt. Adam instinctively reached for a pistol that wasn't there as his heart rate accelerated upwards at two beats for every second that passed. The dashboard display told him that he'd been asleep for nearly twenty minutes and he cursed at allowing the precious minutes of his life to slip past him. The blast of knuckle on glass refocused him in the present. Adam's first instinct of a 'Copper's knock' proved to hold true as the Police Officer's stare penetrated the tinted window to Adam's right.

'Police,' said the man in a firm voice, 'step out of the vehicle.' The request was not a polite one. Adam put his finger to the electric control button and opened the window by a few inches.

'Can I help you Officer?' he asked in the voice that follows sleep.

'Please step out of the vehicle.' Adam held his ground, reluctant to reveal himself and his appearance. The Police Officer barked the command again, this time with the ultimate threat of imminent action.

'Excuse me Officer but you do realise this is a Government vehicle,' said Adam, 'and that I could be on active duty at this moment.' The man didn't look fazed. 'I can give you the direct contact of the Head of the Secret Intelligence Service's Special Operations Unit to confirm this.' The Police Officer pondered the dilemma for a few seconds.

'I don't think we need to disturb Mr Palmer at this late hour,' came the reply finally. Adam tensed. It seemed that Palmer's reach was greater than Adam had given him credit for. The driver's door opened with a soft click and Adam found himself face to face with the Police Officer who either hadn't realised his slip of the tongue, or didn't care.

The Police Sergeant was probably mid-forties and

looked ex-military concluded Adam. To his right stood a younger officer who wore an expression that suggested concern for operating on the wrong side of the law. The anxious officer looked Adam up and down and was unable to conceal his horror as a fresh pool of blood formed at the detainee's feet. Still, the pistol-shaped bright yellow X26 Taser held in his grip was pointed firmly in Adam's direction. The red dot of the laser sight danced on Adam's chest confirming to him that he was the intended target.

'Can I ask why I've been stopped like this?' asked Adam. He directed the question at the younger of the two men, who seemed like he was going to have a hard time justifying the necessary and proportionate use of the Taser in a court of law. The Sergeant butted in.

'We've had several reports of dangerous driving performed by this vehicle in the last hour.' While this was possible it seemed unlikely, thought Adam. He held his gaze on the Constable who was now 'arcing' the hand-held device. The electric current was flowing freely between the barbed contacts at the end of the Taser, lighting up its jaws like some predatory fish at the depths of the ocean. The electricity crackled viciously at the mouth of the weapon in a show of strength by the young officer. The older man shot him an encouraging glance but his young partner wavered as his finger fidgeted on the trigger.

The pair had made no effort to question their suspect or ask for proof of identity. This was a done deal and Adam knew he would soon be on the receiving end of 50,000 volts. The officer stepped forward, Taser raised and ready. The Sergeant gestured again with his eyes. *Now or never.* Adam launched himself at the older man, chin tucked to his chest as the top of his head splayed his target's nose with a sickening sound that reminded Adam of a breaking twig. As the Sergeant twisted and fell back the Taser's laser sighting system jumped from Adam to the man's back, like a parasite looking for a new host, and the bewildered side-kick discharged the electrified barbs between his partner's shoulder blades. A sequence of devastating high voltage pulses coursed through the Sergeant's body relieving him of voluntary muscle control. He hit the ground hard before the younger officer regained his senses and released the trigger.

Adam launched himself over the convulsing pile of flesh towards the Taser-happy officer. A well drilled response kicked in as the younger officer ejected the spent Taser cartridge before thrusting the weapon towards Adam. The angled drive stun was executed with textbook precision as the sparked jaws met with Adam's neck. The one 500th of an amp instantly incapacitated Adam at close range and he fell to his knees. Adam writhed and juddered at the end of the X26; the intense electrical noise from the stun device scrambling his own nerve impulses as he willed his muscles to fight back.

Intermittent pulses thundered through his body causing his muscles to work frantically to the tune of the Copper's finger on the trigger. The glucose coursing through Adam's blood vessels could barely feed his exhausted muscles fast enough and the building levels of lactic acid spilled out of his cells and into his blood stream. The episodic waves of cramp, fatigue and muscle burn gnawed at Adam as he became progressively more disabled but the young Officer persisted, driven by a combination of fear and adrenaline.

As the high-voltage assault continued Adam's heart began to beat irregularly with the rising demands on his body. The young officer was now wild with fury and was no longer concerned for his assailant's condition. A heart attack and likely death where moments away and the lack of coordinated pulses of blood reaching his starved brain loosened Adam's grip on the conscious world. On the verge of passing out, the low levels of oxygen and high levels of acidity in his blood were detected by the dormant Neurotech implant and faint sparks of electrical activity tentatively reached out to the surrounding nerve cells. Just as Adam's world was turning black, the impulses reached threshold and a trail of neural fire blazed from the implant to his right arm and leg. His heart stopped momentarily before restarting itself in normal rhythm. A new surge of adrenaline leaked into his arteries as his balled fist hit the Officer square between the thighs. The Officer recoiled in pain as Adam's right leg involuntarily extended, thrusting him upwards to land another right handed hook on the Copper's left temple. Both men hit the ground almost simultaneously; the Police Officer unconscious; Adam exhausted. In the cold stillness of the late night hour, a fleeting tranquillity settled over the fast-food carpark.

Adam rolled on to his back, feeling every bit of the cold hard concrete floor against his burning back muscles. A pool of blood began to form around him after the intense skeletal muscle contractions had reopened his barely closed wounds. He manged to bring himself on to his elbows only to find the Sergeant towering over him, an extendable baton in his right hand and a look of revenge in his eyes. His nose had come to rest at an obscure angle which gave the older officer a more menacing look than he naturally could have mustered.

'You little fucker,' spat the Sergeant, a splayed nose and a few missing teeth adding a slight whistle to his voice. 'Palmer's put a nice reward sum out on you and I'm going to enjoy cashing it in. And as an added bonus, he doesn't care what state you come back in!' Adam sighed heavily and rolled on to his right side in readiness for the beating. He didn't care anymore. He was spent and once again overpowered. As he lay there beside the younger of the two Police men he recognised the CS spray canister that had worked itself loose from its pouch during the fall. Adam instinctively reached for the spray with his left hand but the Sergeant's baton came down with violent force against his left shoulder. A thousand pain signals exploded in Adam's brain as he rolled back only to see another blow come crashing down. He rolled left leaving the metal rod to spark on the concrete and as the older officer re-cocked his arm Adam rolled to his right and grabbed the CS canister. The Sergeant leaned in and took the full volume of spray to his face. He yelled and cursed, wiping frantically at the excess liquid on his skin. The tough old bastard had a reward on his mind and he launched again at his supine target, but Adam was no longer lying in wait for the next blow.

The red-eyed Sergeant strained through the tears in time to see Adam now lying to the other side of the younger officer, a yellow and black pistol-shaped device held firmly in both hands and restocked with a cartridge. A split second later the two barbs pierced the Sergeant's chest and gave him another massive dose of electricity. This time Adam knew the potential consequences but when it happened it still shocked him a little. The Taser instantly ignited the flammable CS spray, and as the active solvent caught fire the Sergeant's head and upper torso were engulfed in flames. It looked and sounded a painful death, but the heat coming from the burning man did nothing to thaw Adam's ice cold response. Quickly a thick odour of burning flesh and clothing filled Adam's nostrils. He stifled the urge to gag.

The Range Rover tore away from the scene of devastation; one Police Officer dead, one unconscious. Adam glanced briefly in his rear-view mirror to see horrified restaurant workers file out in to the night air, their memories forever etched with the sight of a burnt corpse. There seemed no end to Palmer's necrotising touch and the number of people affected by it. Adam keyed in the phone number again and the touch screen display confirmed that the call was connecting. With barely ten miles between Croydon and Vauxhall, Adam would still be able to make the rendezvous, especially travelling into London at this time of night. Ordinarily he would have been there in good time to stand-off and watch the scene for activity but time was no longer his companion and he would have to take the risk tonight. The ringing stopped and a man answered the call. 'Yes,' said the voice on the other end, this time with more concern.

'The meeting's still on,' confirmed Adam. There was silence again on the line.

'I have underestimated you it seems, Adam. I thought you might have been *detained* en-route,' sneered Palmer.

'This ends tonight. 03:15 hours sharp,' barked Adam before hanging up the call.

Adam raced through the gears of the SUV and prayed that he would live long enough to finish what Palmer had started.

# TWENTY

Twenty minutes later the black Range Rover was rolling down South Lambeth Way in the heart of London. Adam had driven with enough aggression to make up for lost time but had stayed mindful not to attract unwanted attention and further conflict with the law. The last thing he needed or wanted was to expend more time and energy on fighting his way out of another confrontation, and given the outcome of his last ruck, he'd be up against a bigger and more heavily armed force at the next encounter. Instead, every ounce of his remaining strength had been focused on achieving this one goal of getting to Palmer, leaving Adam wondering what he would do once he came face to face with him. Whatever the outcome this would be the last meeting between the two of them, Adam told himself.

With his destination only minutes away Adam's focus turned inwards as he tried to find his inner stillness. It was a ritual he performed before every major contact or operation; that moment when self-doubt was at its peak and a man could slide either side of the ridgeline, tumbling uncontrollably towards fear, or running headlong to victory. His mind was quiet and the mindfulness was reflected all around him as the

SUV wheeled silently through the vacant city streets. The night air breathed gently and seemed to steer him toward his target without any conscious effort on his part, as if all the elements of nature were in tune to this time and place; for a man to meet with his destiny. He instinctively took a left on to Parry Street and then veered right before following the road round towards Vauxhall station. As he approached level with Vauxhall Bridge Adam slowed the black SUV, prowling the streets like a nocturnal predator waiting for its prey to reveal itself. He looked out to his left, scanning for signs of activity or silhouetted figures stepping into the shadows. The bridge looked quiet, perhaps too quiet thought Adam. Would Palmer really come alone?

Adam chewed on his bottom lip as he pondered his predicament. The pools of cooling blood gathering in the relaxed folds of his abdomen forced his hand. He was out of time. Adam's right foot gently built up pressure against the accelerator pedal and the black beast surged forward through the night. He pulled at the wheel to take the right turn leading away from the bridge, the power steering assisting his fading upper body strength. With the bridge disappearing from sight in his rear-view mirror he left his gaze trained on the rendezvous point until it finally faded into darkness. Seconds later the vehicle slowed and came to rest alongside the Royal Vauxhall Tavern at the southerly edge of the Vauxhall Pleasure Gardens. Adam let out a nasal breath, prolonged and gentle. His mouth was closed, teeth clenched and his jaw squared. Silence fell about the Range Rover as the engine cooling system whirred to a halt.

Adam released the steering wheel to reveal imprints in the leather, the recesses filled with a film of sweat and blood. He got to work wiping down any part of the car he had touched, ensuring he left as little trace of himself as he could. Red blood cells lacked a nucleus, and therefore any trace of Adam's DNA, but he knew that the few white blood cells scattered amongst the many millions of red cells could give away his identity in a second.

As he opened the car door there was a sudden pressure change within the cab of the SUV, and the inflow of cool night air engulfed him and pricked at his senses. Adam instantly tuned-in to the concrete jungle's rhythm; the pulse of the capital city throbbing firmly beneath his feet as his brogue boots touched down on the tarmac. He pulled at the blood soaked mat in the vehicle's foot well, making sure there would be no trail of biological breadcrumbs leading back to him.

At the rear of the Range Rover Adam helped himself to a 9mm Browning Hi-Power pistol from the 4x4's cache and 'made ready' the weapon with the hammer cocked, a round in the chamber, and the safety catch on. He stowed the pistol in the back of his waist band and concealed the remainder of it beneath a jacket he had found on the rear seats. It was a leather biker-style jacket and seemed to fit Adam perfectly and conformed to the contours of his body. The extra layer protected his fragile skin from the chilling touch of the ambient air. The falling temperature seemed to pull at the skin still exposed to the elements and his face felt raw as he opened his mouth to inhale fresh air deep into his contused lungs. It seemed ironic to Adam that at a time when he was so close to death he felt so alive. The anticipation of the fight rallied his primal instincts that he had come to accept as part of his genome, and with the adrenaline still heating his blood he made his way on foot beyond the railway lines towards the Thames River. Every successive step loosened his stiff limbs and by the time Adam had reached Albert Embankment his stride had gathered purpose and his cadence urgency. A glance at his wristwatch confirmed it was already 03:12 hours. The lights of a familiar sight were reflected in the sapphire crystal face of the Swiss timepiece, prompting Adam to look up from his Raymond Weil Freelancer and see the iconic egg-box form of the SIS river house. Adam smiled to himself over his choice of venue, and hoped tonight would bring some sort of closure on his fragmented life. His journey had come full circle.

Palmer lit up a cigarette when he saw Adam come into sight. The glow of its tip illuminated the underside of his facial features as he stood otherwise concealed in shadow. From Adam's perspective he looked like a campfire story teller warming up for a ghostly tale. Adam stopped about six feet away from him, the exhaled smoke filling the gap between them. The burning orange hue was enough to confirm Palmer's identity but nowhere near sufficient to reveal him to any near-by surveillance cameras. There was a silence which neither man seemed in a hurry to break.

Adam was relieved to have finally made it here alive, while Palmer seemed to simply be enjoying dragging on his cigarette. Eventually Palmer exhaled words amidst the smoke.

'You are bloody good Adam; I'll give you that. An elite team of Special Forces wiped out by a single man. Shame really when you think about it.' He feigned a tutting noise. Adam tried not to take the bait but he could feel a reaction rising inside of him. He swallowed it down. 'I think you've finally proved your worth,' continued Palmer, goading his opponent. 'You've become the man I always hoped you would be.' Adam's pulse was red-lining and he visualised where he would land his punches to do most damage. Then he reminded himself of why he was here.

'You're right. I have become a better man. But I think we both know what that means.' He left the words to take effect, before finishing, 'and that's why I'm getting out. It's over.' Palmer stepped forward to the edge of the shadow-line that demarcated both men.

'I had a feeling this was coming, Adam; you haven't seemed yourself lately. Perhaps I went about this the wrong way, and for that I'm sorry.' Adam cocked his head slightly to the left to make sure he was hearing the man correctly.

'That's it then?' asked Adam, 'I just get to walk away with no repercussions.'

'Well not exactly,' replied Palmer in a condescending tone. 'You will forever be bound by the Secrets Act, and then there's the issue of your personal safety.' Adam stepped forward to close the gap, the distance reduced so much so that Palmer's stale breath filled his nostrils. The shadows encroached the space and Adam was close to disappearing into the blackness with Palmer. 'Well, you made a lot of enemies out there. I can't protect you from acts of retribution if you choose to leave the Service.' Adam's jaw tightened at the perceived threat. Palmer saw a flicker of doubt in his protégé's eyes.

'You know, Adam,' continued Palmer at the moment of most effectiveness, 'I think you want to see this job out, don't you? Deep down, you know this is what you were meant to do, and perhaps only now we are both realising that fact. Face it, you're a natural.' The change in Adam's expression confirmed the possibility. Palmer stepped back into the darkness leaving Adam on the brink of his thoughts. Elisa Wakefield had been right, and Adam knew it at his core but he hadn't wanted to believe it. Even as Alex Black he felt that his true calling lay elsewhere, and that teaching had been his attempt to run from a part of him he was scared to acknowledge. An indifference to life and death, a matter-of-fact attitude to getting the job done, however dirty that job was. To fulfil a duty. Was this life his true calling? Adam gave it thought and felt himself lean forward under the pull of Palmer's gravity.

'Really Adam, the school run and supermarket shopping on weekends in your shitty little family car. Is that really what you *want?*' Adam was drowning in doubt. As it stood, he was free of the rat race; he held the power of life and death in his hands. The cars. The chase. The kill. He took another step toward Palmer, almost immersed in shadow now.

'What's the offer?' he demanded. Palmer did his best impression of the Cheshire Cat, except that his yellowed teeth made less of an impact against the poor light.

'What do you want?' he asked. 'Your pick of the jobs; training up new recruits, assassination, intelligence? You could have it all.' Adam's heart thumped with anticipation. The whites of his eyes shone brightly in the veil of black.

The belief that he had held so firm twenty minutes ago was now shaken to its foundation. Adam knew less about himself in that moment than he had done at any time in his life. For a moment he was back in that little car, bumping along the road on his way home from a mountain biking session with his old mates; contemplating the possibilities of how his life could have been so different.

Adam backed away from Palmer's faint outline and walking backwards he covered half the width of the bridge, crossing two of the four lanes designated for road traffic. He was momentarily cast in the light of the moon; a silver film illuminating his pained features. The doubt was carved into his face. Adam turned and continued to the east side of the bridge, crossing the remaining two carriageways to reach the steel and iron superstructure.

Once out of Palmer's gravitational pull he was able to think more freely about his future. Palmer's words had struck a chord; killing did come easily to him and the physicality of his new life was a challenge he thrived on rather than a hardship he endured. Yet, despite all of this a deep-seated ache lay within him. He felt overwhelmed with sorrow and loss that churned the pit of his stomach and made him want to throw up its contents. He lurched forward for the arm of the bridge and took several deep breaths to try and settle his nausea. The Thames River thundered beneath his feet, crashing against the massive concrete piers that gave support to the bridge's steel ribs. There was a stiff breeze rising in the night air and it whipped the flow of the Thames into a frothing frenzy. Adam watched the moonlight fragmenting on the water's chaotic surface before it disappeared behind low cloud, scenting the breeze with imminent rain. He stayed there for a minute, propped against the eastern arm of the grade 2 listed bridge, and tried hard to remember his last thoughts as Adam Black.

Palmer's gruff voice burrowed into his thoughts until it reached Adam's consciousness.

'Well Adam, are you on board?' His tone was firmer now and he seemed to be pushing the decision like a determined car salesman trying to close a deal. Adam didn't turn. Instead he stood clinging to the ironworks, mesmerised by the passing river. 'Come on Adam, I don't have all night. And I'm sure you're keen to get back on an assignment.'

The thrill of the chase had now departed Adam's blood stream and in the cold light he considered the harsh reality of his future with MI6 under Palmer's control.

Suddenly there were footsteps to the north, the

heavy pounding of feet in rapid succession. Both men turned in the direction of the sound, their hands reaching for a weapon previously concealed from the other. The late night jogger came quickly into view and on seeing the two men ahead of him he glanced nervously up and down the road before making a cut across the carriageway for the west footpath. The men glanced back at each other, their hearts anticipating action. Neither one of them ignored the signs that the other was carrying a weapon, but then who were they trying to kid. Both men were experts in their trade and a cocked and locked pistol would be the minimum expectation in a scenario like this. When the slapping of tired feet had faded away on the south bank Palmer resumed his pitch.

'Don't waste this chance, Adam. It won't come again.'

Standing in the middle of the east carriageway Palmer had exposed himself to a mix of moonlight and the dull glow of a street lamp further along the bridge. He looked sick, with a complexion and pallor that would have looked much the same in broad daylight. Adam knew he could not have looked much better. Perhaps both men where closer to death than they realised.

Adam stood with his back to the bridge's external ornamental design and looked Palmer square in his sunken eyes.

'I don't remember what it is you're asking me to give up in exchange for a life working for you,' he said. 'But I want whatever it is back and nothing you can say or do will stop me from trying to recover it.' Palmer chewed hard on his bottom lip and Adam watched his fists clench and then his fingers splay.

'Don't be rash Adam, think very carefully about what you wish for. I'm not in the mood for pissing about tonight.' Palmer's tone had turned aggressive and it was clear that Adam wasn't being offered a choice. He didn't care.

'It's over, Palmer. I'm through. And if you've got any ideas about coming after me then think again. You are right; I'm a natural in this business and regardless of what you did to me, the implants and the reconstructions, I'm more aggressive and more determined than you and I'll stop at nothing to be free of this. Nothing.'

'You little shit,' spat Palmer, 'who the fuck do you think you are. I made you, and if I choose, I'll destroy you too.'

Both men were now stood square-on to the other, their feet planted hard and wide in a stable base that suggested they would stand their ground. Palmer slid a pistol from under his mac coat and held it loosely by his side in his right hand. For a brief moment the moon glimmered beyond the low level cloud that had formed and its light reflected from the weapon in Palmer's grasp. A light rain started to fall from the skies and covered both men and the space between and around them in a light film of moisture. With eyes wide open neither man blinked as the rain started trickling down their faces. Both men had a fire blazing within them and the rain was doing little to quench it.

Adam didn't draw the Browning stashed in his waist band. He hoped he could still talk down the situation, perhaps reason with Palmer and find a middle ground that suited both of them. Palmer's stance was aggressive, suggesting that negotiation might not be on the cards. The rain was falling heavier now and Adam could feel the cold liquid finding its way into his collar and down his neck. It trickled down his back, conforming to the laws of gravity. He was shattered, physically and psychologically, and he was bored with killing. He wanted out of this game, and he wanted to get out now while he still had a faint pulse. He wished for one more moment with Amy and the kids.

'It doesn't need to be like this,' he shouted over the patter of the rain. Palmer, who now looked soaked to his bones, strained to hear the words. After what seemed like a few seconds of information processing he replied.

'That's where you're wrong Adam. This is my world you're living in now and I make the rules. Rules which need to be enforced by any means necessary. You are either with me or against me.' Palmer was assessing the man stood ten feet away from him. The leather biker jacket looked slick with rain and it glistened intermittently in the patchy night light. Adam looked weak and distracted, giving Palmer the upper hand on any immediate action he was about to take. 'You were a dead-man and I breathed life back into you. You owe me for that,' Palmer continued.

'Bullshit,' came the curt retort from Adam. 'I was alive. I had a family that loved me and would have cared for me. But you took me away from that. You stole my life.'

The older man shook his head.

'They would have soon got bored of wiping your arse and feeding you blended meals. You should be thanking me for what I gave to you.'

Palmer raised the pistol at Adam and squinted to force the gathering rain water from the wells of his eyes.

'You disappoint me, Adam,' he said. 'So much potential, yet so much weakness. That was the one issue I had with you all along, that one trait that we couldn't remove.'

'Don't mistake my humanity for a weakness,' replied Adam who was now shouting to be heard through the dense rain. 'It was that one quality that pushed me to my limits; that kept me going when I thought I had nothing left to give. Being human is what brought me through hell to be stood before you now. It was my greatest strength and it was the one thing you couldn't give me.' The comeback lit Palmer's torch paper.

'No!' he cried, 'you're wrong! You were our test subject; the one riddled with mistakes. Next time we'll do it right.'

Adam had heard enough.

'There won't be a next time!'

Palmer flicked off the safety catch of his pistol and squeezed the trigger. His body jolted backwards into the middle of the road before falling listlessly. The rain poured down onto his supine corpse; a gaping wound where his left eyeball had been a second earlier. Thick red liquid seeped from the back of his open skull and mixed with the torrents of rain water that ran over the road, diluting the life that bled out of him. Adam's Browning was still level with where Palmer's head had been, his arm steady, his aim true. There was no remorse for this last kill.

Adam let out a sigh of relief but as the air left his mouth, so did a thin line of red metallic-tasting liquid. His legs buckled and he found himself looking for something to hold onto. His brain couldn't compute any more pain than he had already but something was different now. Leaning against the side of Vauxhall Bridge his breathing was reduced to a hollow gasp. Palmer had left his last mark on Adam; a hole in the chest from front to back. The old bastard had still got it. Adam clung with both arms over the iron structure, pulling with his final ounce of strength to take the weight from his folding legs. He couldn't die here. He wouldn't die here. With one massive effort he hoisted his chest and abdomen over the edge of the bridge and hung there for a second watching the blurred boundary between the falling rain and the choppy River Thames. He slid painfully forward another inch until he felt his body reach a tipping point. His head and face swelled with the pressure of hanging upside down before his wet legs slid free of the iron superstructure and eased him head first in to the fast flowing water.

The only witness to the event was a female bronze figure that adorned one of the bridge's piers. Her fixed gaze seemed to follow Adam's limp body as it sank beneath the murky waters. The few remaining molecules of oxygen in his thread-bare bloodstream where quickly used up, but before he died for the second time Adam saw Alex Black's life in full colour. It ended with a crumpled car on a cold night. He felt Amy's touch on his icy skin and saw the smiles of his children. In a fraction of a second he relived the full sorrow of losing the things he loved once again; and the Thames swallowed up his tears.

# TWENTY ONE

The City morning commute was more stressful than usual as exasperated motorists battled to cross the Thames. The lines of slow moving traffic were punctuated by red double-decker buses, all going nowhere quickly. Their usual passage over the water that divided Pimlico and Vauxhall had been unexpectedly closed; the diverted traffic creating bottle necks at the crossings situated north and south of Vauxhall Bridge.

The City's cyclists seemed hardly affected, nonchalantly abandoning the Mayor of London's new Cycle Superhighway 5 in favour of continuing straight up from Wandsworth Road. Others joined the Westminster-bound carriageway from the general direction of Vauxhall bus station, jostling their way across the long lines of standing motor traffic. Their lack of inconvenience and ease of negotiating the bridge closure seemed to punch another nail in the coffin of the floppy-haired Tory's failed cycling initiative.

While the motorists were preoccupied with finding alternate routes and ringing bosses and loved ones to relay their distress, some cyclists, along with many pedestrian commuters passed close to the bridge to get a good look at the drama of the day. They ogled from beyond the blue and white plastic tape that stretched across the width of the Pimlico entrance to the bridge. Stood shoulder to shoulder, not one of them spoke to the other, city-dwellers engaged in their own worlds. The Police cordon danced gently in the light breeze, occasionally cracking like a whip when a rogue breeze blew off the Thames. The sharp sound acted to intermittently disperse the gathering rubberneckers, sending them on their way, only to be replaced by more curious commuters. One woman stood her ground as the plastic tape lapped at her thighs. She strode one leg over the make-shift barrier, careful not to spill the premium Italian coffee from its take-out cup. For a lady in her late fifties she very nimbly flicked her trailing leg over, only to be stopped in her tracks by a male uniformed Police Officer who had been standing sentry at the mouth of the bridge. The officer towered over the woman and cast her in shadow, his thick frame and rotund abdomen eclipsing the morning sun behind him.

'Excuse me Madam but this is a...,' started the copper before a flash of an SIS ID card informed him that she was an Official Representative of the Government of the United Kingdom. The big man's face flushed with embarrassment at his faux pas. 'Sorry Ma'am,' he continued and waved the lady through warmly. Elisa Wakefield didn't seem fazed by the momentary delay; and where others may have pulled rank and given the constable an earful she instead offered a polite smile and thanked him for his diligence.

The early morning sun seemed unusually bright as it peered above the high-rise London horizon. It was now high enough in the sky to cast its glow on the River Thames, which glistened gold for much of its length, reminiscent of a fabled yellow-brick road. It was the type of morning you often got in England in early summer following a heavy downpour the night before. The tension that was in the air the previous night had been cleared, making way for a calm and bright new day. The last of the night's rain was either draining from the bridge's camber or evaporating to the skies from the warming concrete.

A male figure stood alone on the east side of the bridge, by Vauxhall. The sun was heating his back and his long shadow was cast over the corpse that lay in the road in front of him. Lee Dawson looked down at the dead-man's face one last time before the crime scene officers zipped-up the body bag. What remained of Richard Palmer's head finally disappeared from view.

'Tell me everything you know,' requested Dawson of the uniformed man who had just joined his side. The high ranking Metropolitan Police officer was Chief Inspector David Callum; his tall gangly body supported a thin head fronted by a large prominent nose. In spite of his appearance Callum also had a prominent character, and his voice commanded attention when he spoke.

'A taxi driver called it in just after 05:00 this morning. He was bringing his fare over the bridge from Pimlico when at the very last minute he saw something in the road. The rain was coming down so hard it was bouncing off the carriageway and he claims it was difficult to see the road surface.'

'Did he hit the body?' enquired Dawson.

The Chief Inspector picked up his thread.

'No. Stopped just in time. He got out to check what it was, assuming it to be some sort of animal, and that's when the poor bastard got the shock of his life.'

'A bit big for road-kill don't you think?' asked Dawson rhetorically. Both men maintained a professional seriousness. Dawson continued, 'you don't think he's implicated in the death then?' Callum shook his head slowly.

'Both his and his passenger's story check out. And they obviously provide an alibi for each other.' Dawson pondered his next question.

'Do we have an exact time of death?'

'Forensics are still working to narrow it down but given the heavy rainfall and the standing water around the body, we are currently looking at a timescale of approximately 01:00 and 05:00.' Dawson looked at the Chief Inspector more hopefully before asking his final question for the time being.

'Any evidence of the perpetrator?'

Callum shook his head again, this time also scrunching up his bottom lip.

'Only the spent bullet casing; which has been sent for ballistic analysis,' said the officer raising his eyebrows skyward, 'but other than that, very little so far.'

The mature woman had looked on from the east pavement, identifying the body before the zip-bag closed over him. She didn't seem shocked or concerned to see Palmer's cold white body lying face-up in the morning sun. She sipped at her coffee and enjoyed the taste all the more for being outdoors in the fresh air. It was a beautiful morning she concluded as she turned to face the rising sun and let its distant power reach her face. When she finally opened her eyes again she noticed that she had been standing only metres away from a hunched figure in a white cover-all suit. The figure, a man, she deduced from their build and posture, seemed to be focusing on a small area of detail by the eastern arm of the bridge. Wakefield took another dose of caffeine and strode over to the forensic investigator.

'Good morning,' she said with a professional tone. The crime scene investigator looked up briefly from his work, nodded curtly, and then went back to his item of interest. Using tweezer-like structures he removed a small piece of fabric from under the head of a rivet. He held it up to the light to get a better look, and then placed it into a clear plastic bag.

'What do you have there?' enquired Wakefield. The man shot her a glance over the top of his face mask that suggested she and her questions were not welcome. She got the message clearly and was once again impressed with the level of professionalism being shown by the Police. She wasn't however a woman who took no for an answer. She flashed her best smile and her ID card, and repeated her question. It didn't take an expert on non-verbal communication to read the man's response; the roll of his eyes and the almost imperceptible slump of his shoulders gave away his disappointment of being top-trumped. He pulled down his face mask to answer the senior officer.

'My best guess at this moment in time is that it's a clothing fragment.' The man seemed reluctant to offer more but the arc in her eyebrows suggested he should continue. 'Given the orientation of the corpse,' the man nodded his head in the direction of Palmer, whose body was now being slid on to a stretcher, 'I think the killer was along this line of sight, and that he was wounded before escaping over the side of the bridge.' Wakefield pondered the scenario.

'What an interesting imagination you have,' she said before continuing, 'is there anything on the clothing fragment that might help us identify the killer?' The crime scene officer nodded his head enthusiastically, then suppressed his response. 'Come now,' she said. 'This is a matter of state security with possible international implications. It happened on the Secret Intelligence Service's doorstep and involved one of our highest ranking officers. Don't be coy with me.'

There was another roll of the eyes, this time less subtle.

'It looks blood-stained, and unlike the rest of the crime scene that's been virtually washed clean, this cloth should have retained some of the blood in its fibres.' Wakefield took another gulp from her cardboard cup, its contents now cool enough to enjoy fully.

'And who else knows about this fragment and your theory?' she asked.

'Nobody' replied the man looking round. His answer was just what the older woman wanted to hear as she stretched out her free hand. She kept eye contact with the man in his giant plastic onesie, whilst moving her closed four fingers in a flipper-like movement to suggest that he hand over his find. For a second he hesitated. *Bloody secret service*, he thought, before finally obliging the request and passing over the sealed plastic bag.

'Your Country thanks you,' she said with another flash of her persuasive smile.

Wakefield continued her morning stroll over Vauxhall Bridge and drained her coffee cup, savouring the taste of its contents and the small victory she had secured. As she reached Albert Embankment another crime scene investigator had just finished the unenviable job of searching the public waste bin for evidence related to the shooting.

'May I?' asked Wakefield gesturing her empty cup towards the bin.

'Yes,' replied another figure in white coveralls, 'I've finished with this now.' The older woman deposited her empty take-out cup in the waste-bin. Only the cup wasn't empty; inside was a folded plastic specimen bag containing a small blood-stained fragment of cloth. Wakefield looked over to the River Thames that flowed calmly to her left.

'Rest in peace, Adam,' she whispered.

Lee Dawson and the Chief Inspector had stood in respectful silence as they watched Palmer's stiffened corpse be removed from the site of his sudden death.

The rigours that locked his joints gave further evidence to the suggested timescale of the shooting. The pooling of blood in the back of his torso, legs and arms confirmed he had hit the ground at the instant of the post-mortem interval and had stayed there since, undisturbed in his eternal sleep. Once the body had been stretchered out of sight into the back of an unmarked private ambulance Dawson decided he had paid his predecessor enough respect and turned to survey the rest of the scene. By the Vauxhall side of the bridge he could see the familiar outline of a long-serving colleague, Elisa Wakefield, walking away from him on route to the Office. He scanned back to see an empty-handed crime scene officer walking away from the east side of the bridge. The white-cloaked figure looked thoroughly fed-up to have wasted his time hunting for scraps of forensic material.

'Do we have anything of substance to go on here?' he asked with a hint of frustration in his voice. Chief Inspector Callum turned to join Dawson and instantly needed to shield his eyes from the dazzling sunlight that reflected from the river.

Standing there basking in the sun, both men could hardly believe the storm that had preceded the break of this new day, washing away virtually all traces of the darkest of nights.

'Very little,' replied Callum. 'What there is will be in the report delivered to you by lunch time today, but right now we know only that Palmer fired and was fired upon. For all we know his round could have whistled over the Thames. But the gunshot residues over his sleeve and the pistol muzzle confirm a single shot, probably with his arm in an extended position.'

'So you think he fired first?' asked Dawson. Callum shot the man a glance.

'You're taking over the case so that'll be for you to decide.' With that he walked off to finalise Police proceedings.

On entering 85 Albert Embankment Wakefield instantly enjoyed the cool climate provided by the building's air conditioning system. Although the temperature outside was just reaching the high teens of the Celsius scale the direct glare of the sun had been intense and had already left her with a healthy glow across her cheeks. As she crossed the atrium a combination of her clacking heels and her physical presence drew attention and signs of respect from the staff milling about in preparation for their working day. As always, she greeted them all with that eternal smile and used each of their names in a personalised hello.

She had devoted much of her working life to the Secret Intelligence Service and had helped develop a more open and transparent organisation that could still respond to the threats of a modern world. More importantly, she had forged a career path for women in the Secret Service that went beyond sitting behind a desk pouting at James Bond types. One of the ways in which she had shaped the service was by selecting and recruiting the right people for her vision of national security; a skill that she had honed over many years and one that she was renowned for. One of her latest recruits was now rising from a small enclosure of comfy two-seater chairs and was walking across the atrium towards her. She'd noted the GQ magazine he had set down on the glass-topped coffee table nestled between the chairs. She concluded that he could have stepped straight out of the front cover with his tailored navy suit and a crisp white shirt. The look was finished with a knitted texture cherry red tie. He extended out his right hand warmly to expose a strong looking wrist dressed with an Omega Speedmaster watch. Given the SAS soldier's wage the man had been receiving, Wakefield assumed the watch had come via one of those sites specialising in pre-loved quality time pieces. She took his hand in a firm but measured handshake and they exchanged equally self-assured smiles.

'Ma'am,' acknowledged the man.

'Tom,' nodded Wakefield, 'apologies for my lateness, I was delayed across the bridge. You may have noticed the Police circus out there this morning.'

'Yes I did, Ma'am. Thankfully I came up through Vauxhall. It all looked pretty serious; is it anything concerning this place?' he asked, keen to establish the facts rather than the gossip.

'I expect it will all come out in a press release later,' said Wakefield knowingly as the pair headed through the building's security. They were subject to all the usual checks, plus a few additional concerns following the death of a high-ranking SIS staff member on his doorstep.

The pair enjoyed light conversation as they headed through the Vauxhall Cross building toward Wakefield's office. The man beside her lacked any real distinguishing features but he seemed able to exude a physical presence when he wanted to. She fed off his calmness and quiet confidence. He reminded her of someone and after a little thought the irony dawned on her; Tom Austin carried himself with the same purpose and ease as Adam Newman had done when she had passed him in the corridors of the SOU training building several months earlier. He had the same battle-hardened features yet with the same ability to instantly soften them with a well-targeted smile. Their characteristics were uncannily similar she thought and took solace in the idea that she had finally been able to recruit such professionalism to the Office. She didn't believe in fate but perhaps Tom Austin, former Second Battalion Parachute Regiment and later SAS, was destined for service in MI6.

# TWENTY TWO

Lee Dawson was en-route to the Office, having tired of the sterile crime scene. A lack of any substantial evidence and the sudden appearance of the paparazzi had given him more than enough reason to flee the area. He was amazed how the press could find a corpse faster than a swarm of blow flies, clicking and flashing away frantically, all vying for the money shot and the scoop of the day. *Sick bastards.* With the crime scene disappearing over his shoulder the realisation of a new opportunity shone brighter than the early summer sun, and when his mobile phone began to ring in his pocket he seized the moment to promote his new role.

'Acting Director of Special Operations; Lee Dawson,' he said with a beaming smile that rivalled the glistening River Thames behind him. The phone felt warm in his hand having been incubated in his suit trouser pocket. Dawson's puffed up expression deflated quicker than an undercooked soufflé as he listened to the voice on the other end of the line. The clicks and squeaks emanating from the phone's speaker were a story of devastation and horror, revealing the eight bodies recovered from an SIS safe house on the south coast. The newly appointed interim Head of SOU stopped dead in his tracks in front of the MI6 headquarters, desperately trying to make sense of the information tumbling in to his ears. He listened. Then he thanked the caller for their verbal report before hanging up the line. *Baptism of fire!*

'Get me Major Peter Smith,' demanded Dawson the instant the new call connected. There was a momentary pause on the line and Dawson used the opportunity to unleash a hail storm of credentials to reinforce the urgency of the call. Moments earlier he had been shocked to hear how a British Special Forces eight man patrol had been discovered in varying states of death, in the vicinity of a smouldering SIS property. And *that* was the problem. The men had been killed in combat on home soil and the blood was on MI6's hands. The shit was about to blow a hole in the fan. After what felt to Dawson like an eternity the call was transferred and a steady voice echoed over a loud speaker. The man sounded like he was inside a moving vehicle.

'Major Peter Smith. With whom am I speaking please?' The words were clipped and the voice guarded.

'Major, this is Lee Dawson, Director of Special Operations, Secret Intelligence Service…'

'Bullshit,' interrupted Smith, 'put Richard Palmer on the phone. I answer only to him.'

Dawson gave him the bad news straight, with both barrels, and the shot seemed to knock Smith off his perch. There was a silence over the ether but Lee Dawson was all out of respect now.

'What the bloody hell has been going on?' he

demanded, as he probed the clandestine unit's leader about the botched operation. Smith seemed to be in a state of shock himself at the news of the eight deaths, having been wrenched from his sleep in the early hours to be informed of the events. It had been Palmer who had made the call, giving his old mate Smithy a head start on cleaning up the mess or at least getting his story straight. That was the last he had heard from Palmer, and right now he wasn't going to let any of this slip to the jumped-up prick on the other end of the phone.

'I'm en-route from Hereford to the scene now,' said the Army Major. 'I'll need to establish exactly what has happened before I make any further comment. I'm sure you appreciate the critical importance of getting our facts straight on this before we come to any conclusions.' Dawson was pacing along the edge of the Thames, clearly not satisfied by Smith's methodical approach to the disaster.

'Of course I understand that, but what I need to know now,' hissed Dawson, 'was what the fuck they were doing there in the first place and who signed it off?'

'Not over this line,' said Smith, his voice professional and authoritative. 'It's not secure. I'll get in touch with you by the end of the day, and we'll talk more then.' The faint hum from the moving vehicle fell silent in Dawson's ear, leaving him with the tinnitus-like ringing of alarm bells in his own head.

The brass name plate had already been removed from the door by the time Dawson reached Palmer's office, but the newest tenant seemed irked not have his own name in place already. Colleagues he had charged past on his way to the office had mouthed words of condolence to him and expressed their shock at the news of Palmer's death. Dawson had been deaf to the words, seeing only the moving of mouths or the feigning of sad expressions. Instead he was deafened by his thoughts of the trail of destruction left by his predecessor, who had then coincidently wound up dead shortly after. He concluded that he couldn't give a fuck about Palmer's death, but was more concerned about the brewing storm of public account.

Janet Jones was stood by the open door that revealed the vacant office. A slender, well-dressed woman in her mid-40s, Jones had been regarded by Palmer as eye-candy but in reality she efficiently ran every aspect of his official work calendar. As he approached her Dawson wondered how much of Palmer's recent work had actually been 'official'. He doubted that the dead Special Forces soldiers could be regarded as a legitimate use of company resources. Dawson didn't acknowledge his newly acquired Personal Assistant as he breezed past her and slumped in to the heavy swivel chair. He wondered what else could go wrong on his first day of acting-up. Janet Jones knocked at the door to get his attention.

'I have a call waiting for you...Sir,' she said finally having tired of being ignored. Dawson just sat there kneading his temples with his index and middle fingers. 'It's Chief Inspector Callum,' she continued, knowing full well that would get his attention. Dawson snapped out of his trance instantly.

'Well, what are you waiting for?' he said, 'put him through to me.'

'Of course,' replied Jones, an obliging smile forming on her dainty painted lips. The smile faded as she closed the office door. *The king is dead, long live the king.*

Back at the crime scene Callum had seemed equally weary of the fruitless case, but a new piece of evidence had stoked his fire. His voice exuded one-upmanship as he dropped his newest bombshell.

'Ballistic fingerprinting,' he exclaimed, referring to the forensic technique that relied on the markings imparted on a bullet by the barrel of a firearm. Dawson's reaction was one of elation and terror at the thought of matching the recovered bullet casing to the gun that fired it. His morning had already been full of unwanted surprises and he was not sure he could handle another one so soon.

The Chief Inspector continued regardless, in an all-knowing sort of tone.

'A 9mm round was recovered from the scene,' he said. 'Thought to have been fired from a Browning Hi Power pistol.' He let the words hang in the air, and a thousand of Dawson's thoughts filled the space around them. The Browning was a favourite of SIS operatives, but also of British Special Forces. A chill ran down his spine, and some involuntary reaction forced him to stand from his chair. As if reading his panic-stricken mind Callum spoke again.

'I don't suppose you happen to have any of those unaccounted for?' he asked. Dawson gave his best blank expression and thanked God that their conversation was taking place over the phone. It would be a few hours before Peter Smith concluded events at the cottage, and that would include an inventory of weapons. Dawson prayed that a Browning Hi Power would not be missing from the list. But that was not the only kit unaccounted for.

'I hope you're sitting down for the next part,' said the Met Police officer, his words almost a gloat. 'We had another little situation in the early hours.' Dawson leaned in so far that he almost disappeared in to the slim-line mobile phone. 'It took a while to get it out of him, but one of our officers attended to a lone man in a fast food restaurant car park on the outskirts of Croydon. It seems that his partner, an older and highly experienced officer, may have been acting outside the scope of the Force. It's not quite clear how he was put on the job of attending the scene. But in short, he ended up dead at the hands of this lone man.'

'What's your point?' asked Dawson sharply.

'My point is this,' he replied, 'when the younger officer finally talked he described a highly trained man who was badly injured yet still able to take out two officers equipped with Tasers.' Dawson was hooked.

'And?' he said desperately.

'And, he drove away from the scene in a black Range Rover registered as a Government vehicle.'

His jaw was clenched so tightly that Dawson almost broke a few teeth. *What the hell was going on?*

'Who knows about this?' he asked anxiously.

'No one yet,' replied Callum, his tone now very

serious. 'It seems that we have a rogue Metropolitan Police officer acting on instruction from an unknown person to unlawfully detain a highly skilled Government agent; who then killed the officer in question. So you tell me what's going on and how we proceed from here?' It was clear that the Chief Inspector wanted the issue to disappear as much as his Intelligence colleague did.

'Leave it with me,' said Dawson trying to sound convincing, 'I'll handle it.'

Dawson stood by the large window of Palmer's office with its thick tinted panels shielding him from the heat of the sun and the mounting drama outside. He played out hundreds of different scenarios in his head, all with a hundred different algorithms to their conclusion. Whichever avenue his train of thought took there seemed to be a missing piece to the picture. A single man, highly trained. A team of elite British soldiers dead; a rogue Met officer burnt alive; and then Palmer killed with a single targeted shot. Surely not everyone involved had to be dead. He repeated a single question over and over to himself and it burrowed into his subconscious mind as he paced the office; *who or what linked Palmer and the lone man?* A wisp of an idea began to form in his mind, and the more he considered it the more it took shape.

'Dr Grace Quickfall,' he said out loud to himself; the reflection in the window nodding back at him in positive affirmation. Palmer had been keen to have her on house arrest recently but he had never explained his rationale to Dawson. Maybe Palmer had hanged himself with this one after all. He pulled out his mobile phone again and called up the number for his own second-in-command. It rang three times before being answered.

'Luke Lacey. Go ahead, Sir.' The response was short and professional.

'Luke I need you to act on something urgently. Track down Grace Quickfall, the junior officer working for Palmer, and bring her in for questioning ASAP.'

'Yes Sir I'm on it now. And Boss, I'm sorry to hear about the Director.'

'I'm the Director now,' said Dawson firmly. 'ASAP Lacey, ASAP!'

Finally he felt like he might be making inroads in to this deepening mystery and the faint but familiar feeling of control was starting to grow inside of him. He relaxed a little and allowed himself to take a rest in Palmer's luxurious office chair. A subtle odour of stale cigarette smoke rose like the ghost of Palmer from the worn leather fabric. The smell taunted Dawson's senses and he felt acutely out of place; even just sitting back in the massive leather chair he felt like Goldilocks before she found something more fitting. Dawson shook the thought from his head and the odour from his nose and convinced himself that he would grow in to the chair, and the role, with time. And if he didn't, he could always get a new chair. Devoid of all of Palmer's personal effects the office seemed much larger than at any other time he had stood in it. It dawned on Dawson that he had never actually sat in the office before today, because Palmer had never invited him to do so. Dawson had despised the previous occupant, and it seemed the feeling had been mutual, but now he was in Palmer's shoes they seemed rather big and the road ahead rather daunting. It wounded him to acknowledge it but deep down he respected much of the job that Palmer had done with the SOU and the countless successful operations he had conducted in the name of foreign intelligence. It was the methods he had used to get the results that Dawson really reviled. But the events of the last 24 hours were beyond Dawson's wildest notions of what Palmer might be involved in. He would need to do some digging.

He pressed the intercom button on the desk phone and was greeted almost instantly by Janet's perennial positivity. He asked for the tech team to get him access to Palmer's computer files and phone records, stating reasons of national security and to help in the apprehension of his killer. He also ordered a coffee whilst he was at, feeling the need for a caffeine injection to get him through what might lie ahead. Dawson pictured Janet Jones at her own desk responding to his call and as he imagined her flattering figure and long lashes a memory came to mind of him sitting on the edge of her desk promising that one day she would work for him. Then he remembered the conversation that ensued. Lee Dawson sat bolt upright behind the thick wooden desk. 'Adam Newman. Call sign 1.0.' He hadn't intended to verbalise the thought but it was out there now and the words sounded so obvious. Months earlier he had questioned Janet about a man leaving Palmer's office. She had referred to him as a Special Operations Agent within a pilot task force headed-up by Richard Palmer. Dawson renewed the image in his mind of the mystery man's skilled marksmanship at the firing range. He could almost certainly have shot-out Palmer's eyeball at ten paces. Perhaps 'Adam 1.0' had been a live agent after all, working solely for his master. That was, until he killed his master. The kaleidoscope of a million discontinuous fragments suddenly formed a single clear picture. But one question remained; *who was Adam?*

The coffee had been quick to arrive and Dawson drained the last of the cup's contents whilst still standing by for access to Palmer's data files. It seemed that wherever you worked, the IT department had a different version of urgent. The rich filtered coffee taste lingered in his mouth and it prompted him to call through for a refill. Then he sat and waited some more. The shrill ring tone of the mobile phone vibrating across the desk top caused Dawson to jump slightly. He attributed the reaction to the caffeine pricking at his nervous system, but it could equally have been the tension that was straining Dawson's nerves. In his rush to answer the phone he neglected to look at the caller ID.

'Hello,' he answered, not even bothering to confirm his own identity.

'Boss, it's Lacey. I'm at Quickfall's flat.' The very fact that his number two man was not already sat in an interview room with the woman intensified Dawson's adrenaline reaction further. He urged the man to continue. 'No sign of her, Boss. And I mean not a trace.' Dawson was quick to respond.

'Has she run?' he asked.

'No, I don't think so. We've got her passport and we've run a check on her bank account which shows no activity whatsoever over the last week. There are no large withdrawals prior to that either. Her clothes all seem to be here. There's food in the fridge, and even a weekly voice mail message on the home phone from her mother. She seems to have vanished.' Luke Lacey paused for a reaction from Dawson, but there wasn't one. Dawson was falling headlong into the fabled rabbit hole. He wondered what else he might uncover today. Finally he responded.

'Any sign of a struggle? A forced entry?' he questioned.

'No, Boss. Nothing. You thinking she might have been taken, or...' he paused, 'killed?'

'Yes,' said Dawson grimly, 'I think you may be right.'

The scene above the Heritage Coastline was one of utter devastation and reminded Peter Smith of any one of the numerous war ravaged places he had seen in his active military service. The stone cottage was a smouldering shell surrounded by piles of rubble and a bullet riddled Audi R8. This must have been the lone man's vehicle he surmised. He had passed a Range Rover further up the track, and by it the body of his newest recruit to the Increment, Gary Roberts. *This was only supposed to be a bloody training exercise for him.* He cursed under his breath for allowing the mission to go ahead on Palmer's say-so. His old friend had truly dropped him in the shit this time, and several good soldiers had been laid to waste in the process. Further up the track had been a Police cordon, and that was as close as the Police were getting to the scene. This was a black op on home turf, executing a hit on a UK citizen, and it had all gone tits-up. Smith had had to draft in the other guys from E-Squadron to round up the corpses, and they all sported a look of revenge on their faces. There would be some serious drinking at the Newmarket pub in Hereford tonight as the men gave their comrades a proper send off. The impromptu wake would then be followed by some seriously sore heads the next day; but that was the warriors' way. Smith left his men to do the bagging and tagging as he kicked about the ruins looking for spent shells or discarded weapons. He eventually tallied up the team's arsenal and called it in to Dawson over a secure line.

'It's a bloody mess,' he said, 'whoever your man is, he's good!' Dawson was caught off guard by the comment.

'What do you mean by *"your man"*?' he asked, feigning ignorance whilst also inviting Smith to fill the blanks.

'Cut the bullshit,' fired the SAS Major, 'Palmer told me we were taking out a rogue officer of yours – a terrorist threat. You better hope he's dead if this is the level of devastation he's capable of.'

'Can you be sure he worked at the Office?' he asked.

'I'm pretty sure this Audi could be traced as a Company car,' replied Smith in a matter-of-fact sort of tone. Dawson went quiet on the line leaving Smith time to fill the space. 'Perhaps I could trade it for my Range Rover.' The two men talked more and concluded that somewhere close to Vauxhall Bridge would be the abandoned vehicle, complete with its weapons cache.

'I'll put someone on it right away,' confirmed Dawson, wanting neither the Police, the Public, nor the Press to come across the mobile armoury and any evidence it contained. 'One last thing,' said Dawson anxiously, 'might there be a Browning Hi Power pistol amongst the weaponry that's still unaccounted for?' Smith's answer gave him little consolation.

The Army Major's call had interrupted Dawson's search through Palmer's secure files. After putting Luke Lacey and his team on the case of the second Range Rover, Dawson got back down to business at the laptop. The sun had crested the peak of its parabola through the sky and was now heading for the southern hemisphere. Dawson was so engrossed in the folders and files adorning the screen of his computer that he didn't notice the day fading outside his window. After another hour of searching he struck intelligence gold. The file title read 'Project P.' He double-clicked over the thumbnail image and then strained to read the grainy scanned image before him. What he could make out hooked him instantly. '1982. A joint operation between the CIA and the American military codenamed Project P. A Cold War operation to perfect the internal capabilities of the human being.' Dawson's eyes were wide like saucers as his pupils maximised the classified information being relayed to his brain cells.

He read on. 'The Prime Minister of Great Britain rejected the opportunity to further research the SU1 drug in British military personnel. No further action to be taken at this time. This file is to be destroyed.'

Lee Dawson slumped back in his chair, his imagination on fire with the possibilities of the information he had just discovered. It took him longer than it ought to have done to put two and two together and come up with a plausible explanation for the events of the last 24 hours. His search of the files continued with only scraps of reference to a 'Project Adam', and a single word followed by a mobile phone number. Dawson looked at the word and wondered if 'Baker' was an occupation or a code name. He punched the numbers into his mobile and let the call connect. A velvety Scottish inflection sounded on the other end.

'Hello, Dr Kenneth Baker speaking.' Dawson was stuck for a response momentarily and the silence prompted the man to speak again.

'Hello?'

Good Morning. Dr Baker, my name is Lee Dawson. I work for the Secret Intelligence Service.' This time it was Baker's turn for silence. Dawson continued, trying to prevent the line going cold, 'I have very recently taken over the work of Richard Palmer. I think you may have worked with him on a project in the past?' Baker said nothing but he couldn't stop the audible gasp from leaving his tight chest. He was sure the caller could also hear his pounding heart down the phone.

'I…err…I'm not sure I understand what you mean,'

said Baker. The doctor's response was fumbled and his voice sounded strained and higher pitched than it might ordinarily have been. Dawson had conducted enough interviews and interrogations to pick up on the signs.

'It's OK,' he said, 'you're not in any kind of trouble. In fact, I was hoping you and I might work together soon on the same project.' Baker let out a sigh and his vocal cords seemed to relax to their normal state of tension.

'OK...ok,' he stammered.

'Good,' said Dawson, his voice strong and reassuring. 'I'll be in touch again very soon.' He ended the call not knowing fully what he was agreeing to but his instinct told him he was on to something big. There had been many issues that Palmer and Dawson did not agree on regarding the running of the Special Operations Unit, but perhaps this one was an ambition that appealed equally to both men and their inflated egos. Only this time, Dawson would succeed where his rival had failed.

The sun was now kissing the opposite horizon as Dawson drew his working day to a close. He tapped out the final sentence to his press release.

'Richard Palmer, A senior officer with the Secret Intelligence Service was shot and fatally wounded whilst leaving his office of work in the early hours of the morning. The assailant is thought to have been an opportunistic criminal who was unaware of his victim's status and professional background. In the ensuing struggle the attacker was also fatally wounded and fell to his death in the River Thames. The Metropolitan Police and The British Secret Intelligence Service will work tirelessly to recover the assailant's body. The Public can be assured that the individual poses no ongoing threat to their safety.' He hit the send button on the drafted email and watched it disappear to its recipient, Chief Inspector David Callum, with the instructions to disseminate to the Press. Finally, he closed the laptop and cradled it under his right arm as he stood at the window of the office and watched the sun setting on his first day in his new role.

Tomorrow would see the dawn of a new era within the Special Operations Unit.

# TWENTY THREE

The lush green grass was long and thick and peppered with daisies, and it swayed with the breeze that carried the heavy scent of pollen. It was turning out to be another typical British summer with alternating sunny spells and showers providing the energy and water required for plant life to thrive, and the mildly neglected lawn was doing just that. Amy Black looked on her garden as a chore she just couldn't get on top of, having neither the time nor the inclination to work on it. Anything outdoors had always been a 'blue' job in their family and she was having a hard enough time keeping up with what she regarded as the 'pink' jobs, whilst raising two kids and surviving on their reduced income. A life insurance policy had always been one of those things they were going to get, but then never actually did. A bit like a Will, thought Amy with hindsight. But it was too late now for both of those things. Standing in the open doorway at the rear of their family home she leaned up against the frame, cradling a brew, and let out a low sigh that interspersed with the summer breeze before rising on the current of warm air from her mug of tea. Life wasn't always perfect when Alex was around but she missed every aspect of that life now.

Her thoughts of the outdoor to-do list vanished from her mind when a four-year-old boy tore past her, immediately followed by a six-year-old girl. The boy was lean and leggy and for a few seconds managed to keep out of reach of his older sister. She had an intense look on her face that suggested it was only a matter of time before she would take down her target, and before Joe could reach the middle of the lawn Emma had tapped him on the shoulder and both had tumbled exhausted on the carpet of green. The grass still looked a little wet from the night before and Amy felt tempted to shout out for both kids to jump up, but she checked herself and allowed her two precious children to continue having fun. They'd endured so much over the last few years and Amy had struggled to be the best mother she could be. It had been hard for her to come to terms with the loss of her husband and had sometimes forgotten that two innocent children had also lost their father. All too often she had found herself being short with them when they asked about their dad. *Just let them enjoy themselves,* she told herself.

She panned from the movie playing in her mind to the outer world where Joe and Emma were now laughing uncontrollably on the trampoline, jumping or falling about on unsteady legs. Just as one of them seemed to get a bounce going the other would stilt their rhythm and both would collapse in a fit of giggles. Amy laughed too; it was hard not to. They brought her so much joy and every day they reminded her of Alex, whether it was Joe's thick head of black hair or Emma's steely grey eyes. She'd also concluded that personality was as much genetic as it was learned as both children displayed many of Alex's behaviours despite his absence from their early development. Emma would not back down from any fight, often testing Amy to her limits, while Joe had already perfected the charming smile that could get him off the hook for any misdemeanour. In a twisted sort of way Amy considered herself blessed to have lost her man but to be left with his legacy. Suddenly the will and life insurance policy seemed insignificant.

She left the kids to occupy and tire each other in the fresh air whilst she enjoyed a moment to herself. She folded her legs under her as she sat down on the sofa, the soft leather fabric flexing beneath her. The TV had been playing to itself, and for once it wasn't a cartoon or a kids' programme about a Scottish seaside town where everybody lived in a different coloured house. Amy wasn't really paying attention to the national news that was now airing, but was displaying that parental ability of keeping one ear on the children whilst still filtering the TV broadcast. It seemed to be the ongoing saga of the missing body, the one belonging to the killer who'd dropped in to the Thames after shooting dead an MI6 officer. The voice was characteristic of any BBC news anchor with the standard vocal cliff-hangers and exaggerated tone. Flitting between the childish laughter outdoors and the on-screen report, Amy picked up the gist of the six weeks that had passed since the killing and that it was now unlikely that a body would ever be recovered. The male voice continued in the usual lilt, posing sensational questions about where the body might now be; tangled in weeds on the river bed, decomposing in to fish food, or now perhaps dumped into the North Sea. The news reporter seemed to start a discussion with himself about this final option and in a sceptical tone suggested that the body would likely have been recovered at the numerous locks along the length of the River Thames before reaching the open sea. With their report now rising to its over-dramatic crescendo the reporter raised the possibility of a dangerous killer still being on the loose, before concluding that this claim had been dismissed by both the Met and the Secret Intelligence Service. Amy shook her head disapprovingly and wondered what the world was coming to, before switching the TV off and tuning back in to the kids. Squeals of joy emanated from the rear garden and carried through the house on the breeze that blew gently in. Amy smiled again to herself and forgot all about the cruel world that lurked beyond the boundaries of their home.

After draining the last of her tea she set down the sage green Denby mug on a small slate coaster and motioned to stand. The sudden blast of her ringing mobile phone took her by surprise and it ripped her from her private reverie. Her heart skipped a beat, which over the past two years had become a conditioned response to the phone ringing. She checked the caller ID, gave a warm smile, and then lowered herself back into her comfy position to take the call.

'Hi Honey, how are you?'

'I'm fine thank you sweetie,' replied the voice, 'but how are you?' asked the caller with the same tone that everyone used when asking her that question. Jen Shakespeare was one of Amy's oldest and best friends. They had shared all aspects of their lives since their school days, and despite their respective travels in the interim had come to settle within ten miles of each other. 'Aunty Jen', as she was referred to by Amy's children was now a big part of their lives and had helped support them through the darkest times. But recently Jen had urged Amy to start looking forward and to move on with her life. She was constantly reminding her that in her mid-30s Amy was still a major catch for any man, and although none of them would ever be Alex they would at least provide her with a second chance of love, passion, and companionship. Amy knew her old friend was right and was beginning to come round to the idea, albeit reluctantly.

'I've got this fantastic guy I want you to meet,' said Jen excitedly. Amy made the right noises down the line to feign interest but they didn't quite cut it. 'No honey I swear, this guy is the complete package; handsome, kind, professional, funny,' the list went on until she realised she'd overdone the adjectives. 'Seriously girl,' she continued, 'if I were single…' the sentence trailed off into a chorus of giggles from both women.

'I just don't know,' replied Amy, 'I don't know if I'm ready to let go.' She could visualise her friend on the other end of the line banging her head repeatedly against an imaginary brick wall. After Amy had recounted to Jen her experience of 'seeing' Alex at the house two months ago she had declared that enough was enough and that if Amy didn't start moving on she would force her to get professional help. Between them they had decided that the whole event of Alex visiting the house had been a figment of Amy's imagination; that her subconscious mind had constructed the whole thing because Amy had obsessed over the idea that he might one day come back to her. Jen had almost anticipated such an event after seeing the emotional strain grow in Amy. After a few more minutes of selling the latest beau Amy had conceded to Jen and agreed to meet with him.

Amy hung up the line and cradled the phone in both hands. She knew this was the right thing to do, for her and for her children, but that didn't stem the awful sick feeling that filled the pit of her stomach. Moving on meant leaving the memory of Alex behind.

A part of her brain kept tabs on Joe and Emma running wild in the garden, while a large part of her grey matter constructed a future where she might once again be happy and loved. She was lost deep in her thoughts and barely heard the doorbell ring. Ten seconds later she still hadn't motioned towards the door and the bell chimed a second time. Amy partly divorced herself from the mix of guilt and excitement that was conducting an orchestra of hormonal releases deep within her. She rose from the sofa and moved absent-mindedly in to the hallway. Her right leg fizzed with the sudden return of electrical activity that comes after moving off a compressed limb. The sensation filled another section of her chaotic brain.

Still with an ear on the kids, Amy was oblivious to the figure whose fragmented outline was now visible through the textured glass flanking the front door. Even as she reached for the chrome satin door handle Amy had not registered the familiar frame of the man, or his thick black hair; features that were now recognisable through the stipple effect in the glass. Features she would fall in love with all over again.

26088023R00176

Printed in Great Britain
by Amazon